BOOK 1 OF EUPHORIA ONLINE

DEATH MARCH

PHIL TUCKER

DEATH MARCH
Book 1 of Euphoria Online

Copyright © 2018 Phil Tucker

ISBN-13: 978-1723224713
ISBN-10: 1723224715

Table of Contents

DEATH MARCH

1

MY BROTHER'S imminent death had me distracted.
Feet up on my desk, hands laced behind my head, I
watched the wall clock. Two minutes remained till my seventh-pe-
riod students arrived. Two minutes till I swung back into autopilot and escaped my bleak thoughts. Two minutes had never
seemed so long, so when my omni vibrated I gladly accepted the
incoming message without checking who'd sent it.

Want to play Euphoria for free?

I made a face. Yeah, right. Who didn't? What a poor attempt
at spam. Since Euphoria launched I'd received every variation of
that offer through every media channel offering a free weekend
session. My finger moved to the delete button but then paused.
That number. Where did I know it from?

Brianna.

I'd deleted her number after finally—for real and for good and
forever—breaking up with her three weeks ago, and hadn't heard

from her since. In fact, our sole mutual friend, Evalina, had told me that ever since our last falling-out, Brianna'd been waiting for me to call so she could tell me how despicable I was.

'Course, I'd never called her, and it had given me petty satisfaction to leave her stewing.

What the heck was she texting me for?

More importantly, why the hell was she offering a free session of Euphoria?

I bit my lower lip. The voices of my students rang loudly outside my classroom door. One minute till the bell rang and I'd have to let them in.

My thumb hovered over my phone's keyboard. Euphoria. The miracle game produced by our new benevolent artificial intelligence global overlord, Albertus Magnus. It cost three grand for a weekend session. Why was she offering it to me of all people?

Nah. No way Brianna would reach out. Someone had to have hacked her account.

Nice phishing attempt, assholes.

Fine. Forget you, was all that came back. A jolt of adrenaline pulsed through me—*forget you* was Brianna's favorite way of saying goodbye whenever we'd fought. I took my feet off my desk and sat up.

Wait, that you Brianna? I hesitated then added, **And who wouldn't?**

Her response was immediate. **I have a free pass. It's yours if you want it.**

The bell rang, shrill and piercing. The voices outside were raised in laughter, and I knew that even a minute's delay on my part would convince a third of them to simply skip my class.

Especially since they knew the virtual reality units were all out of commission.

I want it, I texted. **I'll call in forty-five minutes.** Somebody pounded on the door. **Last class.** I hesitated and then typed, **Thank you.**

I opened the door and shifted into teacher mode. Even as I called out students' names, told them to quit horsing around and get inside, my mind was scrambling. I was all keyed up. I could barely focus. Euphoria was only eight months old, and the hype was surreal, with its being touted as the first clear sign of Albertus' superiority to mankind.

The forty-five minutes passed in a blur. I ran on autopilot. Classes these days were supposed to be taught in VR, with all kinds of studies touting the benefits of fully immersive learning environments. But I taught in a school with little to no funding and my class's units had broken shortly after I'd started six months ago, forcing me to teach my kids the old-fashioned way: face to face, and with little more than threats, jokes, persuasion and humor to keep their attention.

Once they settled in I resumed drilling them on how to write a five-paragraph essay for the hundredth time, prepping them for their upcoming standardized test which I feared most of them would fail. This was my first year teaching, and already I'd lost all romantic ideals about changing these eighth graders' lives. Crushing bureaucracy and a director's office who sucked up to the parents and sent troublesome kids right back to my class had seen to that.

"All right," I called out as the bell rang again. "Anyone who remembers what a metaphor is gets a whole period next week in the library's VR room. Got it?"

This elicited a chorus of excited shouts, and then all forty-five of them rushed right back out in a storm of backpacks, brightly lit sneakers, glowing AR goggles and laughter.

Last period of the last day of the week.

I was free.

I stood there, simply staring out into space. There was nothing more exhausting than holding the attention of forty-five bored twelve-year-olds for almost an hour. And to do that for seven periods, back to back? I was wiped. The thought of Euphoria brought me back to life, however, and I set my omni on my desk. "Call Evalina."

A blue hologram of a swirling ring of water appeared a foot above it, a small wave rushing around its circumference as it rang. And rang. And rang.

"C'mon, Ev. Pick up already. Come on!" I stared at Evalina's smiling profile pic that hovered above the watery ring.

And suddenly her face animated. "Three forty-six," she said with a grin. "Calling me one minute after class ends? You must be desperate. What happened this time? They demand you do the stanky leg again?"

Ev was my best friend. Perhaps even my only friend, since I'd had practically zero time between teaching and taking care of my brother Justin's case to do anything else.

I'd planned to make this call anyway. Tell her the bad news Justin's lawyer had given me that morning. But now I had a new, desperate hope. The slimmest chance to pull my brother's bacon out of the fire. "I just got a crazy text from Brianna."

"Uh-oh. She threaten to cut the head off your pocket weasel?"

"Just about the opposite. She's offering me a free pass to Euphoria. She's waiting for my call right now."

For once, Evalina was stumped. "She what?"

"I know." I sank into my chair. "You think she wants to try and get back together?"

"Chris, Brianna's an oil fire and you're a bucket of water. No. You're not allowed to get back together. Anyways, you failed to worship appropriately at her altar, remember? Kept trying to treat her like a normal person and not the exalted goddess she really is. You think she'd really offer to spend three thousand bucks on you when she'd first demand you spend ten times that on her as an apology?"

"Well, no," I said. "But… maybe she's moved on?" My words sounded weak even as I said them.

"Uh, no. Not Brianna. That's not how she works. Weren't you the one who called her a manipulative, emotionally damaged psychotic freak?"

"I know, I know." I ran my hand through my hair. "But I was pretty upset when I said that. So you don't know anything about this?"

"No. To be honest, I've been avoiding her since you guys broke up. She's been trying to pull me into one of her schemes to get back at you ever since. So listen. Don't take her offer." A vertical line appeared between Evalina's brows. "I tried warning you the first time and you ignored me. I'm warning you again. Whatever crazy plan she's got going, you're going to regret it. Don't accept."

I closed my eyes. Euphoria. How many nights had I thought about blowing three grand I didn't have just so I could play in Death March mode and earn a full pardon for Justin?

"Chris?" Ev sounded suspicious. "I know that look. You're going to call her, aren't you?"

"Just to see what kind of insanity she's proposing," I said, opening my eyes, decision made. "I won't accept. I'm just… curious."

"Sure," said Evalina. "Curious. That's what you said when you asked me if she was single. Whatever. Why does nobody in this whole world listen to good advice unless it comes from the Universal Doctor?"

"Because Albertus Magnus knows what's up," I said. "Shit. It's three fifty. Going to call her."

"Call me back!" yelled Ev just before I killed the connection.

My heart was racing. I'd sworn Brianna was out of my life for good. I'd deleted her number, erased pictures, removed access permissions, the whole nine yards. Now this?

"Call the number from my last text message."

Her face immediately animated in the air before me. "I thought you were going to stand me up again." Her voice was a shadowy purr, and it brought back all kinds of arousing and uncomfortable memories. And she still looked amazing.

"Hi, Brianna." I tried to keep my voice firm, no-nonsense. "What's this about?"

"Wow, right to business, huh? That's cold. Maybe I'll find another state employee to benefit from my improbable generosity. Have a nice life, Chris."

"Wait—what? What are you talking about?"

She considered me, pretending to debate hanging up. "My father won a raffle at a big fundraiser last night. Three weekend passes to Euphoria, but there's a catch. They can only go to employees of the state of Florida. So I remembered your sorry ass teaching delinquents and thought, hey, maybe I can bring a little fun into his life—"

"They're not delinquents—"

"But I guess I was wrong. I'll just tell my dad to give them to someone else. Bye, Chris."

She hung up.

"Damn it!" I leapt to my feet and began to pace. She was waiting for me to call back. She knew I would. This was just like her. She'd not changed a bit, and the worst part was that she was right.

"Call Brianna," I said. It rang. And rang. And just before it went to her mailbox, her face animated once more. "What?"

"Look. I'm sorry. You're right. That was rude of me. I apologize." I ground out each word, heart thudding in my chest. *Think of Justin. They're just words.* "How are you?"

"I'm fine," she said, voice clipped. "I know you don't really care, but I appreciate the effort."

There was an awkward silence as we stared at each other. She was waiting for me to ask. I wanted to roll my eyes. To hang up. Instead, I forced a smile. "So. You have to give the passes to state employees?"

"Yes. All of my friends obviously already play, and I don't know anyone else who works for the state." *You don't have any real friends,* I wanted to say but held my tongue. "So. I thought it could be my one good deed of the year. You want a ticket?"

Yes, I nearly blurted. My palms were sweaty and my thoughts where whirling. Instead, I forced myself to calm down. "You know I do, but what are you trying to get out of this, Brianna? What are the conditions?"

She gave a dramatic sigh. "Honestly. You'd think I was a Bond villain the way you're acting. Look. I know we won't work out. You're poor, you're rude, and other than your moderately good looks you don't bring anything to the table. And after the way you treated me, dumping me like that? Hell no. So don't worry.

I'm not trying to trap you. Instead, I'd like to use you. I think you'd be a good addition to our team."

Oh man. It took so much effort to bite my tongue. I took a measured breath. "Use me."

"No one can deny you're a talented gamer, Chris. Or were. You'd be amazing in Euphoria, and that's not a compliment. That's a statement of fact. How many Golden Dawn tournaments have you won?"

"Seven," I said.

"Seven. And that's just interfacing through a virtual reality headset. Imagine a true neural connection. You'd be wicked. My friends and I have already hit thirty-fifth level. You'd be coming in at level one, but we'd load you up with gear, help you grind, and within a week you'd be an advantage to our team."

I sat once more and put my feet up on my desk. "Uh-huh. You think I could level up that fast over one weekend?"

"Sure," said Brianna. "Time dilation will make sure that happens. Eighteen to one, remember? Eighteen minutes really is a day in Euphoria. A week of grinding will go by fast, and you'll still have months and months to play at our level and help us compete in tournaments and clear dungeons."

I ran my hand over my face. She was right. I'd been pretty good at Golden Dawn, the virtual reality massive online roleplaying game that had been the ultimate gaming experience until Euphoria had dropped. I'd been living the high life—albeit from paycheck to paycheck—in Seattle off my streaming income till Justin had been caught doing salvage dives on Miami Beach's sunken buildings. I'd blown my meager savings on getting him a lawyer, then once those were gone had moved to Miami-Dade and gotten the first local government job I could find just to get access to their pro-bono lawyers. Well. Pro-bono-ish. My life in Seattle, my life online, the thrill, the power of being the best—it had all faded into a dream.

Brianna was watching me. "You can make some serious money, Chris. Once you level up we'll start doing some cash raids. They'll be tough, but I think we'll be able to pull it off. Chump change to my friends and me, but you could probably use ten grand or whatever, right?"

Right.

That'd be enough to pay off our current debt to the 'pro-bono' lawyer, but that wasn't why my mind was racing. The most controversial aspect of Euphoria was the morbid and inexplicable playing mode Albertus had implemented called 'Death March'. Anybody who survived six months in-game while playing at that difficulty level could ask a single favor of Albertus Magnus, the AI that now supposedly ran the world. A cash payment of up to ten million dollars. Green cards, visas, or citizenships to participating countries. Internships and job interviews at the most prestigious multi-nationals. And, most importantly, pardons for a wide array of crimes.

The downside was if you died in-game, you died in real life. Hence the whole 'Death March' thing.

"What difficulty level are you guys playing at?"

"Soul Grinder," she said. "Bad enough for you?"

Of course Brianna and her friends wouldn't be playing on suicide mode. Why would they? To them, it was literally just a game.

I thought of Justin. Locked up and facing forty years or more in prison due to our idiot governor's draconian laws against looting our flooded coastline. Or, according to the lawyer this morning, the death penalty.

"All right," I said. "I'm in."

"Of course you are." Her sensual lips pulled into a self-satisfied smile. "You'd better hurry, though. Less than an hour for you to get to the docking station before we link up."

"An hour? What?" I lunged for my backpack, scooped up my omni and started shoving my stuff inside. "You serious?"

"Deadly," she said. "If you're not here by five o'clock, you're out." I could hear her smug glee. "See you soon."

"Damn it!" I slung my backpack over my shoulder, sprinted out the door, skidded to a stop, ran back, pressed my thumb against the door pad to lock my classroom, then ran down the hallway again. "Call Evalina," I yelled at my omni.

It rang once before she picked up. "Chris?"

I hip checked the fire escape doors and spilled out onto the brightly lit sidewalk, startling the two armed guards who were sweating like pigs under their slick black body armor. The Florida heat and humidity hit me like a wet brick to the face.

"Ev, you need to help me out here."

"You said yes. I knew it. I knew it!"

"Don't freak out, OK? Just listen. I'm going to call Max—Justin's lawyer—and dictate a new will. I'm leaving everything to you. If you don't hear from me by Monday morning, liquidate all my assets—it's not much—and use them to keep paying the damn lawyer, all right?"

"What?" Shock. "Are you serious?"

Deadly, said Brianna's voice in my mind.

I ran through students, darting like a world-class dodgeball player, and then across the road into the parking lot. "Yes. Please. I have to do this." I was already panting. Six months sitting in a teacher's chair had done nothing for my stamina. I reached my car and simply ran into it. The car sensed my proximity and unlocked the driver's door. "Ev. You're the only one I can ask."

"You're sounding crazy," said Ev. "Please. Stop. You're scaring me. What did she say?"

I yanked the door open and slid in. Pressed the 'on' button, disengaged autopilot, and then forced myself to drive slowly out of the parking lot, even though every instinct urged me to floor it.

"You need to trust me," I said, shoving my omni into its cradle. "I'm going to try for a pardon. I'm going to get Justin off the hook."

"You're going to do that Death March thing? No, no, no. Chris. Stop. Pull over."

"I can't stop." I felt like I was having an out-of-body experience. "I can do this. I know I can. It's what I was born to do."

"Look, I know you were an amazing Golden Dawn player, but you've never—"

"Ev, trust me. I know it sounds crazy, but I'm a gamer. I know I'll adapt fast. Plus, Brianna and her team are going to protect me, level me up, give me elite gear. I'll be safe till I'm ready to mix it up, then I'll kick ass for six months and come back rich and with a full pardon for my dumbass brother."

"And if you don't? If you die?"

I drove up the onramp onto the elevated, flood-proof highway that had been built to replace the old I-95 interstate and punched the gas. I gripped the steering wheel with both hands so hard my knuckles hurt. *If I died?* How to tell her? How to tell her I couldn't stand losing Justin as well?

"Listen, Ev. I didn't tell you, but Max called this morning. He said the prosecution's going to push for the death penalty."

"What?" Her shock was as sharp as mine had been. "That's ridiculous."

"I know. But Max said the government's terrified of mass looting breaking out up and down the coast. That they don't think the emergency disaster legislation is going to cut it. They're going to blame Justin for Sam's death and try to hit him with first degree."

Sam had been Justin's best friend and partner in crime since middle school. His oxygen tank had been faulty and during their dive Sam had drowned while exploring a flooded parking garage. Justin had been arrested after calling 911. The situation was a clusterfuck of bad luck and even worse judgment on Justin's part, and now the government was going to try and make an example out of him to keep all would-be looters out of billions and billions of dollars' worth of private property.

"All the more reason for you to stay, Chris! You're going to leave him alone to go through *that* without you?"

A memory came back to me. My mother in her hospital bed. The tubes. Her sallow skin. The beeping and the smell of disinfectant.

Tears pricked my eyes. I wiped them away angrily. The truth hit me like a blow. I wasn't strong enough to lose him. I'd used up those reserves. I had to do something. I *had* to. Even if the risk was leaving Justin alone if I failed. Maybe it was selfish. Cruel, even. But if it worked? If I came back rich beyond my dreams and with a pardon? Then I'd get to keep what was left of my family.

My throat was tight, so I coughed and sat up straight. "If you can't do this, I understand."

"No. Of course I can do this. It's just that…" She trailed off, and there was silence for a spell. I drove like a madman past cars that were already driving like lunatics. It didn't take much to imagine an accident causing me to meteor through the crash barriers to land in a flaming wreck on the flooded roads and homes below.

The silence over the phone was textured. I could hear her help-lessness. I could hear her struggling to find the words.

"I'm sorry, Ev." I didn't look at her face on the console. Even though I was pushing 120 mph, it wasn't the speed that prevented me. I knew that if I met her eyes, I'd crack. "Thank you."

"You'd better get through to Justin. I'm not going to explain this to him."

"I will."

More silence, punctuated only by the horrific blare of a horn as I slid past an eighteen-wheeler and into an empty lane on the far side. I hit the gas and surged forward. Any moment now, traffic was going to gridlock, and then getting there on time would be out of my hands. I was going to fight for every car length I could until then.

"Take care of yourself," said Ev. She sounded numb.

"One weekend," I said. "You'll hear from me Sunday night. I promise."

"I told you already. Don't make promises you can't keep." Before I could respond she carried on, voice suddenly heated. "And you'd better come back. You'd better."

Then she hung up.

The elevated highway curved to the right up ahead, and as I tore around the huge bend I saw the brake lights. Gridlock, and it was barely past four. I loathed Miami traffic. I eased up on the gas, slowing down, slowing down, then finally came to a stop. I checked my console map. Forty-six minutes till I reached the Euphoria docking station. I glared at the traffic.

"Call jail," I said. I hated that I had Justin's prison number on speed dial.

It took twenty minutes to get through to him. Twenty minutes of being put on hold, ID'd, getting Max on the line to BS a pressing legal issue, until finally Justin's face appeared on my console. He was eighteen, old enough to be tried as an adult. He looked wary and haunted and scared and defiant all at the same time.

"Hey, bro," he said. "I had this crazy dream last night. Remember our trip to Australia when we were little? We were by that lake, but as old as we are now, and these two gorgeous Australian girls wanted to hang out..." He smiled ruefully. "It was a good dream."

I smiled fiercely, tears springing into my eyes. "You keep me out of your dirty dreams, you hear me?"

He laughed. "Yeah, all right. I'm making a note right here on the table with my shiv. So what's up?"

My throat closed up again. I had to cough to be able to speak. "An opportunity's come up. A chance to fix things for us. I'm taking it, and if all goes well, I'll be back Sunday night."

"An 'opportunity'?" I could hear the scare quotes. "Mr. Reggio ask you to help with another truck full of stolen whisky?"

"No, nothing to do with Mr. Reggio." Not a bad guess, though. I'd never met a shadier math teacher in my life. "Look, don't worry about the details. But if things don't work out, you'll be hearing from Ev. She's agreed to make sure Max works his ass off for you."

His face tightened with suspicion, his eyes narrowing as he stared at the side of my face. "What's going on here, Chris? What are you talking about?"

"Don't worry about it," I said. "I just wanted to let you know before—well. Whatever. You'll be hearing from me Sunday night."

"Whatever it is, don't do it." His voice was suddenly heartbreakingly serious. "Please, Chris. Don't do it. Don't get in trouble because of me."

I lowered my chin, grinding my teeth as I fought for control. "It's going to be OK."

"Please. This is my fuck-up. Whatever happens, I'll own it. It's my responsibility. But I can't own you risking your—what? Risking your life? Committing some kind of crime? Whatever it is, I can't deal with you doing that for me."

My throat was getting all tight again. I wiped my eyes with the back of my wrist. "Look, I gotta go. But I'll be back Sunday night, and everything's going to be better, all right?" I knew if I stopped he'd cut in, make things worse. So I bulldozed on. "So just hang in there. It's all going to be fine."

"Please don't," said Justin, his voice thickening with the threat of tears. "Chris?"

"Love you, little brother." Then I jabbed my finger at the red button beneath his tear-streaked face and hung up.

THE DOCKING STATION was one of the few buildings in Miami that really looked like the future we were all supposedly living in. It rose against the skyline like an IKEA store and had the appearance of an Apple product. It gleamed in the Miami sun, smooth and pearlescent, all rounded curves and without any dirt to mar its surface. I'd seen a documentary on its construction and knew there were hundreds of windows in that smooth wall that nobody could make out from the outside.

The parking lot looked normal enough, at any rate. Asphalt bleached and cracked by the sun, and as many BMW's and Zero-Zeroes and Teslas as you could shake a stick at. I expected there to be a security gate or something, but nobody looked twice as I parked my beat-up Honda, leapt out and sprinted toward the front doors.

They were massive, and of course they slid open silently just before I ran into them. I burst into a huge lobby that was easily four stories tall and impossibly elegant, but I didn't have time to take in the decor. I ran up to the frosted glass reception desk and smacked both hands down on its surface.

"I'm Chris Meadows. Brianna Sachdeva is expecting me?"

The young man behind the desk froze, eyes wide, like a cat startled in an alleyway by the sudden flare of headlights. Then he forced an unconvincing smile, like one of those Uncanny Valley HugMe KissMe KillMe Dolls™. "But of course, sir. One moment please." He simply stared at me, eyes glazing over as he waited, and for a moment I thought he was being super passive-aggressive until I realized that of course Euphoria employees would have eye implants.

"Welcome to Euphoria, Mr. Meadows," said the young man with sudden animation. "My name is Carlisle Withers, and I'll be your guide for your onboarding. I see this is your first time visiting. Will you please keep your palm on the glass?"

A white handprint glowed to life on the frosted green glass beneath my hand, and I thought about the famous William Gibson quote: "The future's already here – it's just unevenly distributed." My students were still working with old iPads and dead tree textbooks, and here was tech they'd probably only ever see in movies.

I kept my hand on the print until it pulsed and faded away.

"Very good. I see your session this weekend is being covered by Ms. Sachdeva, and all the paperwork has already been taken care of." Carlisle rose to his feet and walked the length of the desk. I kept pace with him, moving deeper into the lobby. "Which means all that's left to do is process you into the system."

He stepped out from around the desk and gave me an actual bow. "If you will follow me?"

I tried for a smile that in all honesty probably looked more like a grimace as relief flooded through me. I'd made it. Trying to relax, I followed him through another set of opaque glass doors and into the depths of the station.

All the paperwork was already taken care of? That nagged at me. How certain had Brianna been that I'd accept? She'd only asked a couple of hours ago, and I knew how complex the sign-up forms could be even just for public VR stations. Something like Euphoria had to be infinitely more complex, didn't it?

We walked down a broad hallway whose entire left wall was a continuous screen that displayed a forest at what had to be over 8k definition—it looked completely real to my eye, and I had to resist reaching out to touch the trees as we passed them.

"Now," said Carlisle, "Brianna and her friends are awaiting you in the main pod. They've already been vetted and passed their physicals, so we'll just focus on catching you up to speed."

I nodded. There was nothing to say. Like everyone else, I'd geeked out about Euphoria at its launch. A computer game designed by our first true artificial intelligence? You bet I'd devoured every review and playtest. I'd even taken VR tours of the first docking center in Brussels, watched the onboarding videos, and spent countless hours exploring superficial VR facsimiles until I'd grown both frustrated and bored and forced myself to stop researching Euphoria altogether.

So nothing that followed was particularly surprising. First, I showered then changed into comfortable woolens with socks so thick I never wanted to wear shoes again. Then I lay on one of the new bio-reader table things that I'd again only ever heard of but never seen. The table checked my vitals while I watched videos about the Salvation Six coders who had designed Albertus.

When the physical test was complete, Carlisle popped his head around the doorway with a scary amount of animation and beamed at me. "Brianna has instructed us to skip all the orientation materials. She will be taking care of your in-world tutorial, and would like us to expedite the process. Is that all right?"

"Sure," I said, sitting up. "That's fine."

"Then if you'll follow me?"

He led me to an elevator which rose of its own accord to what might have been the third or fourth floor—there were no buttons or indicators—and from there we walked to a set of double doors and entered the pod room.

Seeing this space with my own eyes was surreal after hours spent examining it in VR. Subtle details made it more real, of course, despite the impeccable quality of the VR display; subtle markings on the gray carpet, smudges on one pod, the coolness of the air with a hint of mint, and the soft sound of the air conditioning.

But I noticed all of that in the back of my mind, because Brianna rose to her feet as I entered. She stepped toward me, a smile on her face that didn't touch her eyes.

"Finally! Each minute here is forty-five we're losing in Euphoria." She looked me up and down. "Hello, Chris."

I hated to admit it, but she still looked good. 'Voluptuous' was a word I only ever read and never in my life felt inclined to use, but Brianna brought it to mind in spades. She was shorter than me, her skin a rich brown, her hair so black it had blue tints – and oh, her face. Those lips. The things she had said to me while we dated. The kind of stuff that made you shiver with arousal even as you wanted to rear back in shock. Her eyes, always calculating, always evaluating, even in moments of passion. Everything had always been an act with her. A stratagem to accomplish her next goal.

It was also what made her such a fantastic gamer.

"Brianna," I said. "Thanks for this opportunity."

She waved her hand carelessly. "What can I say? I'm that magnanimous. Anyway, meet the rest of the team." There were five others lounging in white armchairs, three guys and two girls. None of them got up to meet me, though I recognized one of the girls from the first night I'd met Brianna at the club on the beach. They smirked in a way I didn't like until I realized what was up: in their eyes, I was just a level one noob. Of course they were going to give me attitude.

After Brianna rattled off their names, I gave them an ironic little bow. "Pleased to meet you," I said. *Just you wait till you see what I can do, assholes.*

"Now," said Brianna, "let's get down to business. We're all members of the Cruel Winter guild, and we'll be spawning in our safe zone between Castle Winter and its attendant village of Feldgrau."

One of her friends snickered. I frowned at them. What was so funny?

"The best part about Euphoria, of course, is how intuitive it is," said Brianna, ignoring her friend. "I felt like all my time watching the intro videos was a complete waste of money. I know you'll feel the same, given your skills. So. When you enter your pod, select Cruel Winter for your faction, set up your character however you like, and we'll all spawn together and take it from there. I'll teach you everything you need to know in-game."

I hesitated. This was overly simplistic. "Shouldn't we discuss group composition? I should pick a class that rounds out the team, no?"

Another snicker from the same dude. Arvid, was it?

"Don't worry about that," said Brianna impatiently. "This isn't Golden Dawn. Euphoria doesn't work that way. Just make whatever you want to play, and it'll be fine."

"All…. right," I said. *Weird.* "Any advice on my first build? Things I should look for? Stuff to avoid?"

"Didn't you hear her?" This was from Arvid again. I was genuinely amazed at how quickly I was coming to hate this guy. "It doesn't matter. Euphoria'll handle whatever you pick. Go ahead and make something rando if you want. That'll be even better."

Rando?

Brianna walked back to her armchair and then made a *shooing* motion with one hand. "We're all waiting on you, Chris. Sign your last contracts and waivers, generate your character, and then let's go."

I nodded uneasily and turned back to Carlisle, who had remained by the door. He was standing stiffly, brow slightly lowered, but when I stepped up to him he beamed once more. "Very well, Mr. Meadows. Please sign these final release docs. Paper copies. Antiquated, but what can you do? There will be a few more forms once you're in your pod, but you're almost finished."

I signed and then hesitated. I wanted to ask him what was up. Why had he been frowning? Had he had issues with this group before? Was he sad for me that I'd be spending six months in their company? Didn't matter. I wanted to tell him this wasn't for fun. This was for the cold, hard cash and the pardon I'd be walking away with.

"Great," said Carlisle. "Here's your pod, though it's not really a 'pod', per se. Lie down and I'll link you up."

There were six cushioned tables around the perimeter of the room, each a perfect eggshell white. I lay down and found it to be luxuriantly, almost ridiculously, comfortable.

"Now, this can be a little disorienting the first time," said Carlisle from behind my head. "The best thing you can do is relax and focus on your breathing. Euphoria will occur before you know it."

Brianna appeared by my side. She was smiling down at me in a possessive manner, her eyes gleaming with anticipation. "I'm so happy you decided to come, Chris. We're going to have so much fun together."

That look alone nearly made me sit up, but it was far too late. But if things got too obnoxious in there? I'd ditch her and her friends the moment I was confident in my abilities. So instead I smiled right back. "Yeah? So much fun, Brianna. I can't wait."

A warm band pressed around my brow as the circlet was lowered into place. My vision swam immediately. The last thing I saw was Brianna staring down at me.

I blinked, trying to clear away the white light, but to no avail. I was sitting in a cream-colored armchair like the ones Brianna and her friends had been using, but the room was gone. Instead, a white expanse surrounded me without limits or horizons.

Goosebumps ran down my arms. This was it. I was in.

To a degree, this was familiar. I'd been through enough VR character generation rooms that I actually relaxed back into the armchair, but even doing so hit home how amazing Euphoria was: I could feel the texture and coolness of the leather. As advanced as haptic feedback had become in even the most elite VR rigs, they were nothing like this.

I reached down and prodded my leg. I knew my body was lying still in the pod room; that nothing had actually prodded my leg. But my brain couldn't tell the difference. All this was taking place in my mind, controlled by the neural circlet I was now wearing.

Insane.

The gamer in me wanted to laugh in delight. I leapt to my feet and spun in a circle. Friction and gravity were set to earth normal. I pinched my arm. Yep. A little pain there, but nothing too sharp. Speaking of which, I actually felt amazing. I wasn't getting feedback from my actual body, but rather from Euphoria, and Euphoria was telling my mind that I was perfectly rested, filled with energy, and raring to go. I'd not felt this good, this *alive*, since—when? Not since hearing the news from Justin, at any rate. These last six months of teaching and courtrooms and jail visits had been an exhausted blur.

For the first time in forever, I felt like myself again.

Grinning, I looked around, and on cue an outline appeared before me. It cycled rapidly through different forms, all of them shadowy and humanoid, and this time I did give a delighted laugh. *Choose the form of your destructor!* Euphoria was reading my mind, locking in on my preferred tutor's form. I sat on the armchair's arm and watched as the shadowy silhouette quickly slimmed down and became a young, attractive woman.

Her white hair was cut boyishly short, an intricate tattoo of Lovecraftian monsters and flowers wrapped up her left arm, and she wore a wry, teasing smile that made me smile right back. She looked just like the kind of girl I'd love to go on a long road trip with, someone filled with energy, spunk, and loaded with sarcastic comebacks.

"So," she said, looking down at herself. "This is me. What a relief."

"Relief?" Her voice sounded so real. A lifetime spent playing with VR-simulated voices drove home how different a real person's voice sounded to any normal system's mimicry.

"Yeah. You've no idea how often I end up looking like a dark elf blow-up doll. And forced to talk like a child. Honestly, it's really hard to respect you human males when I can see what most of you are secretly looking for."

My smile widened. "I'm impressed. Look at you, already complimenting me and making me feel all shiny and special. I bet you do the same for these dark elf-loving dudes, don't you?"

Her eyes sparkled with mischievous humor. "Of course not. You're the only special guy I've ever, ever met."

This time I outright laughed. I knew she was manipulating me, and knew that she knew I was aware. What was brilliant was that she was purposefully mocking me in a way she knew I'd enjoy, and was *still* able to make me feel special, despite that level of awareness.

"This is great!" I slid off the arm into the armchair proper. "So. What do I call you?"

"My name's Nixie," she said.

"Right." Again, that was perfect. I'd half expected to have the option to name her, but having her own name made her more real. Part of me wanted to stop meta-observing everything and simply immerse, but another part was giddy at how good this all was. How sharp and slick and spot on. It made the prospect of entering Euphoria all the more exciting. Time for a quick test. "Watermelon turkey."

Nixie paused, one finely arched brow rising in confusion. "Excuse me?"

No matter how advanced the games I'd played, spouting nonsense at the NPCs always resulted in them acting weird and breaking their verisimilitude.

"Rotating scrotums." I watched her carefully. Time to see how good Albertus Magnus' AI really was. "Underbelly backwash, please."

She drew in a quick breath, paused as she narrowed her eyes, then gave me a pitying smile. "If that's your idea of flirting, I'm really glad I'm not an actual girl."

"Huh," I said. "Not a bad response."

"Oh…" said Nixie. "You're testing me. Gotcha. Want to spout some more gibberish? I can wait while you get it out of your system."

I gave her a golf clap. "Wow. I mean, really. You're just like talking to a real person."

"Um… yes." She gave me an overly polite smile. "Albertus Magnus, the Universal Doctor? Most advanced AI in the world? Ring a bell?"

"Sure," I said. "But it's one thing to hear about it. Another to actually get to test it out. Awesome. So, Nixie. What's next?"

"Character gen, of course. But first, a few preliminaries." She waved her hand and a blue screen appeared in the air before me. "I'm going to show you a number of pretty boring but life-defining legal docs for you to thumbprint. I advise you to read them all, but I won't be shocked if you skim."

"Sure," I said.

I spent the next half hour actually reading through the small print. Nixie acted quietly impressed, which made me feel savvy and sharp, though I knew—

Enough with the meta-commentary, I decided. I focused instead on what I was signing, and burned through all the pages.

The terms were standard stuff, from the terrifying medical disclaimers that I could die or go mad or suffer from a variety of maladies like 'ludoendocrinal dissonance' or 'glutamate excitotoxicity' to financial stuff that had all been signed already by Brianna. Finally, we got to a simple form.

"So, here we go," said Nixie, perching on my armchair's arm. "This is where you pick the difficulty level of your Euphoria experience. Given your Golden Dawn wins and record, I'm guessing you're going to go with either Maniacal Maniacal or Soul Grinder?"

Both levels glowed on the floating screen, but I flicked my fingers and scrolled past them, down to *Death March*.

"Expand that one, please."

Her playful expression fell away. "You sure?"

"Yup."

New text filled the screen, but Nixie slid off the armchair to crouch before me, reaching out to take my hand and get my attention.

"Listen, Chris. Death March is for real. I don't know what you've heard out there, but if you die in Euphoria while playing on that difficulty level you *will* die in real life. The neural band will fry your brain and there's no coming back from that."

"I, uh, are you supposed to put it that way to me?"

Nixie waved her hand, brushing my words away. "There's no 'supposed' to this. I like you. I know you think I'm just saying that to make you happy and feel special, but I really do. I don't want you to make a mistake here."

"Then why offer the option if you're going to try and argue me out of it? I know what it involves. I doubt anybody would ever pick it lightly."

"True," she said, "but still. We're talking real death here, Chris."

"I know." I clenched my fists and sat up. "If you're so reluctant to let me pick it, why is it even an option? Why did the Universal Doctor program a way for people to die in this game?"

"I don't know." She gave me a sad smile. "I'm part of Euphoria, true, and possess a limited degree of Albertus Magnus' capacity, but not nearly enough to divine his intentions. I don't know why he saw fit to insert Death March into the game, but in his ineffable wisdom... he chose to."

"Wait. You're part of him. How do you not know?"

"It's... complex. Think of it in terms of resource allocation on his part. But regardless, my limited perspective has led me to dislike the option, despite whatever greater purpose it serves. You won't get access to the full menu, in-game tutorials and so much more. Are you sure you want to go that route? You're going to be inside Euphoria for what feels like six months. To date, only two hundred and seventeen people have chosen that difficulty level, and of that number a hundred and thirty-seven have died, seventeen have survived, and the rest are still playing."

My stomach cramped. "I know. But I have to." I felt the ridiculous urge to tell Nixie about Justin. To treat her like a real person. Her eyes were glimmering in that way real people's do when they're feeling a lot of emotion, and her expression was open, vulnerable.

Instead, I sat up straighter and took control of myself. Nixie wasn't real, and I'd come here to work. "Death March, and all its consequent rewards, please."

She sighed. "Fine. There's a *lot* of paperwork to it."

"I'm sure there is. Let's get to it."

I spent the next two hours thumbprinting the densest legalese I'd ever read. When I was finally done, I sat back with a sigh. "Brianna and the others must be going nuts waiting for me."

Nixie smiled in a friendly manner. "For them it's been only a few minutes since you entered."

"Oh. Right. So. What's next?"

Nixie's smile became a grin. "The fun part. Time to make your character. Ready?"

I rubbed my hands together and sat forward. The fugue that had settled over my mind from reading so much morbid paperwork faded away. Nixie wasn't wrong. Character gen was one of my all-time favorite parts of these games.

Nixie bounced to her feet and snapped her fingers. A moment later, her eyes unfocused and she frowned.

"What is it?"

"That's strange."

Concern flickered through me. "What is?"

"I've never seen this before," she said, and then looked right at me. "I'm sorry, Chris. You're not going to like this."

3

I TRIED TO BE calm. Failing that, I tried to *sound* calm. "What's happening?"

"Normally, a new player has access to the full roster of different races, and within those parameters they then have the ability to modify their appearance to their heart's desire. However, it looks like your file's been locked."

"Locked?"

"An avatar has been pre-selected for you by Brianna, your sponsor."

"Oh, crap." I sat back, thoughts spinning. How bad was this going to be? Images of gimps in leather suits along with mewling bat babies and other horrors flew through my mind. Was this the other shoe dropping? Was she going to get revenge on me by forcing me into some horrendous avatar for the next six months?

"Here," said Nixie, and a copy of myself appeared beside her. The avatar was so real that it went beyond a reflection, being three dimensional and vividly real down to the last detail. "This is what she's picked."

I stood and stepped closer. "She's making me look like myself?"

"Almost. She's enhanced your appearance a little. Made you an inch taller, changed your muscle and body fat ratio, minor cosmetic details."

I stared at myself. Nixie was right. This was a slightly idealized version of myself. Perfect skin, stubble just the way Brianna had always said she liked it, hair trimmed, shoulders broad and a little more muscular. No belt of teacher's fat around the hips, no fatigue beneath the eyes. The small, star-shaped scar on the back of my hand Brianna had given me during a particularly nasty fight was also gone.

So this was what I might look like after a couple of months of Hellfit.

"Huh," I said. "That's better than a gimp."

"Much," said Nixie.

"But—why? Does it say in my file why she's forced me into looking like myself?"

"Nope."

I stepped back and slowly sank into my chair. What had at first seemed good news—not being forced to look like a pug or whatever—was starting to freak me out a little.

"My ex-girlfriend is forcing me to look like a hotter version of myself for the next six months." I tried the words out loud to see how they sounded. They sounded bad. I could almost hear Ev groaning and shaking her head. "That's… creepy."

"Brianna is your ex?" asked Nixie. "Yeah. That's definitely creepy."

"Thanks," I said. "Real comforting." I considered myself. I often picked humans as my go-to race due to their inherent flexibility when it came to min-maxing, but I'd kind of been looking forward to doing something completely different this time through. Get away from myself, my life, and spend six months wreaking havoc in the form of a minotaur or half-giant or the like.

But more importantly, my trust in Brianna was rapidly eroding. She was setting me up for something. Was this an attempt to get back together with me? It didn't feel like it. She'd not tried to flirt or ingratiate herself with me, and I knew what she was like when she was turning on the charm. No. Revenge, maybe? But that was ludicrous. Who used a $3000 Euphoria pass for revenge? And over what? My ending a toxic relationship she'd told me numerous times was so awful and pathetic that she didn't even recognize herself when she was with me?

People weren't that crazy and vindictive, were they?

Shit.

"Shall we move on?" asked Nixie.

"I guess. What's the next step?"

"Next, you have to select your class. You've been given free rein here. I'll run you through your options, and then tell you more about whichever classes interest you."

"Sounds good," I said, sitting back and crossing one ankle over my other knee. The sheer fun of character creation had become muted, however.

Nixie cycled my avatar through the fourteen different classes, telling me the class name and a brief description of each as she did so. My idealized self fell into a crouch, dagger held in reverse for rogue; stood straight, shoulders thrust back and a longsword propped on his shoulder for paladin; changed into a threadbare robe with a spell book tucked under his arm for wizard, and so on.

I listened, but not with my full attention. I already knew the basic human Euphoria classes. What gamer out there didn't?

Like I said, I'd obsessed over the tutorials when the game had first come out.

While I usually went for direct roles, opting for rangers or fighters who had the flexibility to work from both a distance and in melee, that didn't seem appropriate here. If Brianna was setting me up, I had to keep her and her friends in mind even more than the monsters and mobs I'd be facing. If this was a trap, then going the fighter route wouldn't help me any. I had to plan long term on dealing with her and her cronies, and direct combat would never be a good option against them all.

No. I tapped my lips in thought as Nixie cycled through the classes for a second time. My usual glass cannon with ranged and melee capacity would be a bad call this time through. I needed something that would allow me to escape her if things turned out for the worst. One of the mage classes, perhaps, or one of the rogues.

I sat up again, uneasy. "Nixie, tell me about the rogue-based classes."

"Sure," she said, and my avatar shifted position, crossing his arms and raising his chin in cold disdain, a curved dagger held in his right hand, a black bandana covering his mouth and nose.

"The three rogue-based classes are straight rogue, darkblade, and charlatan." Three screens opened up before me displaying each class's starting stat modifiers, initial talents and equipment.

"The straight rogue promises a life of endless adventure for those who love to live by their wits. Always one step ahead of danger, straight rogues have the greatest versatility in how they choose to grow. They have the greatest number of in-class skills and talents, and can develop into anything from a thief or bandit to an explorer or sniper."

I nodded. Standard stuff.

"Darkblades tread a darker road, focusing their skills on dealing death from the shadows. They blend magic and illusions with their talent with the blade. What they lose in generalities they gain in specialization: no other rogue class can match a darkblade in stealth, assassination skills, or arcane might."

Interesting. Very interesting.

"Finally, we have the charlatan, whose joy for life is matched only by his ability to convince others to succumb to his charm. Always found in the center of excitement, this rogue class specializes in social interactions, swaying others to his point of view through either diplomacy, seduction, or intimidation. The weakest of the three classes in combat, they instead tend to focus their efforts on alliances, friendships, and acquiring powerful followers."

Nope. Charlatan was right out. While I could see its utility and appeal to certain kinds of gamers, its social focus would only be a handicap if I had to escape from Brianna. Unless I covertly acquired those powerful followers… No. Too much of a gamble.

I had the urge to make my selection immediately, but the experienced gamer in me knew not to rush. I'd have to live with this decision for the next six months, which could be the rest of my life. Instead, I leaned forward and studied each class profile in detail, checking their talent tree progression, proficiencies and possible archetypes. Nixie waited patiently as I read in silence.

"The darkblade class depends heavily on mana points," I said. "Can you tell me more about those? How quickly they regenerate, how I can raise my cap, where I can find more in-game?"

"I'm sorry," said Nixie. "Your file states that you're skipping all basic tutorials."

"I—what?" My heart gave a little painful jump. "No, I mean, I said I wanted to skip that before, but now I definitely want to dig a little deeper. I'm not going to trust Brianna to tell me all this stuff. Please. Tell me everything."

"I'm sorry," said Nixie again with a pained smile. "Your sponsor has stipulated that you're to skip all basic tutorials. We can only do cursory level reviews of all classes, stats, and talents. I can't go into any of the mechanics beyond that."

"You can't…" I sat back, stunned. What the hell? How was I supposed to optimize if I couldn't even learn how Euphoria worked? I recalled Brianna's smirk. *I'll teach you everything you need to know in-game.*

"Crap," I said. How had I let her maneuver me into this situation? Not only was I going to be level one, but I was also going to be completely at her mercy.

I almost pulled out right there. I actually opened my mouth to ask Nixie about withdrawing from the game, but then hesitated. I thought of Justin. Locked up in his cell with his fate closing in on him. Fighting to stay optimistic, cracking jokes whenever we met, but with that growing undercurrent of fear and despair. I clenched my hands into fists. No. Screw Brianna. If she thought she could control me she was in for a huge surprise. I'd find a way to break free if I had to, and would use a lifetime of gaming experience to go it alone if she gave me no choice.

But I was going to win. Whatever she had planned, I'd make her regret it.

"Fine," I said. "Whatever. Let's go through all the classes in as much detail as you can provide. Let's go through the magic users next."

I forced myself to focus as Nixie reviewed the wizards, summoners, witches/warlocks, clerics, oracles, battlemages and enchanters. Nearly half of Euphoria's classes were arcane related, but the more I learned about the class system the more that made sense. The fighter class alone allowed for incredible diversity as you leveled up, making it so that you didn't need a half-dozen combat classes. The same went for straight rogues, wizards, and clerics. These were the four base level classes that in and of themselves allowed for incredible customization down the road.

The more specific classes like enchanter or darkblade needed a unique setup from the get-go; a particular blend of arcane and combat, or arcane and stealth. And of course magic was the most versatile combo maker there was, hence the six arcane classes.

I don't know how much time passed, but when Nixie finished reviewing the last class I got up and started to pace, arms crossed, frowning at the endless expanse of white space.

"It's a big decision," said Nixie, taking my place in the armchair and looping a leg over the armrest. "Want some help figuring out what you should play?"

"No, I think I've made up my mind," I said. "I don't want straight combat, so the knight, fighter, and ranger are out. The arcane classes take too long to become independent, so they're out too."

"You plan to adventure alone?" asked Nixie. "Most players band together to coordinate their skills."

"Trust me, I know. But I may have to hit the ground running and get the hell out of Dodge the minute I spawn. Needing six or seven levels of arcane classes to be able to do so isn't an option."

Nixie shrugged. "Your call."

"Yeah." I stopped before my avatar. "Ranger is tempting for the survival skills. But what's the point of being able to make it alone if I can be easily found? Nope. It's going to have to be a rogue class for me."

General flexibility or a focus on stealth, magic, and assassination? Again, when I really thought about it, it wasn't really a choice. "I'll take darkblade."

"Very well." Gold light shimmered around my avatar, and he assumed his haughty stance once more, curved dagger in hand.

I was starting to grow impatient, which I knew was a bad thing during character gen. But I needed to know what Brianna was up to. What did she have in store?

"Before we get into your stats, I can give you the following introduction." Nixie's voice was all business. "Euphoria is unlike any MMORPG game you have played before. Your every interaction with Euphoria is filtered through your character sheet."

I nodded. Sounded obvious.

"For example, your ability to pick up a stone will depend on your strength score—"

"Nixie, I've played lots of games before. This is pretty obvious."

"Keep listening," she said, sounding annoyed for the first time, "because most games limit your in-game abilities only when it comes to strength, speed, resilience and so forth. Physical characteristics. In Euphoria, your social and mental abilities are also filtered."

This grabbed my attention. I'd never heard of this before. "Wait. You're saying the game will make me dumber if I have a low intelligence score?"

"In a way." She held up her palm, cutting me off. "No, we won't edit your brain or actually lower your IQ. However, a low intelligence score will result in the game making certain things harder for you. The lower your intelligence score, the more complex and hard to understand any text will become. In extreme cases, they might all become completely illegible. A low charisma score will result in NPCs reacting poorly to your presence, and both intelligence and charisma will control what you actually say, regardless of what you *mean* to say."

I let that sit for a bit. "So if I go in there with a super low charisma, I could end up insulting people even if I try to compliment them?"

Nixie flashed me a grin. "I knew you were sharp. Exactly. I've found that most people treat their social scores like dump stats if they're not directly relevant to their class talents. Don't make that mistake in Euphoria. Or, if you choose to go that route, do so knowingly."

"Great," I said. "So as a level one noob, I'm going to be dumb and insulting as well as weak and helpless. Man. I hate level one."

Nixie winked at me. "It gets better as you level up. So. Here's your sheet."

It appeared before me on a slanted blue screen. I read it quickly, devouring it with all the interest and anxiety of an experienced gamer.

Chris Meadows

    Species: Human
    Class: Darkblade
    Level: 1
    Total XP: 0
    Unused XP: 0
    Guild: None
    Title(s): None
    Domain(s): None
    Allies: None
    Cumulative Wealth: 0

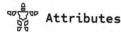 Attributes

Strength: 8
*Dexterity: 10 (+2 darkblade class bonus)
Constitution: 8
*Intelligence: 8
Wisdom: 8
Charisma: 8
Mana: 1/1

 Skills

Stealth: Basic (I)
- The shadows welcome you, and you intui-
tively know how to use them to mask your
presence.
- Basic (I) scales off dexterity and
gains a bonus from wisdom. Allows you
to evade cursory detection if you move
slowly. Unlocks stealth-related talents.

Backstab
- Attacks dealt when an opponent is
unable to defend themselves will strike a
vital spot for extra damage.
- Backstab scales off dexterity and gains
a bonus from strength and wisdom.

 Talents

Shadow Step
- You have the ability to move through one
shadow and emerge from another close by.
Mana Drain: 1.

I looked up at Nixie. "That's it?"

"The beauty in the Euphoria system lies within the interplay of those basic stats," she said. "Unfortunately, I'm prohibited from going any deeper into that aspect of the game. Now, being human allows you to raise a single stat by two points."

My first real decision. I fought hard to keep my disappointment and shock at bay. How long had it been since I'd played a first level character? I was used to sheets that were dozens of pages thick. This didn't even feel like a real character.

Focus, I chided myself. Not that there was much to deliberate. The asterisks next to dexterity and intelligence probably indicated that they were the primary stats for my class. That made sense; I'd most likely be gaining access to my magic a few levels on, which meant my intelligence was going to be key.

But that was a few levels down the road, and right now I needed to survive level one. Boost my con to increase my durability? No. If I got in a fight with Brianna and her friends, I was dead. Boosting my constitution to ten wouldn't make a lick of difference. I needed to max my stealth.

I wanted to laugh. 'Max my stealth'. As if Basic (I) based off a dex of twelve was going to give Brianna any trouble.

I clenched my fists again, then forced myself to relax. I didn't have any hard evidence yet that I was going to be screwed over. All she'd done was make sure I looked like, well, me. That was hardly proof of dastardly intentions, was it?

Who was I kidding.

"Dex, please."

My score pinged and turned into a twelve.

"Woo hoo," I muttered under my breath.

"Most players are despondent when they first view their sheets," said Nixie. "But don't sweat it. All spawning zones feature level-appropriate challenges. Play it smart, play it safe, and you'll find yourself gaining power faster than you can imagine." She grinned. "And as you know, power progression is one of the best parts of the game."

"Yeah, true." I sighed. What had I expected? "All right. What about my gear?"

"It's what you see on your avatar," she said. "You begin with a dagger and peasant's garb."

"Starting gold?"

"None," said Nixie. "Sorry."

"Not your fault. Anyways, Brianna promised me all kinds of loot as soon as I got into the game. Even if she doesn't give me something amazing, I'm sure she'll hook me up with *something*."

Nixie gave me a hopeful smile. "Well, that's about it. All that's left to determine is whether you want to begin the game unaffiliated or as part of a guild. That will in turn determine where you spawn, give you access to guild resources, and modify your interactions with NPCs of different guilds."

"Cruel Winter," I said with a sense of misgiving. Even if she was going to give me a tough time, having access to guild resources and support would be invaluable in Death March mode.

"Very well. Spawning location set." Nixie hesitated. "Best of luck, Chris. I hope Euphoria fulfills your every dream. I'll see you in six months."

"Thanks, Nixie." I hesitated. "There's no way to get hold of you once I'm in, is there?"

"No," she said. "Not at your difficulty level."

That in and of itself made me hesitate. Having Nixie in my corner while dealing with Brianna would have made a huge difference. But so be it. I took a deep breath, squared my shoulders, and gave her a grim nod. "I'm ready."

"Very well. Good luck hug?"

I laughed in sheer surprise, but the concern on her face caused my eyes to fill with tears. What the hell? I rubbed the tears away. Why was it that kindness often hit you harder than cruelty? Nixie stepped into my arms and gave me a tight squeeze. She smelled nice, and for a moment I simply held her tight. Then she stepped back, adjusting her bangs self-consciously, and smiled.

"Insertion beginning in three, two, one…"

My mind stretched nearly to the breaking point as I entered Euphoria Online.

My awareness expanded beyond my body, attempting to encompass an infinitude whose composite elements – mountains, hamlets, the thundering waves of an ocean in storm, the deep silence of an ancient forest – defied my ability to hold them all simultaneously within my mind.

They flashed by, intertwined by bands of golden light, and for a glorious, sanity-threatening second I was a silver fish evading a shadowed predator, a child sitting sullenly in a corner, a rutted street, a morass of broken rock, the sound of laughter on the wind, a bottle half filled with liquor, an algae-covered pond, an eagle spiraling over a battlefield –

I screamed, and my consciousness imploded, reducing to just myself. My mind reeled, and after that brief glimpse of the immensity of Euphoria I felt so painfully limited—and then even that comparative awareness faded. Leaving me standing in a meadow, the sun brilliant overhead, blindingly so.

I raised my hand and squinted against the sunlight. A breeze whispered past, and I thought I heard echoes in its passage, but I was mistaken. Instead, it bore the scent of pine sap, of grass and pollen, of the great wilderness that surrounded me, and I realized that I stood in a highland meadow, tall grass undulating like waves before the wind.

Euphoria.

I was in.

My heart pounded. I turned, trying to contain my excitement, to take in the immensity of the landscape, to get my bearings like a professional gamer and start taking control, but I couldn't focus on any single part.

Snow-clad mountains formed a formidable wall to my left, their slopes scarred by deep ravines and covered in a dark forest that grew right down to the edge of the meadow. A beaten path extended toward a distant lake of hammered silver. A large, ruined building stood a dozen yards off to my right, the meadow ending beyond it at a cliff, past which extended a rolling land made dim by distance, the mountains on the far horizon reduced to pale-blue silhouettes. The sky was vast and filled with towering cumulus clouds like the anvils of the gods themselves.

Exhilaration filled me, and I let out a raucous whoop as I spun and grasped at my head. My VR previews had been an insult to the reality of this place. I'd never imagined it would be this *beautiful*, that the colors would glow, that everything would appear so raw and wondrous and vast.

Grinning like a fool, I turned to examine the meadow's sole building.

That's odd.

What had once been a longhall was all but destroyed. Its stone walls were blackened, and its roof collapsed. A large part of the front wall had been knocked inward as if by a wrecking ball.

I studied it, my elation giving way to confusion.

Had the guild just been raided? If not, what a weird choice for a spawning point. Where were the vendors or the bank?. Even in the most basic games you could expect a quest giver to get you started.

The wind moaned through the longhall's gaping windows, and I felt the first prickles of unease. Where was everybody? For that matter, where was Brianna and her crew? Why weren't they here as planned?

I turned back to the footpath and sighted down its length. It curved past the distant lake to a small village of exceedingly modest appearance, and — looming above it on a mountain bluff—perched a massive castle.

From this distance I couldn't make out much detail, but the building's presence provided a measure of comfort. At least I hadn't been stranded in the middle of nowhere.

Frowning, I approached the ruins, then stopped. The ground was strangely flat, artificially so. I crouched and parted the high grass, revealing slabs of stone under a thin layer of dirt. I yanked out some of the grass and brushed away the earth. White stone, with what looked like a faded crimson stripe, disappeared into the grass on both sides.

Why would the spawning point for the Cruel Winter guild be so completely abandoned?

I strode up to the ruined longhall. The destruction hadn't been recent; weeds had grown thickly inside the blackened walls, and swallow's nests littered the eaves.

Near what had been the front door, I found an old sign. Two rusted chains trailed from its top, indicating that it had once hung beneath a beam. **Welcome to Cruel Winter**, it read in a medieval script with the faded image of a white wolf's head beneath.

I tossed the sign aside.

What had happened here?

I cupped my hands to my mouth. "Brianna?" The vast landscape devoured my paltry yell, and I became painfully aware of my lack of armor and the fact I only had a small dagger for defense. "Brianna!"

Nothing.

I clenched my fists and cursed myself for a fool. Why had I trusted her? Why had I thought she'd play this straight? I'd no idea what she was playing at, but I wouldn't stand around here waiting for her. Games rewarded initiative. I'd head down to the town and discover what was up. As a guild member in my spawn zone, I should be safe. Right?

I crossed the meadow, my awe at Euphoria's beauty replaced by doubt and unease. When I reached the far side where the path sloped steeply down toward the far lake, I stopped.

Something was wrong with the village. Even at this distance, I could tell that half the buildings were little more than ruins. No people walked down there, either. No signs of life at all.

Fear gripped my gut. Forcing myself to take measured breaths, I looked up at the distant castle. No pennants fluttered in the wind. Its drawbridge was lowered over the chasm that separated it from the road. Large holes were obvious in its vine-covered walls. Buzzards circled slowly overhead.

Movement drew my attention toward the tree line. My heart hammered. I rested my hand on my dagger's pommel. It might look pathetic, but it provided a modicum of comfort. "Brianna? What the hell are you playing at?"

Brianna didn't step out from the trees. Instead, two massive figures emerged. They each stood about seven or eight feet tall, with huge sloping shoulders and great bellies under their hide armor. Their skin was gray and splotched with liver marks, but their faces were what evoked terror.

Narrow eyes, bulbous noses, and mouths that were wide gashes filled with sharp teeth and massive twin tusks. Their ears were pointed and tufted with bristly hair, and even from where I stood, their rancid reek of old sweat nauseated me.

I couldn't move. Each of them held a tree limb larger than I was. They stopped and stared back, equally surprised. Fighting them would be impossible.

What the hell are two ogres doing in a newbie zone?

They exchanged a glance and split up, each moving wide to flank me. In their small eyes I saw a terrifying combination of avarice, hunger, and delight.

"Shit!" I started to backpedal. "Shit, shit, shit!"

They moved slowly, not wanting to startle me, but each of their steps was deceptively long. In a matter of moments, I'd be flanked. What could I do? Stealth, Basic (I)? The very thought made me want to laugh and sob at the same time.

Backstab?

Nope. I had only one option.

I spun on my heel and broke into an all-out sprint. Terror gave me wings. The long grass thrashed at my knees as I ran toward the far edge of the meadow. Both ogres bellowed and broke into a run. I felt as if I were trying to outrace an avalanche.

The far end of the meadow ended in a series of cascading cliffs. None of them more than a drop of a dozen yards. If I could get over the edge, drop down into a ravine, and activate Basic Stealth—

Something hit me between my shoulder blades and lifted me off my feet. Pain wrenched my body, and I flew.

I hit the ground, rolled several times, and came to a stop. I couldn't breathe. Couldn't move. I strained, but all I could do was make a high-pitched whistling sound. Pain enveloped me, like I was on fire.

Summoning all my reserves, I flopped onto my stomach and set my eyes on the meadow's edge. I stabbed my dagger into the dirt, planning to use it to haul myself forward, but it hit the flagstone and stopped dead.

One of the ogres laughed gutturally as it loomed. Desperate, I turned over, hatching a wild plan to slice at its palm if it tried to grab me. It didn't. Instead, its head blocked the sun as it lifted its club high.

Panic. Wild, terrifying horror. My chest was still locked up. Black motes danced before my eyes. I glanced around the meadow in desperate hope, but nobody was there. Brianna wasn't appearing to provide a last second save.

This was it? Just a few minutes into Euphoria, and I was going to die? Incredulity and fury filled me. My dagger shook as I raised it. The second ogre stepped up on my other side, club propped over its shoulder.

Nowhere to go. No way to hide. I couldn't even stand. All I could do was lie frozen in the ogre's shadow and stare up at certain death. The ogre grunted, grasped his club with both hands and brought it crashing down with all its strength toward my head.

4

I SCREAMED IN BOTH fury and terror—then sank into the ground. It felt like I'd fallen into a mass of velvet, smooth and delicious against my skin. Darkness embraced me, the world disappeared and took the ogres with it.

A second later I emerged into a vertical crack in a cliff face, sliding out of the shadows to lodge amongst the rocks. I wanted to scream again as pain shot through me, but shock and some vestige of self-control helped me clamp my jaws shut.

My back was killing me. Waves of pain rolled up and down my spine, and sweat burned my eyes and soaked my tunic. With a gasp I fought to remain wedged in that crack and not topple out to plummet to the ground far below.

From over the top of the cliff came roars of anger. The ogres. My chest finally unlocked and I inhaled with a shuddery gasp. I wanted to continue sucking in the air, but the sound was too loud—I clamped my hand over my mouth and tried to bite back my cries.

My vision swam, but some sixth sense told me this was the critical moment. Wedged deep in the shadows as I was, I craned my head back and looked up.

The ogres had stepped up to the cliff edge and were looking around in confusion.

I went to move deeper into the shadows but caught myself in time. I remained completely still. Movement might draw their eye, no matter how small.

Don't see me, I prayed. *Please, please, please don't see me. Come on, Stealth Basic (I). Come on!*

The ogres grunted and turned away. Then they were gone, and a chime sounded, though I couldn't tell from where it came. I allowed myself a hissing inhalation and closed my eyes. I'd nearly died. The knowledge hit me like a cartload of bricks. I said the words to myself again: I nearly died.

I leaned my head back, adjusting my position amongst the rocks. The pain was making me nauseous. Thank god I'd not gone for fighter or wizard. I'd be a dead man right now if I had.

The minutes passed slowly. It felt like an eternity, but I didn't dare try to climb out of the crack and look around. What if the ogres were still there?

I shivered. Euphoria's ethereal beauty had turned cold and cruel. I opened my character sheet. No change other than my mana having dropped to zero. Had I Shadow Stepped? I must have. There was still no sign of hit points or the like. I'd have to take my health cues directly from my body.

"Chris?"

I'd somehow fallen into a doze, and cracked my head against the rock as I startled.

"Chris?" Brianna's voice was incredibly faint as if she were far away.

"Here," I croaked. My voice was little more than a rasp. "Here!"

I forced myself to focus, to assess. I still had no mana. No Shadow Stepping out. With a grimace, I reached up and took hold of a large ridge of rock. I tried to haul myself up and screamed. Or tried to scream. A thin hiss was all that emerged from my throat as the muscles in my back snarled and coiled in agony.

Blinking away tears, I struggled to climb, but could barely pull myself up without fainting from the pain.

"Brianna!" I croaked. I tried again, pain searing my throat. "Brianna!"

Nothing.

I put everything I had into climbing, ignoring the pain and skirting the edge of blacking out. Damn my constitution of eight! Eight strength wasn't helping much either. For all that my hands could find the right ridges and outcroppings, pulling myself out of the crack was a nightmare.

Shaking, shivering, soaked in sweat all over again, I finally reached the top.

Five people stood before the ruined longhouse. They held hands and were facing each other in a circle while wisps of purple and white fire swirled around them.

"No," I whispered. I wanted to wave, but to even let go with one hand would send me sliding back down. "Brianna!"

The fire grew into a funnel, hiding them from sight, and then it collapsed upon itself and was gone, taking the five figures along with it.

I stared, glassy-eyed with shock. A mass teleportation spell. They'd left me.

A cold wind whipped over the meadow, setting the high grass to whispering, and then swirled past me, cooling my brow, and was gone.

I was all alone.

It took serious mental effort to gather myself and finish climbing out of the crack. When I finally cleared the edge I rolled out onto the grass and lay staring up sightlessly at the clouds.

Death March. I was in Death March mode with only a dagger and abysmal stats in a ruined guild site where the wandering mobs were ogre level or worse.

I don't know for how long I lay there, but eventually basic survival instincts kicked in. If I didn't move, I'd be found by something, and I was in no condition to even pretend to resist. With much cursing and effort, I stood and then hobbled back to the longhouse. I slipped in through the toppled double doors, entered the rubble- and rafter-strewn main hall, and then found an out-of-the-way corner from which I could sit and watch the entrance.

Think. I'd spent too much time already in panic mode. What could I do? Brianna wouldn't have abandoned me after a quick search of the meadow. She'd be teleporting around, trying to see where I might have wandered off to.

Or that's what she probably did half an hour ago, or however long it had taken me to recover from the climb. I groaned. Who was to say she hadn't given up?

I could set a fire. Send smoke up into the sky, draw her back. Gamble that she'd return before the ogres.

No. I knew the ogres were in the area. I'd no idea if Brianna still was.

Time to play smart.

First thing I needed to do was heal. If Brianna came back, she'd check this burnt-out building again. My best bet was to rest, regain my health, and hope she'd show. Shock, pain, and exhaustion settled over me like a leaden cape. I stared mutely at the long-house doors until fatigue stole over me and I slept.

Night had fallen when I awoke. I stretched and felt a bubbly sense of energy in my limbs, an eagerness to get going. I paused to marvel; most of the pain was gone only to be replaced with serious hunger pangs.

No sign of Brianna.

I climbed to my feet, crept to the closest window, and peered out to examine the meadow.

The grass was silvered by a full moon that hung low over the western mountain peaks, but right now I didn't care for Euphoria's artistry. What mattered was survival.

After watching the meadow for a good five minutes and not spotting any threats, I checked my character sheet. My single point of mana had returned, so I made my way out the door and along the wall to the building's corner.

Still nothing.

I bit my lower lip. Hang out and wait for Brianna some more, or take the initiative and try to find someone in the town below? Despite its abandoned appearance, you never knew. Perhaps I'd find some food and water.

The thought of food made my stomach growl and that decided me. Hunched over low, I scurried across the moonlit meadow and toward the path that led to town. I kept a wary eye on the forest's edge to my left. The ogres were under no compunction to emerge from the same spot again, but something primal forced me to keep an eye on it.

I reached the path and made my way down. Like the meadow, this stretch betrayed the remains of a once-grand street, and here and there rose ruined, creeper-clad columns that might once have been sources of light or celebratory markers.

The lake gleamed like a silver coin. To my despair, there were few sources of light in the village, and those few were green fires on its far side. I kept going, however. Food. I'd never had to suffer hunger while playing virtual reality games. Sure my character would often become hungry, but me, the player? Never. All I'd ever had to do was pull off my headset and grab a bite. Euphoria Online was a completely different ball game, and getting a sense of all the downsides. Hunger. Thirst. Pain. It was one thing to intellectually know you'd experience them, another to feel your stomach roil and gurgle.

The path entered the forest as it leveled out. Should I leave the path to avoid trouble? With my terrible stats, I'd probably get lost the second I did. So instead I crept forward, listening intently. The woods were quiet. Because it was night time, or because something dangerous lurked close by?

Suddenly, a level in ranger sounded like an attractive proposition.

Nothing waylaid me, however, and five minutes later I emerged back out into the open, the lake before me, the small town on its left shore. I hesitated. The moon was so bright that I doubted Shadow Step would work in the open. Was that someone walking slowly between two of the closest houses? I squinted then shook my head. I looked up at the dark castle. Nothing there, either.

With a sigh, I decided to follow the forest's edge to where it came closest to the village, and only then leave its shelter. I moved at a jog, trying to stay quiet and having a heart attack each time I stepped on a twig or caught my foot on a root.

A splash disturbed the water of the lake. I looked over, expecting to see the expanding ripples that indicated a curious fish, but instead a long, suckered tentacle undulated in the air in the middle of the lake. It slipped sinuously back into the water and vanished.

I stood there, eyes wide. That tentacle had been longer than I was tall. I'd killed scores of underwater creatures like that with my Golden Dawn paladin, but here? With this noob character? I wouldn't have a chance.

I ran my hand through my sweat-matted hair. What the hell kind of zone was this? Ogres? Lake monsters? Where the hell were the cute goblin mobs or rats for me to cut my teeth on and level up?

I ran the rest of the way to the crossing point then spent a good ten minutes nerving myself up for the dash to the closest village building. This close, I could make out more detail. It had the look of a typical medieval town, built where a broad stream flowed down into the lake with a quaint bridge arching over it. The buildings were rugged and made of stone, but about half of them had been demolished or knocked over, leaving a wasteland of ruins from which the few surviving buildings emerged.

No lights. No smell of smoke. Just a clear and aching silence that made me certain of my solitude.

A quick dash would take me to a group of three small homes at the village's edge. They were clustered together as if in fear. I bit my lower lip, took one last look around, then ran hunched over nearly double as quickly as I could.

For some ten seconds I felt heart stopping terror as I ran across open ground, then I fell into a crouch in the shadows of the closest building and tried to listen over my pounding pulse. I waited till I was sure nothing had spotted me, then inched up to the closest window and peered inside.

Darkness and the faint smell of rotting meat. Great. Were the original inhabitants still here? I moved to enter then froze: this was a fantasy world. Who was to say the bodies wouldn't come back to life to welcome me with a big hug? I stared down at my curved knife. How much use would it be against zombies?

A muffled curse sounded ahead and I nearly leapt into the abandoned house regardless. A figure darted through the gloom, briefly visible between two houses close by, followed by what looked like a half-dozen rats. Well, rats if they grew as large as dogs.

Instinct kicked in. I ran closer. Panting for breath, cursing my low constitution, I hit the closest wall, pressed myself against it, then edged along till I could peer into the courtyard beyond.

The figure had backed herself into a corner. She held a scepter of some kind before her, the prongs at the top glowing with a cold blue light, illuminating both her wide-eyed panic and the four rat-dogs that were edging closer.

None of them had noticed me. My throat was dry. Each rat-dog stood taller than my knee, their bodies supple and muscled under their smooth coats, and their tails looked to end in scorpion stingers.

Great.

The woman was jerking her scepter from one side to the other as if trying to keep it directly before each rat-dog. It wasn't working.

Moving as quietly as I could, I ghosted into the courtyard, then ran to the closest rat-dog. My feet barely whispered over the cobblestones, and at the last moment the girl's eyes widened as she saw me. I bit back a cry and stabbed my dagger between the rat-dog's shoulder blades.

The dagger sank in to the hilt and the rat-dog shrilled, spasming and lashing down at my hand with its stinger.

But I didn't wait. The moment my dagger hit home, I yanked it free and desperately thought of Shadow Step, willing myself with all my being to appear on the far side of a second rat-dog that was twisting to face me.

Shadows coiled and enveloped me. For a moment I drowned in nothingness and then I stepped out into the darkness beside my next target.

No time for hesitation. Years of gaming in VR served me in good stead. stabbed the rat-dog's neck. The tip of the blade slid off bone and sank deep; the rat-dog chittered and then its stinger plunged into my shoulder.

I cried out more in shock than pain and leapt back, but already throbbing heat was spreading through my muscle, followed quickly by numbness.

My heart sank: neither of my blows had been mortal. All four of the rat-dogs focused on me, and the closest— the one whose neck I'd sliced—crouched as if preparing to leap right for my throat.

I was out of mana. I couldn't engage Stealth with them all staring at me. No way to Backstab. I shot a desperate glance at the woman. "Help!"

She thrust her scepter into the air. "From the heart of glaciers, blue-green to black, I summon forth the coldest shards and send them to attack!"

The lines were a little cheesy, sure, but I cheered regardless as hand-sized shards of ice rained down upon the rat-dogs with stunning speed and force.

The two I'd wounded quickly succumbed; a dozen new wounds opened across their bodies and they collapsed before the assault. The other two hesitated, then ran off, disappearing into the night without a sound.

When the ice storm ended I let out a shocked laugh and slid down the wall to my ass. A chime sound from somewhere close. My left arm had gone completely numb and I couldn't move it.

"Come on!" said the woman, reaching to hook her free hand under my arm and hoist me up. "What the hell are you sitting down for?"

"Funny way to say thanks," I mumbled. The throbbing heat was now working its way up my neck and across my chest. Whatever the poison was, I'd clearly failed my constitution save.

The woman didn't quip back, but instead hauled me across the courtyard and into a doorway, pausing only to scoop up a hempen sack. I staggered in the dark, but she knew where she was going; we crossed the room, stopped as she lifted a trapdoor of some kind, and then she turned me around.

"There's a ladder leading down. You'll have to descend in the dark. We can't risk being spotted. Hurry!"

I sheathed my dagger and carefully knelt. My foot found the trapdoor's edge, then tapped around till I found the ladder's uppermost rung. With care I climbed down, fighting off the stupor that was stealing across my mind, doing my best with only one functioning arm. Perhaps fifteen rungs down, I hit the floor and stepped away with a stagger.

A small room. I could tell from the closeness of the air. The ladder creaked; the trapdoor closed, a bolt slid home, then the woman climbed the rest of the way down and a small ball of soothing white light appeared over her open palm.

I got my first good look at her. Early twenties, human but with pointed ears, and with shoulder-length black hair held back by a silver band about her brow. She was attractive in a hard-bit-ten way, striking more than pretty, with no softness in her eyes as she examined me.

"Level one?" She sounded like my existence personally insulted her. "You're level one?!"

"Yeah, yeah, try it from this side." I looked around for somewhere to sit. As far as lairs went, it left a lot to be desired. A pallet along one wall. A small chest. A bucket that absolutely reeked, and a small pile of books. One wall was honeycombed with shelving from which the necks of hundreds of dusty wine bottles emerged. "Nice digs. I like what you've done with the place. And wine. Brilliant."

"Sit," she snapped. I didn't resist, and sank onto the small chest. "I don't have any healing spells, but I do have this." She pulled out a vial from a pouch. She shook it till it emitted a soft blue light.

"A glow stick?" My thoughts were racing, making it hard to focus. "You want to party?"

"A healing potion," she said. "One I'd been saving for myself. But you did technically save me, so..." She grimaced, plucked the cork free with her teeth, and held the vial out to me.

I poured its contents down my throat. *Freaking delicious.* Like a carbonated tangerine and pomegranate juice thing. The pain faded along with the numbness; the last tweaks in my back disappeared; and even the puncture mark in my shoulder smoothed over.

"Wow," I said, holding up the potion. "That was great. Can I have more?"

I paused as she frowned at me. That's not what I'd meant to say. Then I closed my eyes and grimaced. "Sorry. I've got a charisma of eight. Didn't mean to say it like that."

She let out a long-suffering sigh, sat on her pallet, and covered her face with both hands.

"Hey," I said. *Don't insult her, don't insult her.* "Uh, you look pretty upset."

She rubbed at her face, then dropped her hands into her lap and leaned back against the wall. "Three weeks I've been fending for myself, and now the first person I meet is a level one noob with charisma eight. Is this a joke? Is Albertus Magnus personally trying to screw me over for something I've done?"

I didn't know what to say. Maybe changing the topic would be a good move. "You a member of Cruel Winter?"

She nodded. "I thought I was the only member left." Her eyes narrowed as she studied me, then she laughed. "You chose to join up? So you're not just a level one noob, you're also an idiot?"

I frowned. "I see you've got charisma eight as well."

"No," she said. "Charisma fourteen."

"Oh. So you were being rude on purpose."

"I'm sorry." She rubbed at her eyes again. "It's been a very long, very frustrating three weeks. I thought I'd surprise my old friends by logging back in, only to discover that everybody's dead, the castle and village are slowly turning into raid dungeons, and I'm stuck here for the next five months unless I decide to end my session early and forgo my payment. I'm this close." She held up her thumb and forefinger with an inch between them. "This close."

"I see. So you don't know what happened here either?"

"No idea. I joined Cruel Winter back when Euphoria first hit, and played two sessions. It was amazing. Then... then work happened, life got busy, and I took a five-month break in the real world. Lost touch with everybody. An opportunity to play with this corporate account came around and I decided to surprise my old guild and just appear—and this is what I've come back to."

"Can't you die on purpose and respawn somewhere else?"

"I'm Cruel Winter. I respawn in the highland meadow."

"Why don't you make a new avatar then?"

She looked away. "My corporate account's locked. I can't make a new avatar."

"Oh." That sounded weird, but she clearly didn't want to elaborate.

"Where's the closest other town?"

She gave a hollow laugh. "Three months away on foot. Euphoria is huge."

"Great." I leaned my head back against the wall. "But hey. I'm glad I ran into you. You may not be excited to see me, but I'm thrilled to have finally met someone else."

She studied me. "What are you even doing here?"

"Long story. I let my ex manipulate me into playing. Turns out she's a lot more vindictive than I thought."

"Oh," said the girl. "Oh. That sucks. I'm really sorry."

"Yeah, me too. But I'm not giving up yet. I've got six months in here and I'm going to make it work."

"That's... optimistic of you. Those draugr we fought are the lowest level mobs here in Feldgrau. I'm level eight and I can barely take a couple of them on myself. I've been killed twice already by wraiths, had my head torn off by a skeletal champion, and that's with staying away from the charnel pit on the far side of town. We're surrounded by the restless dead here. This whole region is full of high-level monsters and mobs. You're not going to have an easy time leveling without dying."

I'd guessed, but hearing it out loud hit me like a blow to the chest. Death March mode meant no second chances. No respawning. No nothing but this one shot.

"My name's Lotharia." She reached out and squeezed my wrist. "And don't worry. Each time you die, I'll head right on up to the highland field to greet you and return your gear. We'll find a way to make this work."

I covered my face with both hands.

"What?" asked Lotharia. "What did I say?"

5

"**Y**OU WHAT?" Lotharia was staring at me as if I had casually revealed that I liked to eat babies. "You came here in Death March mode?"

I decided I didn't have to meet her eyes just then, so instead casually examined the wine bottles. "Yeah. I know how it sounds."

"Absolutely insane," she said. "I mean, Death March itself is one of the most awful concepts ever, but to pick that and come *here*? Didn't you do any research at all?"

"Nope. My ex planned it that way. She called me an hour before we were due to log in."

I risked a glance. She was still staring at me incredulously. "And you wanted to game so badly you threw all caution to the wind and just dove head first into this craziness?"

"Yeah, something like that. I need the pardon."

She snorted, clearly not impressed.

"Not for myself," I said, tone growing hard. "I'm doing this for my brother. He's in serious trouble with the law and it's not his fault."

"Oh," she said. "I'm sorry to hear that. But wasn't there a less… suicidal way to go about helping him?"

"Like I said, my ex lied to me. And to be honest, I was the one who chose to Death March it."

"What a mess." She pinched the bridge of her nose. "What are we going to do?"

"What I always do when I game. Level up. Become the apex predator." It sounded good, but they were empty words. I took down a bottle of wine and stared at it intently. How the hell was I supposed to level up here?

There was a long, awkward silence. To break it, I drew my dagger and plunged its tip into the cork, which I then twisted around and withdrew with a pop.

"You tried any of these yet?" I asked, holding the bottle out to her.

"I—actually, no, not yet. Thanks." She took the bottle and drank. "Pretty good."

I sat as she handed it to me. "So, look. I've played my fair share of games, but you're going to have to help me get a handle on Euphoria. My character sheet is too bare-bones for me to make the appropriate min-max decisions. What can you tell me about the mechanics here?"

"I know. I freaked out a bit when I saw my own sheet three weeks ago. It's been really stripped down since I last played."

"Oh?" That was interesting. "It's changed?"

"Yeah," she said, wiggling her butt a bit to get comfy on her straw pallet. "When I first played, it was much more transparent. You could see your hit points, mana regen rates, plan out your whole skill and talent progressions by researching the relevant trees. Now it's all gone."

"Huh." I took a swig and handed her the bottle. It *was* good. A little sweet, kind of blueberry-ish, but nice. "I wonder why."

"I remember some talk going around before I left the first time. A couple of our members were actually part of the original Euphoria beta test team. They speculated that the AI was trying to find the right balance of immersion and fun. Perhaps he decided having too many numbers on your sheet was ruining the experience. So he cut them down to help people get more 'in character'."

"That's arbitrary, though. I love working my sheet. It's a huge part of any game's appeal for me. If anything, not having that full access has made me really frustrated."

"Yeah," said Lotharia despondently, and twirled a strand of her hair around her finger. For a moment she stared out at nothing, chewing the tip of her hair. "I know what you mean. But what can you do?" Suddenly, she looked up. "Hey, did you hear a chime after the fight? That alerts you to XP gains. You checked your sheet?"

"No." With all that had happened, I'd not thought to check my sheet. I toggled it open before me, then paused. "Can you see my stats?"

She gave a wry laugh. "Don't worry. Not without your permission."

"Not like there's much there. Here, I'll share it with you. How do I... oh." At the thought, a small portrait of Lotharia had appeared in the top right. I reached up and tapped her image. It pulsed gold once and then returned to normal.

Lotharia sat up straight as my sheet opened before her. "Oh, wow. I'd forgotten how awful level one was. Eight, twelve, eight, eight, eight, eight. Ridiculous."

"Tell me about it," I said. Three little windows popped up over my sheet. A shudder of excitement ran through me. Even minor updates were a step in the right direction. I read the first.

> ♔ You have gained 45 experience (15 for sur-
> viving the ogre encounter, 10 for assisting
> in killing of two draugrs, 20 for running
> off the draugr pack). You have 45 unused XP.
> Your total XP is 45.

Lotharia gave a low whistle. "You survived an ogre encounter?"

"Barely," I said. "More luck than anything else."

"Still, impressive."

I examined her surreptitiously through my screen. Was she mocking me? Didn't look like it. I whisked the top window away, and read the second one.

> ✦ Your attributes have increased!
>
> Charisma +1
> Dexterity +1
> Constitution +1 (Con increase is depen-
> dent on one night's good rest.)

> ⚔ You have learned new skills. *Athletics: Basic
> (I), Survival: Basic (I).*

"Not bad," I said, looking up at Lotharia with a grin. "Charisma nine! How do I sound? A little more irresistible?"

"Oh, you're plenty resistible, don't you worry," said Lotharia. "And don't get too cocky. Just saying hello to someone or surviving a fight will earn you XP and new skills at level one. By the time you reach my level, you'll have to do much more to earn the same amount. Killing a draugr pack won't even register for folks around level fifteen or whatever. Enjoy the life of ease while you still have it."

"Thanks. Just the right thing to say to the Death March guy."

Lotharia covered her mouth, eyes going wide. "Sorry."

"Charisma nine joke. All right, one window left. Let's see."

 New talent advancements available!

Adrenaline Surge
XP Cost: 25
- Adrenaline Surge allows you to temporarily boost your physical stats, followed by an extended cooldown period during which you are subject to Exhaustion.
- All physical stats are boosted by +2 for a number of seconds equal to your Constitution x2. This is followed by a cooldown period of -2 to all stats for a number of seconds equal to your Constitution x4.

Sabotage Defenses
XP Cost: 30
- You deal damage to an opponent's armor, lowering their defensive capabilities instead of dealing actual damage.
- All forms of armor can be damaged, reducing your opponent's defensive ratings by an amount equal to the damage dealt.

Uncanny Aim
XP Cost: 25

```
- You can now hurl daggers and other
handheld projectiles with greater accu-
racy at longer distances.
- All ranged attacks with small, handheld
weapons now receive double your dexterity
bonus.

Astute Observer
XP Cost: 25
- You become attuned to your environment,
achieving a heightened state of alertness
and awareness.
- This ongoing passive effect boosts your
perception as if you had Wisdom 14 and
were carefully scrutinizing your environ-
ment.

Minor Magic
XP Cost: 45
- You gain access to magical tricks
common to all arcane adepts.
- You gain access to three cantrips which
you can cast at will.
```

That little thrill became exponentially bigger as I studied my new options. "You see what I'm looking at?"

"The joys of gaining XP. Sure." Was that wry amusement in her voice?

I read through the five new talents again, not skimming this time in my excitement but instead taking my time with the details. Adrenaline Surge sounded great for dire emergencies like being pinned by a couple of ogres—I could really see it helping get me out of a tight corner. But while eighteen seconds was pretty good, the cooldown period could be a killer: half a minute of exhaustion right after.

I skipped Sabotage Defenses. I was nowhere near close to engaging in that kind of tactical approach to combat. Uncanny Aim? I wondered if I could Backstab from a distance. That would be a nice combo—but would result in me losing my knife on my first attack. Nope.

I lingered over Astute Observer. An ongoing passive effect sounded pretty great, and as squishy and defenseless as I was out here, being able to see trouble coming before it hit me could prove crucial. I tapped my lips in thought, then moved on to Minor Magic. Endless cantrips could be useful too, albeit limited. If the Euphoria ones were anything like I'd experienced in the past, their utility would be dependent on their user's creativity.

"I'm thinking Astute Observer." I pushed my screen aside. "What do you think?"

"Strong choice." From the confidence in her tone, I knew she had enough gamer in her to make character progression a worthy subject. "The others are pretty great, but right now you need to focus on not getting killed. None of the others, except for maybe Adrenaline Surge, help you with that. And to be honest, if it comes to your needing Adrenaline Surge? +2s in this zone won't really make that much of a difference."

"That's what I was thinking. Question: can I spend XP on my attributes or skills?"

Lotharia shook her head. "Nope. Those reflect your in-game usage. Spend all day chatting at an inn? Your charisma will go up, and you'll gain basic levels of Carousing or Seduction. Spend weeks reading in a library? Intelligence and skills like Academics, History, or Engineering will bump up."

I gave a long sigh of disappointment. "Makes sense, I suppose. Can I look at your sheet now?"

There was an awkward pause.

"Um. Sorry. Charisma nine."

"Right." Lotharia shook her head. "God, I hope you level up fast. But sure. Let me give you access." She squinted at her personal screen. From where I sat I could see vague squiggles of information, but nothing that gave away even a hint of her stats.

"Here we go." She tapped the screen then sat back, looking both proud and a little nervous.

Her screen opened before me, and I leaned forward, drinking it in.

Lotharia Glimmervale

        Species: Human
        Class: Enchanter
        Level: 9
        Total XP: 832
        Unused XP: 12
        Guild: Cruel Winter
        Title(s): Acolyte of Frost
        Domains: None
        Allies: None
        Cumulative Wealth (GP): 312

Attributes

        Strength: 8
        Dexterity: 13
        *Constitution: 11
        Intelligence: 9
        Wisdom: 14
        *Charisma: 14 (+2 Enchanter class bonus)
        Mana: 0/16

Skills

Survival: Basic (III)
Knowledge (Cruel Winter): Intermediate (I)
Diplomacy: Basic (IV)
Carousing: Basic (V)
Seduction: Basic (I)
Stealth: Basic (III)
Melee: Basic (IV)
Athletics: Basic (I)

 Talents

Spellcasting: Basic
Meditation: Intermediate (II)
Quick Reflexes: Basic

 Spell List

Cantrips: Basic
Frost Armor: Basic
Hail Strike: Basic
Restoration: Basic
Imbue: Basic
Summon Fog: Basic

I gave out a low whistle. "Now that's a little more like it. How long did it take you to hit level nine? And is your name really Lotharia Glimmervale?"

She laughed, a pleasant, rich sound, and for a moment I relaxed, was content to simply take in the sight of her lounging before me. An exposed length of her thigh where her dress was slit caught my eye. *Seduction, Basic (I), huh?* I forced myself to focus.

"No. But Euphoria's more generous with XP if you come up with a new name. It's all about immersion. I used to know members of Cruel Winter who never broke character. No coincidence that they leveled the quickest."

"If they were that hardcore, they might have focused the most on grinding," I said. "That's not exactly 'in character'."

"True. Either way, Lotharia works. And I wasn't really focused on powering up. I spent a lot of time just having fun, to tell you the truth. It was a crazy time when Euphoria first opened up. Everybody was so in awe. So grateful to be here. Like the opening of a new utopia. A magical time." She stared at her bottle of wine, lips pursed, lost in her memories.

I could believe it. Her highest stats and skills were charisma, Carousing and Diplomacy. No wonder she was down about having to hang out with a charisma nine noob.

"Anyways. It's all changed." She took a swig and handed the bottle over. Half the wine was gone. "We won't be able to stay down here much longer. The draugrs will soon work up the courage to come sniffing around once more, and sooner or later they'll either find us or point others in our direction."

"That's too bad. Where should we go?"

Her shoulders slumped. "Hard to say. This was my best hidey-hole yet. We'll have to sneak around during the day and try to find a new basement or the like. It'll be dangerous. Very dangerous."

"What about heading out into the forest?"

"With our Survival levels? We'd be miserable, and would spend half our time starving and the rest of it running away from ogres, demodands, vallomirs…" She trailed off. "No. Best we stay here on the outskirts of town."

"But then where are you getting your food from?"

"Whomever destroyed Feldgrau wasn't that intent on looting. I've been carefully working my way through the surviving homes, finding any preserved goods in their pantries. I've been living off the mayor's house this past week. Here. Look." She took up her hemp sack and began to empty it out. Half a dozen small clay jars, their lacquered surfaces gleaming in her light. A hunk of cured meat, furry with mold. Three waterskins, and six wizened little apples.

My stomach howled and my mouth filled with spit. "I've never lusted after old apples before. May I?"

She laughed and tossed me one, which I immediately bit into. The taste was sharp and tangy and made me moan as the corners of my jaw cramped up in delight. I devoured it in three bites, and nearly ate the core.

"You know, if it weren't for the threat of near certain death, the patrolling undead, the draugrs, and all the rest of it, I'd be spending every moment eating these apples." I dropped the core on the floor and grinned. "I don't think I've ever tasted something so good. Not even in real life."

Lotharia winked at me and cut through the waxen seal over one of the jars. She raised it to her nose and sniffed. "Ah, yes. Pâté. Perfect with... well, cured ham." She used her knife to scrape off the mold, then sliced a thick cut of ruby-red cured meat clear from the bone. She lathered pâté onto it, rolled it into a tube, then took a large bite. "Excushe me," she said around her mouthful, "as I shlowly die of delight."

We devoured it all and finished the wine, too. For a while I lazily considered opening another bottle. Lotharia's light was growing slightly dimmer, more intimate, and I thought that her half-lidded gaze was more appreciative than it had been before.

Who was I kidding? I had charisma nine. Even if I wanted to seduce her, I didn't have the skill, and would probably end up banging my head into her nose or insulting her looks in an attempt to flatter her. I smiled in amusement.

"This is the nicest evening I've had since I arrived here," she said, voice half dreamy. "Talking stats and eating moldy meat. Exactly what I hoped for when I snuck back into my corporate account."

I snorted. "Couldn't agree more. Totally lives up to the hype. This is by far the coziest, most inviting and decadent wine cellar I've ever had to hide in for fear of my mortal life. Ten out of ten." I paused. "Snuck back into?"

Lotharia's eyes widened as she realized her slip, but she covered it with admirable skill. She gave an airy wave of her knife. "Well, I suppose I'm technically no longer part of the company at this point. I was surprised they hadn't shut the account down, to be honest."

I smiled. "You're sneaking in here? Must be a really big corporation for them not to notice an active Euphoria account."

"Yeah, pretty big. I don't miss it." She studied her knife blade. "And it probably wasn't the smartest move on my part, logging back in. But—well. I needed the diversion."

"Why? Your life suck really bad or something?" I winced. "Sorry."

She'd stiffened at my words and her lips pressed into a thin line. "Something like that. I thought some time partying with Jeramy and Hannah and the rest of my old friends would cheer me up. Ha!" She wiped her blade on her thigh and then sheathed it. "Yet another genius move on my part. Some party I logged back into."

I didn't know what to say. Nor did I trust Euphoria to not twist whatever I tried. So I simply sat there, thinking about the second wine bottle, watching Lotharia and wondering what her story was.

Finally, she looked up. "So, what's our long-term plan here?" Strange. You'd think with her higher levels and experience she'd be the one taking control.

"Survival, obviously. But yeah. We need some kind of a plan. I'm hoping Brianna's going to come back looking for me, so I say we leave her a message in the highland meadow. Then we find a new safehouse and hunker down, focusing on smart leveling till she can teleport us the heck out of here."

"Sounds good. I'm suddenly dying to meet your ex." Her eyes were nearly closing.

"Only complete and utter idiots say that," I said, then held up both hands. "Damn it."

"Yeah, yeah. Charisma nine." She grabbed her cloak and pulled it over herself. "Don't worry. Your complete ineptness is kind of cute."

I went to reply, only to realize she'd fallen asleep. I watched her and mulled over the day. I was still alive. That was the most important thing. And I'd made an ally I wouldn't mind spending time with, which was almost as good. While things were still suicidally awful, at least there was a modicum, the tiniest fraction of hope.

Eyelids closing, I realized I'd never actually spent the XP on Astute Observer. Rousing myself, I summoned my character sheet and tapped the talent. It glowed and appeared beneath my short list of items.

And just like that, a number of details about the wine cellar that I'd missed came swimming into view through my lethargy. The third rung below the trapdoor was in danger of pulling free.

Lotharia had brought two kinds of sealed jars: two more tan ones like the first pâté jar she'd opened, and three slightly darker brown ones we'd not tried. A strange seam ran from ceiling to floor down the wall behind the wine shelving. Lotharia's scepter had somehow disappeared altogether, and I'd not even noticed. I could smell draugr blood coming from my sheathed dagger, reminding me I hadn't cleaned it, and I thought I could hear the sound of wind building up above, like a nascent storm.

I sat there, entranced. Anything I stared at seemed to grow slightly clearer, as if an invisible lens had swung before it, giving it a subtle magnification.

I looked closely at Lotharia. Was this what she looked like in real life? Probably not. There was no telling who she really was. But even under my new scrutiny she looked good. *Real*, somehow, and not some idealized and fake beauty. There were a few improbable gray strands mixed in with the black above her temple, which in time might become an actual streak; the hardness that I'd noted in her features had given way in sleep, and I caught a glimpse of what she might have looked like during her happier years here in Euphoria. It made me want to help her escape this wretched hellhole of a village, get her somewhere she could relax again and be herself.

Sleep began to steal over me. I fought it for as long as I could. How long had I been in Euphoria? Six hours? Maybe eight? That meant I'd been lying on my table in the docking station back in Miami for fifteen minutes. Maybe twenty all told.

I shook my head and gave a bemused smile. All this in just fifteen minutes. Amazing.

Warm, well fed, comfortable and with a faint glow of growing confidence, I allowed myself to fall asleep. Sure, I was still a level one noob. But things were looking up.

6

THE SOUND OF scratching woke me. Slight but persistent, and coming from the trapdoor. Lotharia was still asleep. Despite the adrenaline dumping into my system, I couldn't help but feel a spike of satisfaction. Astute Observer for the win.

"Psst," I hissed. Dust was sifting down from between the slats. It sounded like a dog pawing at the wood, trying to get in. "Lotharia. Company."

"Hmmph?" She sat up and automatically activated her screen in the way some people check their phones first thing. "Mana's only at six. What's going on?"

I rose to a crouch. The scratching intensified, as if two sets of claws were now working on the wood. "Draugrs, I'm thinking. They've tracked us already."

"Damn," said Lotharia. "There's no other way out. We'll have to fight them."

"Next base we find will have two exits," I muttered, drawing my knife. My mind was already spinning through our options as I pulled up my sheet. Mana was back to one. Hip hip. That meant I could possibly Shadow Step upstairs and surprise the two draugrs.

No. Bad move. I was assuming there were only two, and Lotharia had said they moved in packs.

She pulled her scepter from somewhere and its pale blue glow filled the wine cellar. "I can buy us a little time. Here." So saying, she extended the scepter to the trapdoor and whispered, "Bind and fasten, firm and strong." The blue glow flowed from her scepter across the surface of the trapdoor and the sound of scratching grew at once a little more distant.

"Imbue," she said. "It's surprisingly handy. Lets me change the nature of inanimate objects to a minor degree. The trapdoor should be as hard as stone for a few minutes."

"Great. Let's grab everything we need. We're not going to be coming back here."

Activity was a welcome distraction. It helped me not think about how I could die down here in a matter of moments. Instead, I shoved the few remaining jars into Lotharia's hempen sack, then held it open for her books and other belongings.

There was a crackle from above, and I looked up to see thin shimmers of black electricity dance across the planks and then fade away. The scratching became much louder, more of a tearing and rending than the tentative explorations of before.

"What was that?"

"Not good. Someone just dispelled my magic."

My blood ran cold. The odds of our surviving had just plummeted. An enemy magic user?

Inspiration hit me. I grabbed hold of the wine rack and hauled it away from the wall. It slid loudly across the flagstones then tipped over altogether, raining bottles onto Lotharia's straw pallet, several of them shattering as they hit the ground.

Lotharia reached for me. "What are you doing?"

"Look! Here, a seam, see?" I jammed my dagger into it at the top then ran the tip down, digging out accumulated dirt and dust. "And there—a second one. Maybe a secret door?"

Planks broke above us and a snout shoved its way through, snarling with hunger and impatience.

"Here, look—might have been a handle once." There was a crude, rusted mechanism visible in a coin-sized hole at about hip height. "Damn it! Looks broken!"

"Cleanse and brighten, fix and lighten!" She waved her scepter, and once again the blue flame from its top spread out, this time focusing on the ruined lock. The metal within took on a polished gleam, and more dust fell from the wall. I shoved my poor dagger into the square hole where some handle had rotted away, dug it in deep, then carefully twisted it.

The mechanism turned smoothly as a draugr fell through the ruined trapdoor, landing hard on its shoulder and scrabbling its claws across the flagstones in an attempt to gain its feet.

I slammed my shoulder into the wall and it opened inwards as if on oiled hinges, revealing a pitch-dark tunnel. Reaching out, I shoved Lotharia inside, threw the hempen sack after her, then stepped right in and slammed the secret door shut as the draugr launched itself against it.

The door shuddered violently.

Lotharia's light spell caused the narrow tunnel to reveal itself. It was roughly carved from the rock and only broad enough for one of us at a time. A few wooden crates nearly blocked the entrance altogether where somebody had used the tunnel for storage years ago.

"Smash a crate!" I yelled as the door shivered again. The draugrs were baying on the far side, attacking the stone door with all they were worth.

Lotharia mercifully didn't ask any questions. She slammed her scepter into the closest crate, shattering it.

"Give me a piece of wood!"

She did so, staring at me as if I'd gone mad, and I wasted no time wedging it tight under the door. The next draugr slam caused the door to open perhaps half an inch, and then it stuck.

I took a step back, hesitant, then the XP chime sounded. I turned to Lotharia. "Now run!"

We bounded down the tunnel, her ball of light dancing ahead of us. The doorway was quickly lost to the darkness, and the stale air filled with the sound of our gasps. The occasional root slapped me in the face, and I stumbled and nearly fell when an explosion sounded behind me.

Somebody had blasted the door in.

Draugr howls echoed behind us, sounding like the stuff of nightmares. My breath was already burning in my throat, my legs cramping, my brow wet with sweat. Lotharia pulled ahead of me, running with greater confidence and ease. The difference between my con eight and her con eleven was becoming apparent. Only my new skill of Athletics was allowing me to barely keep up.

I darted a look over my shoulder. The eyes of the draugrs loping after us burned red in the darkness. They were gaining, fast.

"Can you collapse the tunnel?" I shouted.

"No!"

It has to come out somewhere.

I gritted my teeth and put on an extra burst of speed. Adrenaline Surge would have been awesome right about now. Dagger in hand, I considered turning and fighting the lead draugr before it could leap at my back. Suicide. Literal suicide!

"There!" shouted Lotharia. Wooden slats came into view, nailed into the tunnel's side up ahead. "Pass me!"

She stepped to the side, turning as she did so, and raised her scepter. "From the heart of glaciers, blue-green to black, I summon forth the coldest shards and send them to attack!"

She screamed the words so quickly I could barely make them out. I leapt and grabbed hold of the highest slat as a storm of icy shards rained down from the tunnel roof right before Lotharia. The lead draugr snarled as it tried to leap through and was pummeled down to the dirt, shards tearing open its hide. Four more skidded to a stop before the ice storm, lunging and snapping their jaws.

I could just make out a figure emerging from the gloom behind them. The sight of the man made my blood run cold. Twin specks of burning red light burned within the empty sockets of his eyes, his face little more than dried skin stretched tight over his angular skull. A dark hood was draped down low over this nightmare visage, and he walked slowly, staff tapping on the dirt as he drew close.

That was enough for me. I shoved at the trapdoor above and threw it open, then clambered up into the open air and turned to reach down for Lotharia. The sound of the ice storm abruptly cut off as I grabbed her by the wrist and hauled her up, shoulder burning from the effort.

Lotharia stumbled up and out into the ruined building and I slammed the trapdoor shut.

"Here!" Lotharia struggled to lift a large block of stone. I hurried to help her. Grunting, we hauled it over and dropped it onto the

scarred trapdoor. Only then did I stumble back to look at where we'd emerged.

Dawn was breaking over the mountains, filling the ruined village of Feldgrau with a soft, dusty gray light that bleached the surroundings of all color. Not that there was much to bleach. We stood in the ruins of a house, the walls ragged and mostly toppled around us, the ground covered in the collapsed remnants of the roof, the furniture shattered beneath it.

"Oh no," said Lotharia, drawing close. "We're out in the open."

We were surrounded by other shattered buildings, and to my right I could make out the remnants of a stone tower, broad and squat. "That way?"

"That way? No! Never! Come on!" She grabbed my hand and we ran out of the house, leaping and hopping over the fallen rafters as the trapdoor behind us erupted in a torrent of green flame.

I turned, wide-eyed, as the last of the viridian gout curled away and disappeared in the morning air, but Lotharia grabbed me by my collar and hauled me on. I twisted and ran after her, out into the street.

I'd seen photographs of villages like this in the real world. Villages that had been bombed into ruin during the world wars of the twentieth century. Gaping, empty windows, stone chimneys rising up impossibly straight while the rest of the home had fallen. The street was filled with rubble, abandoned carts, rusted lengths of metal that might have once been swords. What the hell had happened here?

Lotharia gripped me by the wrist and ran. We pounded down the narrow street, hemmed in on both sides by the ruins. The baying of the draugrs grew loud once more. They must have somehow climbed out of the tunnel. We sprinted around a corner onto a new street only to stagger to a stop at the sight of a skeleton swaying as it limped toward us.

I must have killed literally thousands of skeletons in all the different games I'd played over the years, and always thought of them as little more than annoyances. In Golden Dawn I could unleash a channeling blast that would demolish hundreds of them at a time.

But here, now, staring at the moss-covered bones of an actual animated skeleton, its jaws clacking unnervingly as it reached for us and stumbled forth? Every detail made painfully clear by my new talent, from the remnants of a torn dress about its legs to the dried blood and flesh that hung from its unnaturally long talons?

Horrific.

Still, you spend enough time gaming, you develop the right instincts.

I sidestepped into the shadows beneath the closest wall and activated Shadow Step. It was more intuitive this time, and I emerged a dozen yards down the street, elbowing my way out of the coiling darkness that filled a doorway. I immediately ran back to the skeleton, trying to move on the balls of my feet, and slammed my dagger as hard as I could down on its skull.

The tip of the blade sank in perhaps a quarter of an inch and stopped, but the force of my attack wrenched its head around regardless. Then Lotharia was there, swinging her scepter like a baseball bat right across its head, and with a crack she sent its lower jaw flying free.

The skeleton wasn't finished. It reached for her, grabbed hold of her shoulders. I slammed the heel of my foot into the back of its calf – uh, tibia? Fibula? Whatever, its lower leg – and drove its knee down hard onto the cobbles.

Lotharia tore herself free, raised her scepter overhead with both hands and brought it crunching down. Its skull fragmented and it collapsed, all of its bones losing cohesion.

I grinned at her, elated, almost manic as the distinctive XP chime sounded. Then the draugrs came racing around the corner, trying to turn at full speed, one of them losing traction and slipping onto its side, the second leaping up to run along the far wall for a beat before dropping back down to the ground.

"Here they come!" I turned and ran on. "You have any mana left?"

"All out!"

"Damn!" I opened my character sheet even as I ran, the pale screen allowing me to make out the street through it, and checked the pop-up window:

👑 **You have gained 35 experience (10 for evading the draugr ambush, 25 for defeating the peasant skeleton). You have 55 unused XP. Your total XP is 80.**

I swiped it away, nearly tripping as I did so, and swiped away two more screens before getting to the window advertising the new talents available to me. I could barely make out their titles, but I knew exactly what I was looking for. I selected Adrenaline Surge without any hesitation and a new entry appeared at the bottom of the list.

Ledge Runner
XP Cost: 30

I had enough XP left over, and instinct made me select it without even reading the description. The text glowed gold, but I dismissed all the screens to see that Lotharia had pulled ahead by a good ten yards. Looking over my shoulder, I saw the draugrs right on my heels.

Cursing, I activated Adrenaline Surge. Fire flooded my veins, my lungs expanded with fresh air, new energy filled my muscles, and a dizzying sense of exhilaration flooded through me, as if I'd just pounded six black coffees back to back.

I tucked my chin and sprinted all out, leaving the draugrs behind and swooping in behind Lotharia. She turned to look at me even as I scooped her up in my arms, carrying her with ease.

"What are you—"

Her scream cut off as I ran right at a tumbled wall and leapt. Every second was precious. Every moment of fiery energy was crucial. Even with her in my arms I was able to reach the top of a ragged chunk of wall, and before I overbalanced I hit my newest skill and activated Ledge Runner.

I found my balance immediately, as if the earth had become magnetic and the soles of my feet were made of iron. Adrenaline still pumping through my system, I grunted and ran up the precarious wall, fleet as a fox and high up onto its jagged top.

Lotharia held tightly onto me, staring wide-eyed over my shoulder, but I didn't hesitate. How many seconds did I have left? Five? Ten? I sprinted with everything I had along the six-inch-wide wall, striding over gaps and cracks, right up to where it ended at an alley. A charred beam extended between the two houses across from me, and with a strangled shout of fear I leapt.

There was no way I could land on that narrow beam. A lifetime spent in my real body made me feel nothing but sick with horror for even attempting it. But somehow my feet found the four-inch-wide beam, and somehow the balls of my feet stuck, arresting my momentum so that I fell into a cat-like crouch some fifteen feet above the ruined interior.

I could feel Adrenaline Surge fading. Grunting with effort, hoping Ledge Runner wasn't on an even shorter time limit, I raced along the blackened beam to its terminus, ducked my head and collapsed forward through the window and into a dark room.

Lotharia rolled free of my arms as soul-crushing exhaustion and nausea overcame me. The draugr barks were faint, still coming from the street over, and growing fainter.

"How— Never mind," said Lotharia. She ran to the window, pressed her back to the wall alongside it and then carefully peered out. "I'd forgotten how quick you earn XP. Good thinking."

I tried to rise and instead threw my arm over my eyes. "Not like you were about to do anything."

"We've got to work on that charisma," she said distractedly. "It sounds like they're looping around the block. They may have lost our scent for now, but they won't give up." She came back from the window and crouched by my side. "You all right?"

"Gah. No. I feel like I was out drinking for three days straight." My head pounded, my muscles ached, even my lungs were cramped and tight. "Shouldn't... shouldn't last long." I knew I should be looking around, investigating our new digs, but it was all I could do to stop the room from spinning by lying still, eyes closed.

Lotharia move around, and then, like a sweet benediction, the nausea and exhaustion fell away. It felt like a fever breaking, and with a deep breath I sat up.

We were in a small attic, the ceiling sloping down on both sides, our window the sole source of light. A faded rug lay over the warped boards, and small cupboards lined the low walls beneath the angled ceilings. A narrow door stood shut across from the window, and what looked like children's toys – wooden blocks, faded dolls, toy soldiers – lay strewn across the rug under a thick layer of dust.

"Kids?" I picked up one of the dolls. "Can players—"

"No, but the NPC families usually had them."

I moved to the window and listened. The draugr barks had grown faint, but peering outside I saw that our activity had stirred up the dead. I caught glimpses of skeletons filling the street we'd left, some of them armored and moving with greater purpose. A lone draugr was sniffing at the rubble directly beneath us, its stinger tail dragging over the rocks like that of a rat.

I crept back to Lotharia. "Looks like the whole area's riled up."

She pinched the bridge of her nose and nodded. "We'd best stay quiet and stay put. Things will quieten down in a few hours."

"What are the chances they find us in here? Will they search every house?"

"Possible. The draugrs have terrible eyesight, and usually track by scent. Going high was perfect. But the wraith that was coursing them? If it saw us go up, we're done for. But if it was still around the corner, we could have thrown him off, too."

"A wraith? I'm guessing they're hard to kill?"

"Way beyond our paygrade." Lotharia moved over to the cupboards and began opening each one. "They're level twenty-five, minimum, and immune to normal damage. Even if I used Imbue to enchant our weapons, we'd not be able to scratch it. My Hail Strike would probably just tickle it."

"What was it doing coming after us?"

Lotharia pulled out a broad, narrow box and blew dust from its surface, revealing primary colors and figures dancing along a crimson road. "Probably wanted to drain our mana and raise us as minor wraiths. Which would have well and truly sucked."

"That can happen? We can get raised as undead?"

She set the box on the floor and pulled the lid off, revealing a board and several small pouches. "Yeah. Only really powerful undead can do it, and it can be reversed by other players with the right magic. Course, if that happens to us, nobody would know to help us out. We'd spend the next six months with our ability to control our avatars seriously modified to the point where most people just give up their session and log out."

I stared right through her into the middle distance, horror filling me. "What would happen to someone on Death March if they got raised as undead?"

"I… I don't know." Lotharia blinked. "At a guess? They'd be killed by Euphoria when their six months were up if nobody rescued them. Turned into permanent undead NPCs."

"Great. I'm going to make it a point to avoid wraiths."

"Then you need to get out of Feldgrau," said Lotharia matter-of-factly. "This place is crawling with the undead."

"And go where?" I asked, trying not to feel exasperated with her. "The castle?"

She paused in the process of laying out the board. "I don't know. I've not been up there."

I took one last glance out the window at the undead milling below, then uneasily sat across from her. "Not once?"

"No," she said. "I just assumed it would be more dangerous than Feldgrau itself. Though, to be honest, I've not had much of what you might call 'a plan' since I logged in three weeks ago."

"Then maybe we should go take a look." When she didn't answer, I continued. "Look, there's a logic to these kinds of situations. In games like these, nothing is truly random. Something happened here. Somebody is in control of these undead. I'm willing to bet there's some kind of final boss here in town. That wraith coming after us today means we can't count on being ignored any longer, and if the final boss is interested in us, then we've got to get out of Dodge."

"Feldgrau," said Lotharia, not meeting my eyes.

"Whatever. Let's wait till things quieten down outside and then head up to the castle to explore. Maybe we can hide out there for a spell. Maybe we can find clues as to what happened to Cruel Winter, or some useful items."

Lotharia rattled a pair of dice inside a leather cup.

"Unless you want to try your luck again the next time that wraith shows up?" I continued. "Last I checked, the undead have a remarkable ability to focus exclusively on any one given task. If the big boss ordered it to find us, it won't stop looking."

"Fine," she said.

I studied her as she busied herself placing tokens on the board. "What is it?"

"What's what?" She still wasn't meeting my eyes.

"Why are you so resistant to going to the castle?"

"I said fine, didn't I?"

"Yeah, technically. But you're acting like a four-year-old who doesn't want to have a bath."

She snapped her head up and glared at me.

"Sorry," I said. "That could have come out better."

Lotharia sighed, shoulders slumping. "You're right. I don't want to go up there. Some of my best memories are from times spent in that castle. Best memories of my life, even. To go there and see it all ruined, destroyed… It's irrational, I know. But I was just trying to preserve those memories, and not overwrite them with horror."

A burst of compassion for her passed through me, and wanted to put my hand over hers. But knowing me, I'd accidentally clock her in the face while trying. I'd never appreciated how important social stats could be if they were actually taken seriously.

"I hear you," I said, focusing on my words, trying to not let them wriggle out of my control. "And I'm sorry. But I still think it's our best bet."

"Yeah," she said, staring glumly at the board. Then she took a sharp breath and sat up straight, visibly perking herself up. "And who knows? It might not be as bad as all that."

"Right!" I tried to smile, but doubted the expression was convincing. "Who knows what we'll find?"

"A party, just waiting for us!"

"A feast!" I said.

"A weapon rack loaded with legendary artifacts!"

"A swimming pool filled with liquid XP!"

We grinned foolishly at each other, then both slumped.

"Guess we'll find out," said Lotharia. "Ready for a round of Candyland?"

"Sure. I love playing minigames while the undead hunt for my immortal soul. Roll 'em."

B Y MIDDAY, the undead furor outside had died down. From our window I could still make out the occasional skeleton or worse monstrosity amble past the alleyway between the closest homes, but the sense of being searched for was gone. Lotharia meditated till all her mana returned (my entire point did so of its own accord), and then we headed out.

The front half of the house we'd been hiding in had collapsed into the street, making our descent from the little attic room rather more adventurous and exposed then I'd have liked, but we scrambled down the remains of the stairs and into the shadows of the ground floor without being noticed.

From there, Lotharia showed me her patented technique of getting around Feldgrau without being discovered. It basically involved short sprints from one hiding spot to the next whenever the coast was clear, which meant it took us nearly two hours to finally leave the village behind us. On the plus side, nothing spotted us in the process.

Those two hours gave me ample opportunity to observe the current denizens of the town, and I tallied up six different kinds of wandering mobs. You had your basic draugr pack, which tended toward five or six individuals. Then you had your lone peasant skeletons who staggered around like drunks looking for their car. There were these horrific zombie creatures that scared the pants off me: they had the zombie look, but were all hunched over and moved with unnervingly sudden jerks of speed. They'd sniff at things, too, which made me think we were done for, but luckily their sense of smell had to be rotten because they didn't pick up our trail.

Draugrs, wandering skeletons, and creepy hunched zombies and plague zombies surrounded by clouds of buzzing flies. Those were the most common. Then there were the six-armed skeleton champions. I saw only two of those, but that was more than enough. Eight feet tall and wielding rusted scimitars, bands of platinum around their brows, they made me want to nope the hell out.

Even worse was what could have been a banshee or wraith variant that floated down the street right at the end when I thought we were in the clear. She had that classic, never out of style look where your legs fade away into mist below the hips, a ruined wedding dress and hungry way of leaning forward as she went, hands clutching and clawing at the air.

Yeah. Pretty awful.

The final mob I saw looping erratically around was as disturbing as it was weird. It looked like a rhino—which was already pretty weird—with a massive bone ribcage emerging from its neck instead of a head. Or a bone flower that was curled up tight? I couldn't really tell. It just drifted forward, bone head-thing pulsing.

When we finally cleared Feldgrau and could relax, I turned to Lotharia. "What the hell was that rhino?"

She looked as spooked as I was. "Rhino? I guess it looked like one. I don't know. I've only seen it once at night with its head unfurled. It has like six red tongues a yard long that float up and dance in the air. I didn't stay to learn more."

I ran my hands through my hair. Despite our slow pace I was drenched in sweat and my heart pounded as if I'd run a marathon. "And you've been living in there for three weeks? How've you not gone mad?"

Lotharia gave me a shaky grin. "I thought I had at some points. Still, I'm really warming up to your idea of leaving town. Genius. Surely the castle can't be as bad."

We both looked up the overgrown road that curled amongst the foothills and led to the castle barbican. It was one of those realistic looking castles, the kind that was built to resist sieges and not host fairy princesses. The exterior curtain wall – what was left of it – rose some forty feet and looked as dense and impenetrable as a cliff face. Of course, the gaping holes put the lie to that. The barbican was a brutal outpost that defended the approach to the drawbridge and gatehouse, and it too looked battered and savaged. I could see a blocky keep rising behind the walls, flat-roofed and with arrow slit windows, while three round towers rose up from inside the curtain wall.

"That looks like the kind of place a warlord would love to hang out in," I said. "Complete with fifty or sixty murderous soldiers and a dozen killer knights. Not a place for parties and fun."

Lotharia gave a one-shouldered shrug as we made our way up the road, gravel crunching underfoot. "We had a couple of wizards who specialized in illusion magic. Jeramy was an archmagus, even, so powerful we even forgave his obsession with awful puns. They'd decorate it every night in a different way. Make the stones look like gleaming white marble, or glass cubes filled with water, all kinds of wonders. And inside there's a large courtyard – the bailey – where we had a stage on which we performed plays, held dances, and we strung lights everywhere, invited all kinds of mythical creatures to come party and play with us..." She smiled sadly. "It all feels like an impossible childhood dream now. We once even hosted the Silver Flame herself. She came down with a dozen of her Argent Exarchs. I can barely believe I was part of all that."

I sensed something up high and off to my left. On instinct, I took hold of Lotharia's arm and pulled her off the path and behind an outcropping of boulders. She followed, not resisting, and when we crouched behind the rocks she joined me in staring up at the sky.

Dragon.

It had emerged from the clouds and was gliding in a lazy circle far, far above us. It tightened its approach into a downward spiral, looking majestic and at ease in the sky, growing ever larger, and then flew down onto one of the castle towers with a massive, jerky flapping of its wings to arrest its momentum and disappear from view.

My stomach cramped and I clenched my fists. "Well. So much for that idea." I wanted to give up right there and then.

Lotharia was pale beside me. "If I met your Astute Observer talent at a bar, I'd let it buy me a drink and take me home." She gave me a shaky smile. "You can believe it's next on my shopping list."

"But what are we going to do? How the hell do we tackle a *dragon*?" I knew the answer. We didn't. We couldn't.

"That wasn't a dragon," said Lotharia. "That was a wyvern. Far smaller, and did you see it only had two legs?"

"All right, fine. Wyvern. Still way out of our league."

"True," said Lotharia. "But wyverns are dumb as bricks. They're like really ferocious cows. We should still be able to poke around if we're careful."

I raised my eyebrows. "Did you just compare that thing we saw to a cow?"

She gave a nervous laugh. "Yeah. Maybe not the best comparison. But do you really want to go back down into Feldgrau?"

I studied the small village that lay below us, a morass of ruin, debris, and wandering dead. "Not really."

"Come on. Let's keep going. We'll play it safe. You're the one who woke up all my old memories. Now I want to take a peek."

"And if it spots us?"

"I'll Summon Fog. That should give us enough time to hide."

I rubbed my face vigorously with both hands. "And I'm still just level one." I wanted to laugh; wanted to cry. "Fine. Let's keep going."

We made our way up alongside the road, keeping an eye on the tower top and making sure we were always close to some kind of cover. Feldgrau grew ever smaller beneath us, until finally the road leveled out and ran straight toward the barbican.

It was basically two round towers connected by a short, heavy wall, the road running through an archway in its center. Behind it the land dropped off into a ravine, over which lay the drawbridge that led to the actual castle gate.

Off to the sides, I could make out two broad siege bridges made of bound logs laid over the ravine, leading up to where entire chunks of the curtain wall had been demolished.

"What do you think?" Lotharia bit her thumb. "Direct approach, or do we try for a siege bridge?"

"Going straight through the gate's just asking for trouble," I said. "Let's try to sneak in through the side."

We ran off to the left, avoiding the barbican altogether, watching the battlements anxiously until we reached the first bridge where we crouched down once more. It was massively built, each log about three feet wide, and lashed together with huge amounts of rope. Its surface was scarred by countless blows, blackened by attempts to fire it and stained with dried blood. It led over a gut-wrenching chasm to the base of the curtain wall, where huge blocks of masonry had toppled down everywhere, even out onto the bridge itself.

I peered through a hole in the wall at a section of the inner courtyard. Nothing was moving within. Nobody was up on the battlements. The wyvern was quiet atop its tower.

"Ready?"

Lotharia nodded.

I considered activating Adrenaline Surge to speed us across, but then decided to save it. Taking a deep breath, I bolted forward and up onto the bridge, which was so massive it didn't even flex beneath my weight. I tried to imagine what it'd be like to cross it while under fire from the walls, shield raised to protect my head, arrows and stones and boiling pitch raining down from above. The screams and shouts, the fear and panic.

I reached the far side and leapt down to hide between two huge blocks, Lotharia squirming in right behind me.

Nothing. No shouts, no alarm raised.

Heart thudding, I weaseled through the fallen remnants of the wall until I found a good angle to see into the whole inner courtyard.

The first thing that struck me were the massive wooden spikes that had been driven through the flagstones everywhere, each at least four or five yards tall, their tips carved to wicked points. There had to be scores of them, all of them pointing straight up.

"Defense against the wyvern?" I asked.

Lotharia shrugged. "Could be. None of my skills cover this kind of stuff."

I looked closer. There were no corpses, but plenty of debris everywhere. The wind blew through the ravine beneath us, sounding a haunting dirge.

I shivered. "Ready to take a closer look?"

Trying to remain as close to the shadows as possible and praying that Stealth: Basic (I) would suffice, we moved through the wall and into the bailey. The space was huge. You could easily gather several hundred people within the walls. The keep rose like a stone gauntlet into the sky, four stories tall. Interestingly enough, someone had nailed huge planks across the doorway and ground floor windows.

I nudged Lotharia and pointed. "That's not ominous at all."

I knew a fair bit about castles, having owned my own in Golden Dawn and spent perhaps a little too much time working on all the details. Castles were meant to be self-sufficient, to be able to withstand sieges for months if not years. The bailey contained the burned remains of what had probably been the smithy, the stables standing beside it miraculously untouched. Doorways led into small buildings set against the inside of the wall, most of them in decent condition. There'd be a chapel, a bake house, a granary, servants' quarters perhaps. The kitchen, pantry, great hall and private chambers would all be in the keep.

"Over there," said Lotharia. "See the stables? Looks like someone took extra time to fortify them."

She was right. The huge stakes were tightly clustered around the stable building, with some of them even emerging through its roof.

"Think someone's using that as their base of operations?" I asked.

"Looks like. Though why they'd insist on staying with the wyvern up top…"

"Let's take a closer look," I said. "Seems all quiet for now."

Together we snuck along the inside of the wall. I had my dagger out, Lotharia her scepter. I kept shooting glances at the wyvern's tower, then over to the stables, then back to the ruined gatehouse. I felt like I could die at any second.

Which is why when the rat suddenly ran past me I didn't hesitate, but stabbed down and ran it through.

The XP chime sounded and I grinned. "Finally! A level-appropriate monster!"

"Uh," said Lotharia. "There's more of them. Run!"

"What?" I straightened, flicking the rat off my blade, then froze. A thousand beady eyes stared at me from the doorway of the small building we were passing. With a chittering shriek they poured forth, a swarm of rats, their black bodies gleaming as they plunged toward us like an animated carpet.

"Argh!" I hopped back, thought about using Shadow Step to escape, then instead simply turned and ran after Lotharia who was darting away between the upraised stakes.

The ground was torn up, entire flagstones pulled aside, with huge footprints here and there, each the length of my arm. *Giants?* I wondered, and then a ghastly roar bruised the air, clotted and deep, and I ran straight into Lotharia.

I clawed my way free. An ogre was running right at us. A dead ogre. Its skin was gray and green, huge holes in its side and chest revealing bone and rancid flesh. Worse, we had no time to escape. It bellowed and raised its arms high, ready to bring both fists crashing down, then slammed to a stop as if it had run into an invisible wall.

A huge collar was affixed around its neck, a chain as thick as my wrist running from its back into the dark doorway of the building closest to the stable.

Lotharia and I both tripped over each other, throwing ourselves back and crashing to the ground. The ogre bellowed again, chunks of its throat or vocal chords spattering out of its maw, and swung its arms at us, trying to grab us.

We backpedaled on our asses, shoving with our heels, but then a second roar sounded from overhead.

"Oh, come on!" I shouted. The wyvern had appeared at the tower's edge, wings spread wide. It dove off the tower right at us.

Instinct urged me to use Shadow Step, but that would have meant abandoning Lotharia out in the open. Instead, we both flipped onto all fours and threw ourselves toward the base of the closest spike.

"Obfuscate the keenest eye, blanket thought and hide from sky!"

Thick, white, cottony fog boiled forth from Lotharia's scepter, gushing out like a hydrant gone mad.

The ogre bellowed and flailed at us, but with the shock of its appearance now gone, I was able to tune it out. Besides, the chain was clearly keeping it at bay.

Instead, I watched as the wyvern dove and then banked to swoop over the stakes, wings causing the fog to swirl in mad arabesques. It shrieked in frustration, circled around with much awkward maneuvering within the bailey confines, and then hovered above us, jerking up and down with each frantic beat of its wings.

Then the fog closed in, and I couldn't see it any longer.

Lotharia and I were of the same mind: we scampered on all fours across the ground, weaving between the stakes until we reached the castle wall. No, the front of one of the many little buildings.

Praying it wasn't filled to the brim with peckish rats, we both hurried inside and split, me going left, Lotharia going right, so that we could place our backs against the wall on either side of the door.

The fog quickly dissipated. I listened, staring at the gloomy interior of the building but not seeing anything as the wyvern flew about for a minute or two. With a final squawk of dismay or frustration it climbed for altitude. I dared to peer outside and watched it ascend to the tower top and disappear.

We were safe.

My XP chime sounded, as did Lotharia's. So as to distract myself, to calm my thundering heart, I opened my character sheet.

⌂ You have gained 25 experience (5 for killing a rat, 10 for surviving your encounter with the undead ogre, 10 for evading the wyvern attack). You have 25 unused XP. Your total XP is 105.

Congratulations! You are Level 2!

Tiredly, I swiped the window away, barely feeling the flicker of triumph.

Your attributes have increased!

Mana +1
Wisdom +1
Dexterity +1
Constitution +1 (Con increase is depen-
dent on one night's good rest.)

 You have learned new skills. *Dodge: Basic*
(I), Athletics: Basic (II), Stealth: Basic
(II)

I sat up. That was good news. I glanced over at Lotharia. She was reading her own screen. Back to the next window.

**There are new talent advancements available
to you:**

I scrolled past the ones that were still familiar: Uncanny Aim, Sabotage Defenses and Minor Magic. Two new ones caught my eye. Looked like I'd always have five talent options available.

Double Step
XP Cost: 55
- Your understanding of the shadows
grows, and you can now delve into their
depths not once but twice in quick succession.
- Mana Drain 1

Distracting Attack
XP Cost: 35
- A successful blow will befuddle your
opponent, causing them to momentarily

lose track of you and opening them to a
Backstab.
- Mana Drain: 1

My finger hovered over Double Step, but instead I dismissed
my sheet and looked over to Lotharia. "You're not grinding with
a level one noob any longer."

"No?" She smiled and dismissed her sheet in turn. "That's a relief.
Any new talents? Here, I'll take a peek."

I watched as she scrolled through my sheet then dismissed it.
"Going to wait to spend that XP?" she asked.

"Yeah," I said, "and I'll tell you why in a second. What about
you? Any new abilities?"

Lotharia shook her head. "By the time you hit my level, you
don't get rewarded for this kind of stuff. A little XP here, a little
there, but nothing yet. I'm saving up for a new spell."

"Fair enough." I peeked outside. The undead ogre had disappeared,
a coil of chain emerging and then looping back into the doorway
of the little house set next to the stable. "It's time we approached
this situation professionally."

"As opposed to what we've been doing?"

"For sure." My confidence was starting to grow. Was that the bump
in my wisdom? "We've been reacting, running from one encounter
to the next, simply trying to survive. I think now we need to take
the initiative and focus on leveling up. This castle is perfect for that."

"It is?"

"Yeah. If we play it smart. There looks to be plenty of rats. We—"

"I don't get XP for rats."

"No, but I do. If they respawn, they can prove just what I need
to acquire some quick levels and plenty of new talents."

Lotharia nodded. "Remember, be careful: this area is slowly turning into a raid area, which means random traps and monsters."

"Sure. All the better. Because once I've gained more power, we go for the undead ogre. It's an easy kill if we set things up right. That should give even you a good boost in power."

"True enough."

"From there, we scout out the wyvern tower and plot a way to kill it. You're right. It's as dumb as a barrel full of rocks. Once we kill it, we'll be ready for our next big mission."

Lotharia raised an eyebrow. "Which is?"

"The keep. Whatever's boarded up in there is probably worth a ton of juicy XP. We're just going to have to keep an eye out for whatever's in the stables. Something I plan to do now, actually, with my raised Stealth."

"You actually look excited," said Lotharia.

"I am." I drew my knife, wiped its blade on my pants leg and grinned at her. "I'm finally starting to feel like myself again. Hungry. Eager for a challenge I can defeat with a combination of wits and power gaming. The monsters in this castle have no idea what they're in for."

My confidence must have been contagious, because Lotharia gave me a shark-like smile. "Did your charisma go up?"

I laughed huskily. "Not yet. But just you wait. I feel like I'm finally starting to get the hang of this."

8

I GAVE THE WYVERN five minutes to settle down and get lost
in its book or whatever before I slipped out the doorway and
back into the courtyard. Whomever was living in the stable could
come back at any time, so I kept a weather eye on the front gate
as I moved forward.

I couldn't help but grin. My body had adopted a more intuitive
understanding of how to move from shadow to shadow. A sixth
sense was developing within me, helping me place my feet just
right to avoid crud on the floor, helping me angle my body just
so behind different objects, and picking the best path forward.

The closest I could compare it to the real world was the way I
knew how to move my shoulders when walking quickly through
a crowd. That intuitive sense that helped me avoid hitting other
people. Except now it guided me toward the shadows.

Enjoying my soundless approach, I hurried from stake to stake
like a flitting shadow and eventually reached the fullest extent the
undead ogre's chain had allowed it to go. I hesitated, peered care-

fully at the dark doorway into its den, studied the loop of chain, and then took a deep breath and pressed on.

The stable was a large building, with double doors on one end through which to lead horses. As I drew close, the smell hit me like a rotting wet towel to the face: the rich, nauseating scent of feces, the stink of old sweat, and greasy reek of rancid fat.

I knew that smell.

I slunk up to the doors and peered inside through the cracks. Light filtered into the interior through large gaps in the tiled roof, revealing a squalid campsite – if you could even call it that. A large firepit had been dug in the center aisle that ran between the stalls, and over this a massive spit rested, the remnants of a deer charred and half eaten still on it. A mass of old furs were arranged in one corner, looking something akin to a fetid nest, and sacks of what looked like coins and other loot sat close by. Bones lay everywhere, along with unrecognizable hunks of flesh and gristle.

No sign of horses.

My eyes were watering from the stench. I looked around for a moment longer, and then backed away. Forcing myself not to be hasty, I slunk back across the courtyard to the small building in which Lotharia waited.

"And?"

"Ogres," I said, and spat in an attempt to clear my mouth of the taste. "Maybe even the pair that tried to kill me in the highland meadow."

"Huh," said Lotharia. "And the undead ogre?"

"An old friend, maybe?" I shrugged. "They're clearly using it to guard their lair."

"But why go through all the effort of lairing here?"

"If this were any other game," I said, "I'd not look for much reason. But this being Euphoria… you think the AI thinks things through that deeply?"

Lotharia gave me a bemused nod. "Hell yes it does."

"Then… who knows? Maybe they've always coveted the castle and dreamed of living here, and now they're in they're not going to let the wyvern drive them off."

"As good an explanation as any. So what now?"

"Now I'm going to do some leveling and exploring. You're welcome to join me if you want."

"Killing rats? No thanks." She hefted her hemp sack. "Though I would like to try to get into Jeramy's tower." She thought about it, then made a face. "Too bad I don't know the password to get in the front door. Never mind. I found a comfy corner in the back over there where a ray of light comes in. I'll catch up on my reading. I want to raise my intelligence for my next purchase."

"Sounds good. If you hear me screaming at the top of my lungs, come running, though it'll probably be too late."

She laughed and swatted me, and I stepped back outside.

There was a lot to explore here. Maybe six more little buildings along the inside of the wall besides the rats' nest and ogre lair. The two non-wyvern towers. The gatehouse itself. But before I found something I couldn't handle, I'd work on that which I could.

Time for some good ol' fashioned rat killing.

I studied their lair. Built of the same gray stone as the other buildings, the roof was partially sunken in, exposing the rafters amidst the skewed tiles. There were maybe twenty-five or thirty yards between the roof and the parapet above.

I snuck over to the wall and then followed it to the rats' house, my blade drawn. Every few seconds I checked the gatehouse and wyvern's tower, but nothing stirred.

When I drew close to the rats' lair, I slowed down and watched. Nothing at first, but then a black-furred body emerged from a gap and hurried along the wall toward me. I held completely still, and when it noticed me I lunged forward and stabbed at it.

It gave a strangled squeak, spasmed, and went still. The XP chime sounded and I grinned. Oh, the memories of grinding in my older games!

I used to love the old-fashioned Multi User Dungeons when I was a kid. While everyone else was playing advanced online multiplayer games, I'd be hunched over my phone, reading that old school green text on a black background. Text-based rooms with basic commands and a player base of perhaps seventy. Peanuts compared to what everyone else was playing, but for some reason it fascinated me. I still recall the joy of typing 'n' for north, entering a new room, skimming the description and going right to the mob line: "You have encountered a RAT!"

How the world had changed. Phones had been replaced by omnis, for one. I sighed, flicked the rat's corpse off my knife and opened my sheet.

⟐ You have gained 3 experience (3 for killing a rat). You have 28 unused XP. Your total XP is 108.

Huh. Down already from the five XP I'd earned as level one. Still, that meant I only needed to kill thirty-two and a third more rats to hit level three.

I chewed on the inside of my cheek as I considered my sheet, then waved the window away, scrolled down to my talents section, and tapped Uncanny Aim. While I was still looking to get Minor Magic and unlock the darkblade's arcane abilities, nothing would help as much with killing rats as throwing pointy things at them.

Case in point: a second rat had emerged from the same gap in the wall and was staring right at me, doing that nose wrinkly thing they do, whiskers twitching. There was no way I could reach it before it ducked out of sight. I slowly crouched down and scooped up a rock the size of a tennis ball. I drew my arm back very, very slowly, and activated my new talent.

A thin silver thread appeared that began at my rock and arced over to the rat, locking in on its snout. My eyes widened, then I grinned. My arm whipped forward; the rock sailed through the air and *cracked* into the rat's head.

The rat fell back in through the hole, and I heard my XP chime.

I cast around. There were dozens of suitable rocks at my feet. Perfect.

Another rat appeared in the hole. Dumb idiots. I scooped up another rock. My talent was still active, a new thread lining up, but the rat was moving. My thread tracked it down the wall even as a second and then a third appeared. Suddenly they were boiling out the hole, with more pouring around the building's corner, emerging no doubt from the doorway.

I'd attracted the attention of the swarm.

Now, normally I'd deal with something like this with a fire storm or the like, wiping them all out at once, but such were the travails of a low-level character. I launched my rock at the first rat and scooped up a second rock immediately.

The silver thread leapt from whichever rat's head I was looking at to the next. I threw, scooped, threw again.

Ding. Ding.

Six XP right there.

I backed up quickly, grabbing rocks as I went. I targeted the lead rats now, and my aim was amazing. I merely had to look at my target and I could hit it no matter which way it darted. Six. Seven, eight.

There were hundreds of them, maybe even more than a thousand.

More rocks. Eleven. Twelve. Thirteen.

The swarm flowed over the corpses of their brethren without hesitation.

Fifteen. Sixteen. My back hit the wall of the next little building.

I turned and grabbed hold of the rough rock, fingers digging into a crack, and hauled myself up. Athletics, Basic (II) for the win! Still, it was hard work, and I had to kick and grit my teeth to reach the top, finally pulling myself over onto the roof.

Which immediately began to collapse under me.

Eyes widening in panic, I activated Ledge Runner and caught my balance right at the edge of the roof as a half-dozen beams clattered down into the room below. Perfectly poised, I scooped up a clay tile, turned, and dashed it down upon the swarm climbing up after me.

Ding, ding, ding, ding.

Another tile, then a third and fourth. I was in love with my aiming thread. No movement from the wyvern's tower. The coolest part was that now, with a larger tile, the thread split at the end into four or five different lines, each linking to the closest rats.

Gasping for breath, I stepped up to where the roof met the castle curtain wall and found a broader beam to stand on just as Ledge Runner ran out. My legs grew a little shaky, and when I tried to activate it again nothing happened.

Ah. Cooldown period.

Uncanny Aim also stopped working. Same deal. I tried throwing a couple more tiles, but my aim was off and it felt like trying to hit them with bent frisbees.

The swarm flowed over the edge onto the roof and came right at me.

My smile slipped and I considered my options. The roof looked scary. One wrong step and I'd plunge into the room below. And into the swarm too, no doubt. I shot a terrified look upwards. An oblique line of holes perforated the wall high above me, running from the bottom left up toward the higher right where they met with the battlements some twenty yards above. Most of them had planks of wood jutting right out of them. The remnants of a staircase?

The first rats reached my feet and I lashed out, kicking them over the edge. I sent perhaps five flying before they began to scurry up my legs, biting and clawing at me.

Time to go.

I activated Adrenaline Surge, crouched down, and leapt. The fire in my veins made me feel like I'd soar right up into the sky, but instead I only leapt high enough to dunk. My fingers closed around the uppermost edge of one of the wall's huge masonry blocks, and not wasting any time, I began to climb.

What I lacked in skill I compensated for with sheer strength and adrenaline. Sweat stung my eyes as I hauled myself up the wall, fingers digging into each crack, the rough masonry working in my favor. The rats grabbing the front of my legs chittered furiously as I smashed them into the wall, and then fell away.

Up I went, block by block, till I reached the first of the shattered beams of wood. I grabbed hold of it, praying fervently that it wasn't rotten, and boosted myself up to land on it in a crouch as if I were a ninja.

I paused as I realized how high up the curtain wall I was, what a drop onto the swarm and ruined roof would do to me, and the enormity of what lay ahead.

I had seconds before Adrenaline Surge left my system and I collapsed. Desperate, I tried to activate Ledge Runner again – and it worked.

I bolted. Straight up the ruined steps, taking them three at a time as the adrenaline fizzled in my blood, my balance that of an Olympic gymnast. I placed my feet flush with the wall where the wooden beams emerged for maximum security, leaping the gaps where they'd fallen away altogether, going so fast my feet blurred.

I was five steps from the top when Adrenaline Surge gave out, and exhaustion clamped down on me like the world's heaviest iron hand.

With a desperate cry, I threw myself upward. The last of my strength disappeared. For a sickening moment I was stretched out over the void, forty yards above the bailey. Then my waist slammed into what was left of the wooden platform at the top.

I scrabbled at the weathered wood, trying to find purchase even as my gorge rose in my throat, my muscles cramping, my body sliding down.

No shadows to sink into. Summoning the last reserves of my will, I managed to wedge my fingers between two planks and throw a knee up and over. A grunt, every fiber in my being protesting, and I rolled up onto the wooden platform.

Which immediately creaked and sank beneath my weight.

Terrified, I rolled onto my stomach and frog jumped onto the battlement as the platform gave way and fell into nothingness.

I lay on the stone wall, heaving for breath, then rolled onto my side and puked. The distant crash of the wooden beams hitting the bailey below floated up to me, but couldn't make myself care. For what felt like hours I lay there shivering and shaking, covered in a cold sweat, every muscle cramping up – and then the pain receded and I was fine again.

"Gah," I said, sitting up and wiping puke from my chin. I was staring to hate Adrenaline Surge as much as I loved it. I crawled to the edge and looked down into the bailey. I could barely make out the rat swarm far below, fading back into its little house. The undead ogre had emerged from its lair but was staring around vacuously, trying to locate the source of the sound.

Only then did I raise my head and stare at the top of the wyvern tower.

I fully expected to see it rousing itself, spreading its wings, staring right at me – but the tower was still too tall for me to make out much from where I crouched. I could see the top of a massive nest, woven from thick branches, but no sign of the wyvern itself.

I breathed a sigh of relief and scooted back, along the top of the wall and to the mangonels themselves, against which I sat, catching my breath and wiping the sweat from my eyes. With a grin, I opened my character sheet.

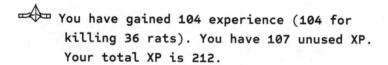 You have gained 104 experience (104 for killing 36 rats). You have 107 unused XP. Your total XP is 212.

Congratulations! You are Level 3!

I let out a whoop of joy and then clamped my hand over my mouth. Why risk your life fighting peasant skeletons for twenty-five XP a pop when you could wipe out a bunch of rats with much greater ease? Ah, the joys of low-level grinding. So much easier than going after massively more difficult opponents.

I was about to move on to the next window when I paused. One hundred and four XP for thirty-six rats? That was off. I did some quick calculations and then realized what had happened: the rats had gone from three XP a pop to one XP a pop as soon as I hit my new level. Dang. Reaping that reward was going to take a lot more work.

I swiped eagerly to the next window.

 Your attributes have increased!

> Mana +1
> Strength +1

 You have learned new skills. *Climb: Basic (I), Athletics: Basic (III)*

Only a boost to my mana and strength? While that was really welcome, I couldn't help but feel a pang of disappointment. I'd been growing used to broad stat boosts. And while the Climb and increase in Athletics were also great, I was still a little miffed. And it looked pretty official now: I was gaining a mana point each time I leveled.

I gave my head a good rub and swiped the window away. Lotharia had warned me about getting used to the early rewards bonanza. Looked like things were already getting a little stingier.

There are new talent advancements available to you:

This was the good stuff. Minor Magic, Sabotage Defenses, Double Step, Distracting Attack—those were all still there, along with a new talent:

```
Pin Down
XP Cost: 35
- A judicious application of your weapon
to a foe's foot, clothing, or other part
will result in them being trapped in
place for a variable amount of time.
- Pre-requisite(s): Uncanny Aim.
```

I chewed on my lower lip as I stared out into the sky. I could go big with this purchase. One hundred and four XP was more than I'd ever had to throw around. Looked like it was time to get Minor Magic at last.

Which was really exciting. A major reason I'd picked dark-blade as a class was for the arcane aspect, and while the Shadow Stepping had already proven pretty sweet, I was eager for more.

I reached out and tapped Minor Magic.

The letters glowed gold, and then the world fell away from me.

My sense of self bled out of my head, like water sloshing out of a bowl. I became aware of the rocks around me; of the battlements; of the air, of its substance. Of its commonality.

More accurately, what they all shared in common. An essence. A flow. A force.

My awareness spread out even further, incorporating the entire curtain wall. I could sense where it was smooth, still well structured, the golden glow of its essence bright. Could find countless areas where it had been dented or ruptured, the golden glow growing diffuse and torn.

The landscape opened before me. I was at once flying above and flowing through the ground. Up into each tree, into each blade of grass. I was the rocky roundness of pebbles, the silvery, mercurial sweep of the stream. A brilliant knot of golden light hopped, stopped, and turned to look at me. An animal, a *rabbit*, but so much more.

The experience was dizzying. Everywhere and everything was suffused with this golden light. What was living or orderly glowed brightly. What was torn or broken bled the light out into the air.

I swept down to Feldgrau, which was chaotic to my new senses: fragments of bright gold rising up where walls yet remained, but everywhere else the dark, jumbled mess of destruction. Rubble and detritus, ruins and chaos.

Even as I explored Feldgrau, the rest of the world around it continued to open up to me, a golden expanse, the fields, forests, cliff faces, the clouds and sky—

But something caught my attention. A figure walking through Feldgrau, glowing with a cold, icy blue energy. The opposite of the gold. Unlike the animals and plants, I couldn't flow up into it; I tried to touch its essence and was burned by its awful cold. There were more of them, countless of these icy blue figures stumbling and stalking through the ruins.

The undead.

My mind rose up over the village, and I saw a great pit of churning blue in the town commons, deep like a whirlpool and swirling as if full of broken ice. Beyond it, the remnants of a tower, and within it, a presence, an intelligence.

I hovered before the tower, and a presence noticed me. I felt its attention rise to match my gaze, twin ice-blue eyes staring at me from its dark interior.

Noting me. Sensing me for the first time.

I recoiled, screamed, and with a start I was back in my body, high up on the battlements.

I passed a shaking hand over my brow. What had just happened? Where had that come from? I squeezed my eyes shut and then it hit me: I'd just learned Minor Magic. Was that vision a sense of the magic in Euphoria?

I picked up a shard of rock that lay next to me. It was gray, dusty, unremarkable. Yet in my mind's eye it had glowed more precious than any gem. Everything. Even the very air. Laden with that golden magic. That potential.

I opened my character sheet and scrolled to the bottom. A new section had appeared, similar to Lotharia's:

 Spell List

Cantrips: Basic

I tapped the word "cantrips," and three spells appeared, nested beneath that title:

> *Light:* Summon a small sphere of illumi-
> nation with the power of a well-burn-
> ing torch. This sphere can be directed to
> follow you at a fixed distance, or moved
> as you desire up to a distance of twenty
> feet.
> *Mage Hand:* Lift and move a small object
> by simply pointing your finger at it and
> focusing. You can manipulate objects

within twenty feet of you, though the
closer the object, the greater the weight
you can lift.
Detect Magic: Detect the presence of
enchantments and sorcery within a range
of twenty feet. The strength and nature
of the magic will be indicated by the
brightness and color of its glow.

Nothing earth shattering, but still a start. Suddenly eager, I pointed my finger at a pebble a couple of yards away and focused. In my mind's eye the pebble glowed golden, connected to my finger by a thin golden line. I pointed up, the line flexed, and the pebble rose smoothly into the air.

I snapped my hand into a fist, severing the line, and the pebble fell with a clatter. I could cast magic. What had that unlocked?

I swiped to a new window:

There are new spells available to you:

Death Dagger: Craft a blade from the
essence of night. This spell allows you
to summon a small blade imbued with the
essence of the dark, dealing negative
energy damage to your foes.
- Mana Drain: 3
- Cost: 75 XP

Night Shroud (I): Envelop your immediate
environs in a pall of inky night, dousing
flames and blinding all those who depend
on natural light for sight.
- Mana Drain: 2 to summon, 1 to maintain
for every additional minute
- Cost: 75 XP

> *Ebon Tendrils (I):* Animate a length
> of shadow so that it obeys your will,
> growing up to a length of five yards and
> with half your physical stats.
> - Mana Drain: 1 to summon, 1 to maintain
> for every additional ten seconds
> - Cost: 65 XP

I whistled. Those all sounded amazing. I leaned back and played out each spell in my mind. I was starting to get a sense of just how lethal an assassin a darkblade could become. I loved it. But the XP cost! No wonder Lotharia's talent list was so limited; she'd been saving up for her spells. They changed everything, but came at the expense of normal talents.

Originally I'd intended to splurge and buy Double Step too, but now I wasn't sure. Should I save up for one of my true spells? I spent several minutes pondering, then decided Double Step was the smartest move. It would allow me to move into an attack, and then escape right away. At the moment, regular Shadow Step served to either get me out of trouble or simply into combat. Having that versatility was key. After all, I was still only level three.

I sighed wistfully as I read the spells again, then tapped Double Step. The talent glowed a beautiful gold – a gold I now better understood – and appeared under my list of talents.

Time to continue exploring. I rose to my feet and looked both ways along the battlement. One side curved around to the wyvern's tower. The other ended thirty yards away at a second tower, its arrow slits dark, the door that opened to the interior hanging ajar as if it had been nearly smashed apart by a fell blow.

I rubbed my hands together. Time to explore.

9

I MOVED QUICKLY along the wall, peering between the crenellations at Feldgrau far below until I reached a mangled wooden contraption that filled nearly the entirety of the wall top. It was some kind of war machine, but had been badly battered apart, with entire chunks shattered and fallen. I bent down, peered at it from different angles, then realized with a start what I was looking at: the remains of a giant ballista.

It listed badly from the swivel pole on which it had been mounted, its huge boxy head banged in and the thick ropes that had twisted the stubby bow arms now hanging loose like mop-heads. A number of spear-length bolts lay on the walkway beside it, and the bowstring wire seemed to be in good condition.

Curious, I ducked under the end of the long stock, where a groove was cut out and lined with leather padding. With a grunt I rose to my feet, barely able to take the weight, and then lowered it once more. A stronger person than I would be able to aim the ballista where they wanted, using the swivel pole as a fulcrum. I reluctantly stepped around the broken machine. I wouldn't even know where to start fixing it.

Instead, I continued on to the next tower top, and slipped up beside the door to take a good listen. Nothing from within except perhaps the play of wind through the narrow windows. I ducked my head around and peered inside: pretty dark, but after a moment my eyes adjusted to the gloom and I made out the contours of an empty chamber. Nothing moved, nothing made any sound, so I stepped inside to examine things more closely.

The floor was littered with rusted blades and dented armor, most of it splotched black with dried blood. A horrendous fight must have taken place here. A hole larger than me gaped in the far side of the tower where something akin to a magic cannonball must have burst inside. The far wall of the tower bulged out as if the projectile had nearly gone through it as well.

A stairwell descended to the next level, and I was about to take it when a column of shadow moved with a leathery rustle.

I nearly yelled. Instead, I jumped back against the wall, my newly intuitive stealth helping me avoid kicking metal debris. I stared at the long shadow, trying to make it out.

Slowly, its features resolved themselves. A huge bat, nearly as tall as I was, suspended upside down with its black wings wrapped about itself.

I remained frozen. It had stirred but not awoken. How had I missed seeing it? Some magical or monstrous property? If so, that meant it would be a wicked predator at night, swooping in unseen. And at that size? It wouldn't be hunting moths.

I licked my dry lips. What to do? I loathed the idea of killing an animal while it slept, but even from where I stood I could make out the massive fangs that emerged from its foxlike muzzle.

What would be best: killing it while it slept and feeling guilty, or trying to fight it at night by waving my dagger in the air in the hopes of scoring a fleeting hit as it attacked me?

I hardened my resolve. First, it wasn't a real animal, just a creation of Euphoria. Second, it was clearly a monster, and would have to be dealt with sooner or later. This was my opportunity to take care of it now, on my terms. As a hardened gamer, I knew what I had to do.

I crept with exceptional care along the wall, and as I drew close I finally smelled it: a warm, musky smell, with hints of cinnamon. It smelled nice, actually, which kind of threw me off. I was used to monsters smelling like rotten meat or mold.

I inched forward and positioned myself behind it and to the left. That way I'd be able to reach across its throat with my right hand and slit it with one pull. I took a measured breath. I'd have one shot. I was counting on Backstab, but I'd need to take extra precautions.

Adrenaline Surge hit me like a flash flood roaring down a slot canyon, filling me not only with physical might but also with renewed confidence in what I was doing. I made a mental note to consider that later: did it have a secret effect on my mental stats?

I gripped my blade tight. Took a deep breath. Reached across the bat's neck. Its long muzzle was tucked up, making my angle of attack narrow. One last breath, and then I stabbed in as hard as I could and *yanked*.

Adrenaline Surge made all the difference, for the bat's hide was as tough as a leather couch. The point of my dagger struck true, sank in an inch or so, and then I ripped it free in a welter of blood.

The room exploded into chaos as the monstrous bat flapped its wings with a high-pitched keen, falling to the ground and thrashing around. I leapt back, right into the stairwell that curved down to the next floor, and ducked out of the way. No sense in taking a random buffet or blow.

The bat hissed and gurgled and flapped for what seemed like ages until finally it went still. My XP chime sounded in the resultant silence, and I slowly stood to peer back into the room. The bat lay on its back, one massive wing rising up the wall, the other half furled by its side.

I found that I didn't want to stare at it. As necessary as the attack had been, I still felt dirty for killing a sleeping animal. *Sleeping monster*, I corrected myself. I shrugged my shoulders, cleaned my blade on my thigh, and tried to put the thought aside. In an attempt to cheer myself up, I opened my character sheet.

 You have gained 35 experience (25 for killing a dire bat, 10 for your first assassination). You have 42 unused XP. Your total XP is 247.

You have learned new skills. *Backstab (II)*

My first official assassination. That did and didn't make me feel better. Apparently, that kind of kill was sanctioned by my character class – obviously – but that didn't assuage the unfairness of it. I rubbed at my jaw as I made my way down the stairwell to the next floor. I'd have to work on reconciling myself to life as a darkblade.

The stairs opened onto another chamber that took up the entire width of the tower. Faint bars of light filtered in through the arrow slit windows, barely enough to make out anything in the gloom, so I focused my thoughts and cast my Light spell.

In my mind's eye gold light coalesced in my palm, grew extra bright, then broke free and floated up to become a radiant ball. Interesting. Powered by my own life force? My innate magic? Either way, it filled the chamber with a cool, eggshell-white glow, banishing the shadows and revealing the contents.

A metal spoke in the middle of the chamber rose from floor to ceiling, dozens of short rods of different lengths extruding from its body. It turned slowly with a subtle grinding sound, as if some sand had drifted into its works.

What the heck?

I fell into a crouch as I considered it. How was this part of the tower's defenses? The floor was bare and clean, almost as if it had been swept. The walls, however, were scored with deep, blackened gashes, as if the stones had been slashed at by a blade so hot it could cut inches into the rock. Horizontal slashes, most of them a yard long or so, all at different heights.

This was a puzzle. Some kind of trap room. But what was it doing here? Lotharia's warning came back to me. The castle was slowly devolving into a raid area. Perhaps this revolving column was a new addition. Something to challenge ruin-exploring adventurers. Either way, I'd have to get past it if I wanted to keep going down.

I studied the rods that extended out from the column's surface. They were plain, about a foot in length, but their circular ends had been painted in different colors. Greens, blues, yellows and reds.

One thing I'd learned over my years of gaming was to not rush trap rooms if there was no need. So I settled down to think this one through. Examine every facet. I'm embarrassed to admit it took me five minutes to realize that the horizontal slashes in the wall lined up with the rods.

Huh. So something activated them, causing them to shoot beams of rock-melting energy. That wouldn't be good.

Through painfully slow process of elimination I tried to match up the different colored tips to the slashes on the wall. I quickly connected crimson with the deepest gashes. Yellows clearly lined up with their own set of cuts, too. I wasn't a hundred percent sure if the greens lined up with any, and was pretty sure the blues didn't. But was I willing to bet my life on it? Try to sneak through the room, only crossing before green and blue rods?

Nope.

I dismissed my Light spell and Shadow Stepped across the room into the opposite stairwell. I ducked down out of sight immediately, but no slashes of fire split the air. My XP chime sounded. Surprised, I opened it up.

> You have gained 5 experience (5 for evading but not defeating the tower trap). You have 47 unused XP. Your total XP is 252.

Rats. Almost enough for a spell. I just needed a bunch of rats to push me over and I could get Ebon Tendrils. For a second I was tempted to try and solve the trap room, but the depth of those slashes in the rock convinced me to keep going. I could always come back with Lotharia for her opinion.

Down to the next floor.

This one was lit by a faint blue radiance, the kind of light you might see if you shone a flashlight through a thick curtain of clear ice. It stemmed from a translucent cylinder that filled the center of the room, its interior rippled but not opaque. I'd never actually gulped before, but the sight of the cylinder's interior made me do so.

It had to be some kind of time-stop effect. But only one person had been completely contained by the cylinder. A half-dozen others had been partially caught, and those parts of them had been perfectly preserved. The parts of them that had remained outside...

Disgusting.

They hadn't rotted off but rather it looked like something or someone had harvested the flesh that had remained free. Thus within the cylinder I could see legs, arms, parts of torsos, even two shoulders complete with necks and heads. The rest of their bodies were missing. Just rotted stumps, cut clean as if by cleavers.

Were those two men with their heads in the time-stop still alive in some sense? If so, they'd die horrifically the moment the spell ended.

Shuddering, I peered past the victims at the edge toward the man in the cylinder's center. He was a young black guy, late teens perhaps, and clad in a combination of chain and plate armor. He was frozen in the act of yelling his defiance, an arm outstretched to shield his face, probably from the incoming timebomb that he'd seen hurled his way.

He looked so alive. Eyes narrowed in anger and defiance. As if at any moment he could have snapped out of his trance and finished his yell.

"Damn," I whispered. "Whoever you are, I'm sorry."

I was about to turn my scrutiny to the rest of the room outside the cylinder when I saw something lying on the floor before the armored youth. An intricate little sphere of blue enmeshed in silver wire.

I activated Detect Magic. The time-stop cylinder was blindingly bright, and for a moment I had to shut my eyes, dazzled by its power. By slow degrees however I was able to squint at the cylinder through my fingers, then drop my hand altogether.

Fascinating. The closest comparison I could come up with was those drawings of the earth's magnetic poles, where the north and south pole were connected by continuous lines that bulged out around the planet. In this case, the lines were a soft, robin-egg blue, and energy was pulsing out of the top of that magic apple, circulating around the cylinder, then feeding back into the apple's base.

Huh. If I could destroy the apple, or dispel its magic, I'd free the prisoner. But it was protected by its own effect. Out of curiosity, I picked up a pebble with Mage Hand and flung it at the cylinder.

The pebble hit the cylinder's exterior without a sound and stopped, half embedded. So much for that.

"Sorry, buddy," I said to the young knight. "Wish I could help you."

I forced myself to look away. The rest of the room had been scavenged pretty thoroughly; a heap of trash had been swept up into one corner, while the rest of the floor was bare. Giving the cylinder a wide berth, I walked around to the next stairwell and made my way down.

I emerged onto the ground floor chamber, and someone – or something – had converted it into a den. Old sheets and blankets had been stretched out to form a small tent-warren, so that I couldn't make out the actual floor. The broad doorway leading out into the bailey was blocked by numerous stout timbers jammed between it and the floor, while a largish gap in the wall led out onto the berm that hugged the castle wall just within the ravine.

As I crept down the stairs, I heard voices raised in argument. Three troglodytic humanoids, squat and small, clambered in through the gap, sacks over their shoulders.

"Ain't worth it, I tell ya. How many of us are left now?" This was the smallest one, his skin the lightest green, his head hairless and his ears massive.

"Seventeen," said his plump companion with beatific confidence.

"You always say 'seventeen'," snarled the little guy. "You don't even know what that means!"

"Seventeen," repeated the plump goblin with obvious wicked delight.

"Enough!" This was the third goblinoid. She wore what looked like a beaver skin over her head and draped down her back like a cloak, and had painted her face bone white with little black lines to indicate skull teeth over her lips. "We've brought back loot and food and more loot time and again, ain't we? Quit yer yapping, Dribbler. We got a good thing going."

"All I'm saying," said Dribbler, dropping his sack as soon as he made the interior of the tower, "is that this ain't workin' in the long run! Where's Hootie got to?"

"Dead," said the plump goblin.

"And Licky-lick?"

"Eaten by the night terror."

"And Snot-Boogie?"

"Snot-Boogie," said the plump goblin sadly, as if pained by the memory.

"And Red Bean?"

"Also eaten by the night terror."

"And—"

"Yes, yes," snapped the female, leaping down off the last ledge to land next to Dribbler. "We've lost 'em pretty good. Don't mean we're gonna all get lost. And look!" She opened her sack and pulled out a glittering dagger that looked like a shard of ice. "Lookit!"

"Oooh," said both Dribbler and his plump companion.

"Mine," said the female, jamming it into her belt beside numerous pouches. The blade cut the leather easily, and her belt and pouches fell to the floor around her ankles.

This cracked the other two goblins up to the point that Dribbler fell on the floor while the plump goblin clutched his belly and squeezed his eyes shut, crying.

I took a step back up out of view. Goblins. More monsters. Should I attack and kill them? They were walking treasure troves of XP. And that dagger *had* looked nice. Could I take them? Even if I could, was it right to kill them just for the XP?

Dang it. These kinds of questions had never plagued me in Golden Dawn. There, goblins had simply screamed and attacked on sight, or wandered around their little camps looking lost and confused till you attacked, at which point they switched into murder mode.

But here? Dribbler? Snot-Boogie? Expressing concerns and humor? They seemed all too real. I stared down at my dagger. I couldn't just *kill* them. That'd be murder.

They were apparently going about making lunch. Dribbler was telling Barfo – that had to be the fat one – how to light a fire. Barfo was ignoring him altogether, and would only reply with 'seventeen' on occasion, much to Dribbler's fury.

I rubbed a knuckle into my temple. These guys were cute. Funny. They had freaking personality. God damnit.

Well, how was I going to get out, then? The windows were too narrow. The only exits were the goblins' blocked door or heading back up to the wall above and trying to find another way down.

"Oi," said the female goblin, staring right at me from the base of the steps, eyes wide. "Who are you?"

"Ah," I said, rising to my feet. "Um."

"Intruder!" she screeched, and ducked back out of sight into the main room. "Human in the tower! Murder and anarchy! Death and blood!"

"What?" Dribbler sounded taken aback. "Here, like here-here?"

"On the steps!"

"Should we run away?" That was Barfo's slow, cautious voice.

"Run away? This is our den, our castle, our queendom!" The female knocked something over with a crash. "Shhh! He can hear everything we say. Shh!"

I stood there, nerves taut, not sure whether to laugh or run. "Hello?"

Dribbler screamed, and more crashing ensued. Sounded like he'd run into something.

"He's casting a spell!" yelled the female. "Cover your ears or he'll turn us into toads!"

There was a tense, expectant silence.

"Um, I'm not casting a spell," I called out. "I don't want to hurt you. If I did, I could have slit your throats already." I slammed the base of my palm into my forehead. *Damnit!*

"See? He wants our blood!" The female was working herself up. "He wants to *bathe* in it!"

"He does?" Barfo sounded confused. "Why's that, Kreekit? That wouldn't make him clean."

"'Cause that's what humans do." Kreekit sounded furious and very excited. "They bathe in it and blow bubbles and it makes them want *more,* more and more till they become demons!"

"Ohhh," said Dribbler and Barfo in unison.

"That where demons come from, then?" Dribbler sounded curious.

"Some of them," said Kreekit. "Some of them, oh yes."

"I don't want to become a demon," I called out. "Or bathe in your blood! I, ah, just want to get out of the tower."

"Get out of the tower, he says!" Kreekit's scorn could have etched metal. "With all our loot, I bet. Our hard-earned loot—"

"Scavenged," said Dribbler.

"Our scavenged loot. No! He doesn't get our loot, and he doesn't get our blood!"

"I'm keeping my blood," said Barfo sullenly.

There was another pause. The ball was in my court.

"Um." Not a very authoritative start. Something they'd said earlier caught my mind. "Can I ask a question? What's this night terror that got some of your friends?"

I heard hissed whispers as if they were conferring, then Kreekit's voice. "Why's you want to know?"

"Well, I might have some good news for you."

"I like good news," said Barfo.

"It's a giant flying demon," said Dribbler excitedly. "He swoops down on you in the middle of the night if yer out taking a pisser or mooning around watching the stars—"

"Not that we do that anymore," said Barfo.

"No, no, of course not, goes without saying," said Dribbler. "He's the goblin-bane, the... the... what's another good name for 'im?"

"The sun of death," said Barfo solemnly.

"What?"

A beat as I imagined them both staring at Barfo.

"Yeah, maybe not," said Barfo.

"He's the death bat," said Kreekit. "Summoned from between the stars! Sent by elder witches to bathe in our blood..."

"Well, good news!" I tried to inject some cheer in my voice. "I killed him."

"You what?" asked Kreekit. "You never."

"I did too. He's up in the top room, dead and cooling down."

This time the silence sounded impressed.

"You sure?" asked Dribbler at last.

"Yep."

"Words are easy," said Kreekit, suddenly dismissive. "Look: I killed Mogr the ogre lord!"

"You did?" asked Barfo.

"No! But it's easy to say, innit?"

"Ohhh!" said Dribbler. "Like...I killed the Dread Lord!"

"Shhhh!" Kreekit sounded horrified. "Don't you never say that!"

"But—"

There was the sound of a smack. "Never!"

"Sorry."

"Look," I said. "If you want proof, I'll go get it. Give me a moment."

I ran up the steps, rounded the time-stop cylinder, up the next set of steps, Shadow Stepped to the far side of the room, then back up to the top. I was gasping for breath by that point. Wasn't my constitution supposed to have risen? Oh – that's right. It had been conditional on my getting a good night's sleep. Something I hadn't had since arriving in Euphoria.

I crouched down next to the dire bat and set to cutting its head off with my blade. Doing so was grisly, hard work, and took me far longer than I expected. My shoulders were burning by the time I was done, my hands drenched in sticky blood, and fat blisters had been rubbed into existence along the inside of my thumb. With a grunt I rose, lifted the head by the thick fur on top, and then paused.

I had one mana left. Which meant I'd be trapping myself below with no way to skip the revolving column if this didn't pan out. A real risk. The goblins were humorous, but I had no doubt about their ability to attack and kill. Was this worth it? What was I trying to gain?

I looked down at the bat's head and clenched my jaw. Somehow this felt right, even if I couldn't tease out why. So I made my way down, taking the steps two at a time, and Shadow Stepped. When I finally reached the goblin floor I slowed, caught my breath, and called out, "Here it comes!"

"Here what comes?" asked Barfo.

I threw the bat's head down the last of the steps and into the room.

There was a chorus of screams that all cut off as one. Footsteps padded closer, and then there was a sticky sound as if the head had been prodded.

"It's the sun of death," said Barfo. "Isn't it?"

"The demon of stars and blood has been slain," said Kreekit, voice awed. "Human, you did this?"

"I did," I said. I thought of embellishing my claim, but decided not to trust my charisma nine. "That was all me."

"I can't believe it," said Dribbler. "Our friends are avenged!" There was another wet, sticky sound, and the head slid into view as if it had been kicked.

"Can I come down now?" I asked. "I promise no funny stuff."

"Come!" said Kreekit. "We celebrate! Come! Join our feast! Barfo, hurry with the cooking!"

I stepped down warily into view. The three goblins grinned at me with their ferociously pointy teeth. Dribbler ran forward, hand extended.

"Shake! Human shake! Hand to hand, goblin to man! Shake! Shake! Shake! Shake!"

I took his wiry, heavily callused little hand in my own, and he pumped my arm furiously, leaping up and down to do so.

Kreekit spread her arms, extending her beaver skin behind her like a cloak, and intoned gravely, "The feast begins! Throw the head into the pot!"

Oh, great. A goblin feast. What had I gotten myself into?

10

BARFO'S DIRE BAT head soup turned out to be surprisingly tasty. When he first ladled the gray slop into my bowl, complete with tubers and gristly bits, I gave him a glazed grin and felt like I'd stumbled into some cannibal camp out of a nineteenth century Victorian dream. *Eat the flesh or be eaten in turn! Tekeli-li!* But a cautious sip turned my grimace into a surprised smile: it tasted delicious!

I had three bowls, and I think that made me Barfo's best friend for life.

Kreekit chose to stand on a stool and orate as I ate, waving a wooden spoon with grave dignity to punctuate her points.

"We are all that is left of the mighty Green Liver tribe! Once, when the sun was made, which was a long time ago, we were made too! We were as many as the leaves on the trees, and we were happy, and spent all our time eating and sleeping."

"And mating," said Barfo. "That's important to me."

"But then the good times, they ended," said Dribbler.

"Yes, I was getting to that," said Kreekit. "The humans came and built this castle, and built their village. They killed many Green Liver goblins. They get so mad! We steal a little food, they kill. We take a few of their people to eat, they kill! We set fire to their house and roll cart full of dung into their party? They kill!"

"No humor," said Barfo sadly.

Dribbler leaned forward. "But humans get in trouble."

Kreekit threw her spoon at him, but missed. "My story! Humans, you see, they get in trouble. A terrible bad evil dead man come, and he destroy everything!"

I thought of the icy blue eyes that had stared out of the ruined Feldgrau tower at me. "Is that the Dread Lord? The one who lives in the village?"

"Shhh! Don't say his name, never say his name, or you will bring him here! But yes. The Dread Lord come and bring ruin and fire and kill all the humans and take the castle. Then he try to dig under castle for a long time, but finally he give up and go away, going back to village to rule the village."

"Huh," I said. "There are tunnels under the castle?"

Kreekit gave me a pitying smile, the kind I tried not to give my slower students when they said something unintentionally hilarious. "Are there tunnels? There are dungeons! Many many! Previous Green Liver chieftain, Fire Toe, he lead many goblins into the keep to see what was in dungeon after Dread Lord leave. He never come back, so now Kreekit is the chieftain."

"And the Dread Lord – what's he want down in the village?"

Kreekit shrugged. "Don't know. He is not Kreekit's friend. He doesn't tell me his secrets."

I couldn't wait to share this with Lotharia. "How long ago did this happen?"

"Seventeen days ago," said Barfo.

"Many moons ago," said Dribbler.

"Many years!" Kreekit threw her arms open wide. "But now the Green Liver tribe is very small. Demon death bat eat us, dead humans in village kill us, ogres in castle throw us for fun. Very sad time for the Green Liver tribe."

"The ogres," I asked. "They live in the stables?"

"Yes," said Kreekit. "There are four of them. Mogr is their boss. They are cruel and stupid."

"I bet. And the undead ogre? What's up with him?"

"Once, the ogre clan was five. But the Dread Lord killed one, and turned him undead. That was Mogr's mate. He go down into village and capture her, bring her back, try to heal her."

"True love," said Barfo with a sigh.

"But it not work. So Mogr chain his mate to keep her close to him, and he grow even meaner and cruel ever after." Kreekit sighed and sat on her stool.

"All stories have lesson," said Barfo, leaning in conspiratorially. "This one: avoid true love. It make you undead in chains."

I snorted. "Yeah, good advice. And the wyvern?"

"The dragon?" asked Dribble.

"Right. The dragon. When did it show up?"

"Seventeen days ago," said Barfo.

"Many moons ago," said Dribbler.

I cut in. "Got it, got it. What about the keep? Why's it boarded up?"

"Bad things in keep," said Kreekit darkly. "Mogr close it up after Fire Toe go in with many Green Liver goblins. Bad things inside. Must say, pretty good move of Mogr."

"Much approval," said Dribbler.

"I see." I set my bowl aside. "One last question. Can I come back with a friend? I want to show her the blue light upstairs."

Kreekit narrowed her eyes. "Who your friend? Mogr?"

"No, no, no, no. Not Mogr. She is another human. Very nice. Lotharia. She likes goblins. A *lot*."

They glanced at each other, then Kreekit shrugged. "If she your friend, and she likes goblins, then she can come."

"Great. Thanks." I stood. "And, ah, mind if I open the door to the bailey? I'd like to get out."

Barfo stood and dusted off his bandy legs. "I open it. Come." He pulled the propped beams away and set them aside, then peered out through a gap in the wooden door. "No ogres. Dragon sleeping. Safe time to go. Be careful."

"I will. Thank you for the delicious dire bat head soup," I said. Inspired, I bowed low to Kreekit. "And thank you, Green Liver chieftain, for your kindness and wisdom."

Kreekit adopted a severe scowl. "You are welcome, human."

I hid a grin and stepped outside. Barfo closed the door behind me, and the beams scraped as they were pulled back into place.

My XP chime sounded.

Not wasting any time, I jogged quickly around the inside of the castle wall, skirting around a few small buildings we'd yet to explore. I darted by the rat swarm home before they could notice me, then stepped into our little base.

My eyes adjusted quickly to the gloom. Lotharia was asleep in the back, curled up against a pile of leather saddles covered in dusty blankets, a thick ray of sunshine splashing onto her lap where her book lay open.

"Working hard, I see," I said as I walked up.

"Hmm?" She cracked open an eye, then gave a feline stretch, groaning as she did so. "So you weren't just a low-charisma dream of mine." Her smile was mischievous. "You know, life doesn't have to be all about leveling. There can be moments in which to simply nap in the sun while pretending to read a really dense treatise on the arcane."

"Says the lady who's not on Death March mode." I sat on a crate. "I've discovered a lot while you slept. I'm level three now! And look what I can do." I focused my energy and used Mage Hand to poke her in the ribs.

"Ah!" She startled upright and then narrowed her eyes at me. "A single Mage Hand?" Six handfuls of straw rose up from the same bale and flew at me, exploding at the last moment in a flurry of gold.

I laughed and fell off the crate, tipped it up onto its side and used Mage Hand to pelt her with everything from scraps of leather to small chunks of wood. She laughed, retreated behind her saddles and did the same, and for a few minutes we engaged in the arcane equivalent of a snowball fight.

"All right!" She held up both hands. "A truce! Or you'll provoke me into escalating to Hail Strike."

"Fine, fine." I grinned, coming up from behind my crate and setting it back down so I could sit. "A truce. But wow – did you see the same thing when you first acquired your magic?"

"The golden light that flows through Euphoria? Yes." She pulled a strand of straw from her hair and returned to her nest amidst the blankets and saddles. "There are many names for it, but I've always preferred Prime energy. It's the life force of Euphoria. Not to be confused with animal or player 'life' as we understand it, but rather the animating force exerted by Albertus Magnus to shape the world we see and experience."

"And magic allows us to use Prime?"

"Exactly. A friend once explained it to me like this: magic represents our ability to 'hack' Euphoria. To step into Albertus' shoes in the most insignificant way possible and break the rules, shape the world as we see fit."

"Well, not as we see fit," I said. "We're constrained by the nature of our spells."

"Sure," said Lotharia. "We low-level dweebs are. But once you hit level fifty you get access to archspells. Those are much more open-ended. I only met one archmagus while I was here before, but... wow. The things Jeramy could do."

"'Jeramy'?" I asked.

She laughed. "Yeah. His full name was Elmanderyn Phlogiston Magnifico the Gray, but everyone just called him Jeramy. Really weird, really fun guy. He was the one who made Cruel Winter happen. The whole guild kind of coalesced around the parties he'd throw. Kind of like if you mixed Gandalf and Gatsby."

"Huh," I said. "Sure would be handy to have him around now."

"Yeah." She chewed on a strand of straw. "I wonder what happened to him."

"Well, I may have found out." So I told her about Kreekit and her goblins, and what she'd relayed to me about the fall of Cruel Winter.

Lotharia sat up in shock. "You had lunch with goblins?"

"I've never been the kind of guy to go for escargot or head cheese or blood sausage, but yeah. Dire bat head soup? Pretty damn good. Except for the bristles getting in your teeth. Could use some kind of filter to— ah, never mind." Her face had turned a little green. "But yeah. A 'Dread Lord' came and wiped everybody out."

"Must be the power that resides in the tower in Feldgrau. I wonder why. For something under the castle? And if he was that powerful, what stopped him from finding it?" She shook her head slowly. "It's like one answer only creates two more questions."

"And I think he saw me," I admitted. "When I discovered my magic, my mind went down to Feldgrau and he looked at me from within his tower."

"That's not good," she said.

"No, I can't imagine it is. Felt very Sauron-y of him. And you know how that turned out for Frodo."

"I don't like that metaphor," said Lotharia. "That would mean I'm Sam."

"Or Gollum, if you prefer."

"Even better. Raw fish and lots of talking to myself sounds like a wonderful way to spend the next six months."

We sat in companionable silence. It was the first moment of true peace I'd experienced since arriving in Euphoria. The evening in Lotharia's cellar had been good, but the threat of imminent death had loomed. But here? I could almost imagine we were safe.

"Why did you leave your job?" I asked, sliding down off the crate to sit in the hay.

Her expression changed subtly. She glanced away and her shoulders grew a little more tense. "Why? I've asked myself that more times than I can count. A guy, of course. Don't all the pathetic stories of women sacrificing their careers involve a guy?"

I winced in sympathy. "Must have been a hell of a guy, then."

"I thought so." She looked down at her hands, where she was pulling a piece of straw apart. "At the time, anyways. He was the lead singer of a band." Her smile became self-conscious, as if she were laughing at herself. "I'd been supporting him for a couple of years, but finally things seemed to fall into place for him. They started booking bigger gigs. Started traveling across the country. There was talk of their playing at one of the Albertus Magnus inauguration ceremonies."

"That's pretty amazing," I said.

"Yeah. And it was. I quit my job, and we and the rest of the band traveled around for six months. We went to Europe, there was talk of heading to Australia, but that crazy June wildfire killed that idea. It was amazing. Until... it wasn't."

"What happened?"

She tossed the piece of straw away. "You ever seen a surfer try to catch a wave? He'll wait out beyond the breakers for a good one to roll in, and then will start paddling really hard, trying to catch it so he can jump up on the board?"

"Yeah?"

"Well, Paul's band was like a surfer who almost caught his wave. But it slipped by, and after a lot of paddling they were left with nothing to show for it. The band fell apart, we moved back to San Francisco, then Paul told me he wanted to start seeing other women and we broke up."

"Shit," I said. "What an asshole."

"No, not an asshole." Her voice sounded worn out beyond belief, sad and soft. "He never lied. He was always upfront with me. When I offered to quit my job and help, he told me to do so only if I really wanted to. It hurt at the time – I thought he'd be thrilled – but he made it clear it was my decision." She tried for a smile. "A big life lesson for me, I guess. Though I'm still trying to figure out what I learned."

"And your old job didn't want you back?"

"They filled my position within a month of my leaving."

"But didn't cut your access to Euphoria."

"But didn't cut my access to Euphoria." Her smile became wry, a smile that was becoming familiar. "So I came here. To party, to be with old friends, and to spend six months figuring out what I want to do next."

"Well, you came close. Instead of partying you get to spend each waking minute fighting for your life, talking to an insulting noob, and spending the next six months figuring out what you want to do next. Close!"

"Yeah, real close," she said, and looked away.

We sat in awkward silence for a beat. I took advantage of the moment and opened my character sheet quickly to see what my XP chime had signaled.

You have gained 20 experience (20 for befriending the Green Liver tribe). You have 67 unused XP. Your total XP is 272.

Your attributes have increased!

Charisma +1

You have learned new skills. *Diplomacy: Basic (I)*

"Hey!" I said, swiping my sheet closed and grinning at her. "Notice how I haven't insulted you since I got here?"

"Actually, yeah," she said. "You've been surprisingly fun to talk to."

"Charisma ten, baby! And! Diplomacy!" I leapt to my feet and did a little shuffling dance from one side to the other. "I should party with goblins more often."

"Now that *is* good news! Charisma ten makes you practically bearable." She smiled.

"Oh, and there's more. I want you to come back with me to the goblin tower."

"OK, your diplomacy just failed you."

"No, not for head soup. Though you're missing out. I found this weird time-stop spell thing I want you to look at. There's a guy trapped inside it. He looks kind of awesome, and I'd love to figure out a way to free him."

"Oh?" She sounded suddenly very interested. "What did he look like? Maybe I knew him."

I described the guy, but Lotharia shook her head. "I'll have to come take a look. Maybe he joined after I left."

"Well, let me spend this delicious XP and we can go. I've actually got enough to buy my first real spell."

"Oooh, now we're talking. Lemme see." She keyed open my sheet and scrolled down. "You're growing *fast*. Nothing like a noob leveling in a ridiculously dangerous zone."

I opened my sheet again and scrolled down to the available spells. "I've been working on defensive and evasive talents so far, but maybe it's time to pick up a little offense? Death Dagger sounds pretty sweet."

"Yeah, but that'll eat up all your mana, meaning you can't Shadow Step in for the kill and get back out."

I frowned. "True. But doesn't your Summon Fog kind of make my Night Shroud redundant?"

"My fog doesn't douse flames, which is useful. And I think you can dispel your shroud, whereas my fog lingers after it's cast. Hmm. Ebon Tendrils looks like a pretty good utility spell that might double as an attack. Half your strength and dex would give it strength four, dex six. Not the best, but enough to maybe help you flank an opponent, opening them up for a Backstab."

I sat back and pondered my options. Out of curiosity, I opened my available talents window to see what had replaced Minor Magic and Double Step.

Sabotage Defenses, Distracting Attack, and Pin Down were still available, but there were two new additions:

```
Darkvision
XP Cost: 100
- The darkness is no barrier to your
sight, and reveals its secrets to those
with the means to probe its depths.
- Mana Drain: 1 to activate, 1 to main-
tain every ten minutes.

Wall Climber (I)
XP Cost: 75
- Vertical surfaces can now be scaled
with alarming rapidity, allowing you
to climb them at four times your normal
speed.
- Pre-requisite(s): Ledge Runner
```

"Did you see my new talents?" I looked up at Lotharia. "Darkvision sounds amazing."

"But you see the XP cost? Welcome to the bane of reaching ever higher levels. I'm warning you. Things are going to start to slow down, and soon all those tantalizing goodies are going to haunt you, floating just beyond your character sheet but feeling forever out of reach."

"What are you saving up for?"

Lotharia sighed, swiped away my sheet, and opened her own. "This beautiful, insane spell called Ice Grip. I've been wanting it since I arrived in Feldgrau. One hundred XP to coat the ground in ice that traps all enemies in its grip for a short period of time. It would have made all the difference in escaping the draugr and skeletons down there."

"You still want it?"

She nodded. "We're so underpowered here that anything that lets us get away would be key."

"True enough." I examined my options again. I really wanted Death Dagger, but I was ages away from level four and earning more mana.

Was it worth grabbing a couple of talents now, and one spell upon leveling? Or should I save to get two spells in quick succession?

Planning far into the future when in Death March mode felt futile. After all, a single mistake could kill me today.

Lotharia closed her screens and stood. "Ready?"

I selected Pin Down and closed my screens too. Better to make sure I lived today than plan big tomorrow and not get there. "Actually, mind doing a little more reading? I'm all out of mana and could use a nap in the sun over there."

She patted the straw by her side. "Come on over. I'm going to have to teach you how to meditate soon, but for now I'd love to read this chapter again for the third time. Maybe I'll even understand it this time round."

I grinned and threw a saddle blanket over the straw next to her, then lay down and wiggled till I was comfortable. It was indescribably delicious to stretch out in the sunshine beside an attractive young woman and allow myself to sink into a doze. I opened my eyes once as I fell asleep and caught her watching me. We smiled at each other and then I drifted away.

When I awoke I saw that I'd regained two mana points. Good enough. We hurried back around the castle bailey perimeter, and were almost at the goblin tower when bellows echoed from within the ruined gatehouse. I ducked down into a crouch and moved as quickly as Stealth allowed me to, Lotharia following my lead. Not being able to sprint was agonizing.

Four ogres entered the bailey, and I immediately could tell which one was Mogr. He stood a foot taller than the other three and must have weighed an extra couple of hundred pounds. His skin had darkened to an ashen gray, and his teeth were so large they practically looked like tusks. Bones were tied into black, greasy hair, and he carried a huge double-headed battle ax propped on one shoulder.

I ducked my head and focused on reaching the tower door. Each time I moved quicker I felt Stealth giving way, the shadows receding from around me, my intuitive sense of hiding slipping. Each time, I forced myself to slow.

Luckily, it sounded like the ogres were arguing. I couldn't understand their harsh language, but it Mogr was angrily refusing what the other three were demanding. Perfect.

I reached the door and knocked anxiously. "Barfo!" I hissed. "Kreekit! It's me! Let me in!"

Barfo's eye appeared in the knothole. "Mogr!"

"Come on! Please?" I glanced over my shoulder. The ogres had stopped amidst the stakes to face each other in an angry circle. "Open the door a crack!"

"But Mogr is out there!" Barfo sounded genuinely distressed.

"I'll— I'll bring you whatever head you want to cook with if you let me in. Promise!"

"Promise?" Barfo hesitated, then pulled the beams away, and a moment later Lotharia and I slipped inside.

I nearly collapsed in relief. The thought of trying to evade four ogres in a closed bailey was not an enticing one. "Thank you."

Lotharia ran her sleeve across her brow. "Yes. Thank you."

Kreekit emerged from one of the tents, Dribbler close behind her. "You the friend?"

"Yes," said Lotharia, and had the wit to bow low. Ah! The wonders of charisma fourteen and Diplomacy (IV)! "I am honored to make your acquaintance, grand chieftain of the Green Liver tribe. I've heard of your bravery and am very impressed."

"Yes," said Kreekit, clearly surprised and pleased. "Of course you have! I have a lot of bravery to be heard about. Good, good."

"Soup?" asked Barfo, raising a ladle from his black pot and wiggling it enticingly at Lotharia. "Some ear in it!"

"Why, yes, please!" Lotharia rubbed her tummy enthusiastically. "It smells delicious!"

Barfo beamed even as I stared incredulously at Lotharia, but she ignored me.

"But my friend here wants to show me something upstairs," she said. "Could I eat your delicious soup when we come back down?"

Barfo paused, considered, then nodded. "I save your soup right here. It stay hot for seventeen minutes."

"Come," said Kreekit. "I show you the sticky light."

"Sticky light?" I asked, following the little goblin up the steps.

"Yes. You touch it, your hand sticks. Happened to Red Bean. Very funny! He was stuck for days before he cut his hand off." She shook her head fondly. "Stupid Red Bean."

We rounded the curve of the stairwell and emerged into the second-floor chamber. I stepped aside, giving Lotharia room to approach.

"Wow," she breathed. "This is some crazy advanced magic." She walked around it. "And you're right. It's being generated by that sphere on the ground. This won't run out for centuries – its own magic is working on it, making its mana burn exceptionally slowly."

"And the guy in the center? Do you recognize him?"

Lotharia shook her head sadly. "No. But he's wearing the uniform of the Winter Guard. From the amount of chain he's wearing as opposed to plate, I'd guess he was a squire. That'd put him at about my level, maybe a little higher."

"And if we freed him? Would the player still be around to play his avatar?"

Kreekit frowned up at us. "Avatar?"

"Yeah," I said. "I mean, would his spirit come back to his body?"

"Oh, of course," said Kreekit. "Even if not, the All Soul would provide."

Lotharia smiled. "She's right. If the original player has signed off, Albertus would step in to simulate how the character behaved before."

"Huh," I said. "Fascinating. But that's all theoretical. How do we switch off the time-stop?"

Lotharia studied the frozen man, frowning and chewing on a lock of her hair, then drew her scepter out from under her cloak.

She turned to me, eyes lighting up. "Luckily for you, I'm an accomplished enchantress. I think I might have just the spell."

I tried to remember her options. "Restoration?"

"Nope. Imbue. It's a surprisingly versatile spell, and ultimately it will be what I level up the most. It allows me to change the state of any object, even to give weapons temporary magic bonuses."

"How does that help us here?"

"I can also imbue items with anti-magic." She winked at me. "See what I'm getting at?"

"No… wait. You could enchant something so that it wouldn't be affected by the time-stop?"

"You're not as dumb as you look." She looked around. "Now we just need a long enough stick to smash it with."

"Ooh!" Dribbler hopped up and down. "I have a big stick!"

"You do?" Lotharia smiled encouragingly. "Great. Could you get it for me?"

"Sure!" Dribbler's beam was rapturous, and he began fumbling at the leather cords that held up his knee-length trousers.

"No!" I stepped between them. "Dribbler! Ah – we need a different kind of, um, stick – like a wooden one?"

Dribbler's face fell. "Sure?"

"Yes," said Lotharia, eyes wide. "Oh, god. How did that almost happen? Yes. A stick made of wood."

"Hard wood?" asked Barfo, eyes gleaming.

"Watch it," said Lotharia, pointing her finger at him.

"Dribbler happy to watch," said the smallest goblin, and then cracked up. Barfo joined in, and the two of them rolled around on the ground, giggling like four-year-olds.

"How have I been outwitted by goblins?" asked Lotharia, shaking her head in wonder. "How?"

Kreekit kicked them both till they stopped laughing and climbed to their feet. "Enough! Enough! Go get wood stick, now!"

Still hiccupping with laughter, the two goblins ran downstairs, and moments later came back, carrying one of the heavy beams that had held the door closed. "Here," said Dribbler. "Not as big as my stick, but still pretty big."

"Yes, I'm sure. Now, put it down there and step back."

The goblins did as they were told.

Lotharia moved her scepter over the beam. "I abjure thee, I compel thee, to resist with disdain, all manner of wonders and miracles arcane."

Blue light streamed down from her scepter to soak into the wood, which quickly took on a silvery sheen as if it had been laminated.

"There," said Lotharia. "It's done, but hurry. It won't last long."

I tentatively touched the beam, but nothing happened. I gripped it with both hands and grunted as I lifted it up. "Do I just smoosh the time-stop bomb?"

"Yeah," she said. "But be prepared to jump away if you knock it closer to us. The field will move with it."

I hesitated. "You think there's a way we can turn it off and use it ourselves against an enemy?"

"Sadly, no. That would require handling it and using magic to stop its flow. It's pretty much a one-use item as a result of its very nature."

"Too bad." I hefted the beam and stepped up right next to the glowing blue light. I tried activating Uncanny Aim, but the silver thread kept slipping off the enchanted beam of wood. No go. "All right. Swing number one."

I lined up the beam and brought it down hard. It hit the blue light and sank through it as if it weren't there to crash next to the blue orb. Miss.

I dragged the beam back out. "Just a test run. Here we go. Number the two." I swung again, and this time I connected. The blue orb shot out from under the beam, badly dented but not destroyed.

"Watch out!" I yelled as it skittered off to the right, taking its field with it. Chunks of bodies that had been trapped in the left side of its field fell to the ground. The goblins shrieked and danced away, but the field moved too quickly – Kreekit and Barfo were trapped as the blue light washed over them, parts of their bodies still sticking out into the air.

"Hurry!" shouted Lotharia. "They'll die if their blood can't circulate back into their bodies!"

I ran around the cylinder to where the blue orb now rested just shy of the trapped squire's feet. If only I could use Uncanny Aim! I raised the beam high, then brought it crashing down with all my strength.

The blue orb crunched in a truly satisfying manner. The blue light flickered and disappeared. Kreekit and Barfo screamed as they staggered over and fell to the ground, surrounded by body parts that rained down alongside them.

But my eyes were on the youth in the center. His roar of defiance cut off as he staggered back, eyes wide, trying to adjust to how the world had changed in an instant. One moment he was in the midst of a horrific battle, then here we were. For him, not even a second would have passed.

"Invaders!" he shouted, raising his bastard sword high overhead. "Death to you all!"

11

"WAIT!" I SHOUTED, throwing my hands up in an attempt to placate him. "We're not your—"

The youth roared. I mean, literally. He threw his head back and let forth a terrifying roar that no human should have ever been able to make. It sounded more like a lion, some massive predator that was about to demonstrate why it ruled the apex, and echoed off the tower's walls.

Despite myself, my knees turned to jelly, my throat closed up, and I staggered back, overwhelmed.

The squire leapt forward, moving with ease despite his armor, and brought his glittering sword swinging around to take off my head. Panicked, unable to form a coherent thought, I activated Adrenaline Surge and brought my dagger up in the most insane attempt to parry.

Strength flooded my arms, and with both hands gripping my blade I blocked the squire's swing – only to feel the force transfer through my blade, down my arms, and hit me in the chest like a wrecking ball. I lifted off the ground and flew through the air to collide with the wall three yards behind me.

I think I bounced, then crashed to the floor. I don't want to think how bad that would have been for me without my adrenaline coursing through my veins.

"Stop!" yelled Lotharia. "We're—"

My vision cleared to see the squire point his blade at her. "I challenge you to combat! If you have any honor in your soul, then get over here and fight!"

Lotharia's eyes widened in panic and she mechanically marched forward, scepter held at the ready.

I activated Detect Magic. Thick cords of gold extended from the squire's blade to wrap around Lotharia's body, compelling her forward to fight him.

"Armed by the heart of glaciers, I cloak myself in the frigid north!" Her voice was barely audible as she spoke through her terror, but a moment later frost flowered across her body, forming crystalline patterns that quickly thickened until her chest, shoulders, and limbs were covered in thick plates of ice.

I had to get up. Any moment now my adrenaline would pass, and I'd be useless. And we'd be dead. Shaking my head, still feeling dizzy from the sheer force of the blow, I rose. What the hell could I do?

"We're on your side, you idiot!"

The squire ignored my yell, and when Lotharia was close enough he lunged forward, spearing his blade straight into her chest. The icy breastplate shattered, huge chunks raining down, and Lotharia staggered back, uninjured but now vulnerable to his next attack.

Kreekit began to dance, hopping from one foot to the next, waving her hands and calling out in a sing-song voice, "Ribbits and giblets, froggies and fire, spirits of goblins, hold onto this squire!"

Ghostly forms appeared around the youth, foggy and insubstantial, but they latched onto his limbs and arms, and tittering mutedly as if from a great distance away.

The squire tried to shake them off, but would have had more success trying to shake off glue. Growling, he took a deep breath, and his muscles swelled with his lungs; veins appeared down the side of his neck as his shoulders grew broader, and he powered forward as if charging through mud to where Lotharia was helplessly shaking her head.

"Don't make me hurt you!" she yelled, backpedaling.

I activated Pin Down and hurled my dagger. A silver thread guided its path right at the squire's legs, and for a second I thought the talent was going to take him in the back of the knee, but the squire moved forward so that the dagger slammed into his boot, sinking through the back of the heel and into a crack in the floor.

The squire yelled in fury as he fell face down, armor ringing out on the stone. Barfo ran forward, snatched up the bastard sword that had fallen from the squire's hand, then ran off with it down the stairs.

"Enough!" I shouted, moving forward but wary of coming too close. "Listen to me! We're part of Cruel Winter!"

The squire yanked his foot free of his boot and then hesitated. He looked from me to Lotharia. Turned to stare out the arrow slit windows, then around the room at the fallen body parts. "What— what is going on?"

"Oh, thank god," said Lotharia, sinking down into a crouch, head in her hands.

"You were frozen in a time-stop bomb," I said. "Years have gone by. The castle and Feldgrau are abandoned. We three are the last members of our guild."

"We lost?" The squire stared at me with wide eyes, and suddenly he seemed quite young.

Exhaustion hit me like a hammer to the back of the head. Nausea rose up in my throat as my legs gave way, and I sat heavily. It took all my strength not to lie down.

"Yes," said Lotharia. "We lost."

"But— but—" With effort, the youth stood and moved toward one of the windows. He peered outside, craning from side to side to try and see as much of the land as possible. "They're gone," he whispered. "All gone."

"I'm Chris, by the way." I gave up and lay down. Twenty or so more seconds to go. "Though I should probably come up with a fantasy name soon."

"I'm Lotharia Glimmervale, enchantress and Acolyte of Frost."

"Falkon Alastoroi," he said, voice distant. He turned, set his back against the wall, and then slid down to sitting. "Frost Squire."

My gorge rose up in my throat again and I turned onto my side. The dire bat head soup wanted out.

"How many years have passed?" he asked.

"We don't know." Lotharia sounded dejected. "But they're all gone. Ragnar Wyvernsbane, Jeramy, Cassandra Flameheart, Lokoko, the Emerald Twins – all gone."

"Impossible," said Falkon. "They were all here. Just— just seconds ago."

"Gah." I spat what tasted like bile onto the floor and then forced myself to sit up. My arms were throbbing painfully. "You hit really hard."

"I'm glad I didn't really hurt you. The vigor one feels in combat is both the best and the worst, isn't it?"

"No kidding. That what got you all pumped up there?"

He nodded. "I can feel the excitement about to pass. Won't be able to talk much for a while."

"You've still got it running?" I was amazed. "What level you at?"

"Level?" He frowned, but then his eyes glazed over, his face turned waxen, and he keeled over slowly in the goblin spirits' grip with a groan.

"I hate Adrenaline Surge," I said. "Right up till I need it, then it's the best."

"Human a friend now?" asked Kreekit.

"I think so," I said.

"Then goblin spirits begone." She waved her hand, and the smoky apparitions around Falkon faded away.

We sat in silence while Falkon shivered and shook, and after a couple of minutes he sat up again, wiping the back of his hand across his mouth. "Sorry about that."

"Trust me, I understand."

He examined Lotharia and me with narrowed eyes. "So how come you two are here if everyone else is gone?"

So we told him. Lotharia went first, explaining how her surprise return had proven to be a disaster, and I gave him a superficial version of Brianna's duplicity.

"I'm not sure I understand all that," he said. "But it looks like we're all that's left."

"Yep. And, ah, I know this is a weird question, but, uh… are you, like, the real you? Or are you being run by Albertus?"

Lotharia glared at me. "Chris!"

"What?" I raised my eyebrows at her. "That's not a fair thing to ask?"

Falkon watched us in confusion. "I don't understand the question."

"Which is all the answer you need, Chris. Drop it."

"Fair enough." I had to admit I was disappointed. It would have been nice to have another player with us, but given how long Falkon had been frozen? That'd been really, really unlikely.

"So what's the plan?" asked Falkon. "Are you two working toward some goal?"

"Survival," I said. "It's pretty nasty out there."

"Ogres, wyverns, skeletal champions, wraiths – we're out of our league here." Lotharia blew a lock of hair out of her face. "We've been taking it moment by moment."

The goblins were seated together in a row, chins on their knees, listening avidly. "Kreekit the chieftain of the Green Liver goblins," she said. "This here Barfo and Dribbler."

"Ha," said Falkon. "I remember you guys. We used to… never mind." He blushed. "Sorry. Any chance I could get my sword back? It's mana enhanced. I'd rather not lose it."

"We lost it," said Dribbler innocently. "No way to get it back."

Barfo gave a shrug. "Gone forever and ever. Sorry."

Falkon gave them a deadpan look. "Really?"

"I….ah… maybe we can look again." Dribbler jumped up. "And earn reward for finding it!"

"Reward!" said Barfo, and they both ran off down the stairs.

"We're working on clearing the castle," I said. "We've got an ogre problem in the bailey, a wyvern nesting atop one of the towers, a second tower we've yet to explore and a boarded-up keep apparently filled with evil monsters that leads down to all kinds of dungeons."

"Ambitious," said Falkon.

"Don't forget your pet rat swarm," said Lotharia.

"Right. I'm using it to level up. I'm only level three."

Falkon's brow contracted in confusion. "Level three?"

Lotharia sighed. "It means he's considerably weaker than we are."

"Will you help us?" I asked. "Clear the castle?"

"Need you ask?" Falkon gave a bitter laugh. "I'm a Frost Squire, and you tell me Castle Winter has been overrun with monsters. Of course I'll help. It would be my greatest honor. What is our first objective?"

Before I could answer, Falkon went rigid. His eyes glazed over, his mouth went slack, and then he simply froze.

"Uh…" I looked to Lotharia. "What just happened?"

"I don't know. Falkon?" She moved over to him and tried to shake his shoulder, but he was immobile. "Falkon?"

"A glitch in Euphoria?" I asked.

"Never seen one before," she answered.

Suddenly Falkon relaxed, blinked a few times, and then looked at us with avid curiosity. "Hey." His voice sounded the same, but was sharper now, more alert. "Who are you guys? What happened? I thought I died."

I shared a confused glance with Lotharia. "We… just covered all that?"

"Oh, well, not with me. I got a notification like ten seconds ago that my avatar was freed up while I was doing some playtesting in a beta zone. Did you guys get me out of the time quake?"

"Oh!" Lotharia sat back on her heels. "You're Falkon's player!"

"Yeah, name's Lisa." Falkon gave us both a wide smile. "Falkon was my favorite avatar till I lost him. What did you guys do?"

"I cast Imbue on a beam of wood, which Chris here used to crush the time quake generator."

"Well done!" Lisa climbed to her feet and looked down at herself. "Urgh. I feel the aftereffects of Adrenaline Surge. Did I spaz out and attack you guys?"

This was kind of weird. Like talking to the ghost of someone you knew before they died. "Yeah. But it was kind of understandable."

"Well, doesn't look like I killed anyone. That's a relief." She smiled again. *Amazing*. Lisa's smile was completely different from the AI Falkon's grin. "So, I'm Lisa. I work for Euphoria. Are you guys Cruel Winter? Looks like it. Can you catch me up on what happened?"

So we did. For a second time. We went into more detail this time through. Maybe because Lisa – Falkon – was such a good listener. She was really empathetic, nodding and making under-standing expressions as we caught her up to speed.

When we finished, she leaned back against the wall. "So we're basically screwed."

"Yeah," I said. "That's a good summary. You work for Euphoria, though. You didn't know?"

"Nah. The Universal Doctor's really good at keeping folks who are out of character from learning what's happening in-game if it doesn't affect their active avatars. I thought Falkon was lost for good. I've been meaning to bring one of my other avatars here to see what happened, but it's so far away from anything that I never got round to it."

"So what did happen?" I asked. "What's the last thing you remember?"

"It's a lot like you said. A huge undead army showed up without warning. They must have killed our patrols, though those were all NPCs 'cause who really wants to spend time riding around in circles when you could be living it up in Castle Winter? In retrospect, it makes me wonder if a player was directing it, but I don't see Albertus giving anybody that kind of power. I don't know."

She – I mean, he – made a face and gazed off at nothing. "Anyways, they attacked from three directions. Rolled through Feldgrau, speared straight up to the barbican, and had some fliers to strafe us from above. The scene was pretty nuts. I've not seen a fight like it since. We had some real heavy hitters – Jeramy alone could handle almost any threat – but I don't remember him taking part in the fight. I was told to hold the tower while Ragnar and Cassandra and the others planned out our defenses in the keep. I remember Ulfsted on the wall, exchanging crazy spells with the Dread Lord, as you called him." Falkon rubbed the side of his face, reliving the battle. "Everetos was also missing. Huh. So, yeah. I was part of the contingent holding this tower. I was squired to Sir Kay—"

"I remember Kay!" said Lotharia. "He was the best!" She smiled at us both. "This one time— well, anyway. Never mind. But yeah."

I watched her process her emotions, smiling then shaking her head as her eyes teared up. She finally smiled again and nodded to Falkon. "Go on."

"Well, we were hit hard. This green glowing ramp let the enemy charge up over the ravine right at our tower top, and we lost a ton of people trying to push them back. We were driven down through the tower. I lost sight of Sir Kay, and then it was just me and a bunch of regular guards here when a wraith magus threw that time quake at us. And that was it."

He snapped his fingers. "I hung around for a few hours, waiting to see if it was a short duration spell, but after a while I got really bored of seeing nothing but gray static outside the spell perimeter. So I logged out, waited a day, logged back in. Nothing. For a while there I would log in every week, but it was always the same deal. I think the last time I checked was maybe three or so months ago."

Lotharia gave him a sympathetic nod. "I know how that feels. When I was pulled away from Euphoria by real life it nearly drove me crazy, but after a month or so I kind of got over it. It all began to feel like a dream. You going to stick around and help us, or go back to your other avatar?"

"Well." Falkon looked down at his hands. "I'm technically supposed to be working right now. This is the equivalent of my taking a bathroom break."

I couldn't help but frown. I much preferred Lisa-Falkon to the stuffy AI version of himself. "We gotcha."

"But." Falkon frowned as he thought it over. "I could maybe put in a request for some personal leave. It's not like I haven't racked up the hours."

"You sure?" I asked. "I mean, it would really mean the world to us." *I'm playing in Death March mode*, I almost added, but that would've been unfair on Lisa. It would have pressured her to help, and that very pressure might have made her resent my situation, even change her mind and say no.

"Yeah, sure." He pulled up her character sheet. "Aw, Falkon was only level nine. So cute! Look at those baby stats." His punched up another window. "And my code of honor." He scrolled through it, a sad smile on his face. "I remember taking ages to write this all up. Kay was a big help. And my squiring ceremony was so awesome." He dismissed all her windows. "Yeah, I think it would be cool to come back. Plus it sounds like one hell of a challenge. Clear the castle? With all of us being only level eight or nine?"

"I'm level three," I said, trying not to be apologetic.

His eyebrows went up. "And you're still kicking? Damn. That's pretty impressive."

"Thanks," I said, enjoying the warm glow of pride.

"All right. Let me go speak to my supervisor and see if he'll give me the time off. If so, I'll be right back. If not, then Falkon will wake up as his AI self, and you'll know I couldn't swing it."

"We'll wait with our fingers crossed," said Lotharia.

"OK. Hang tight." Falkon lowered his head and went to sleep.

"Your new friend," said Kreekit. "He haunted by spirits. He need exorcism."

"You're not wrong," I said. "But I think we should leave him alone for now."

Kreekit shrugged and stood. "I go check on others. Make them find sword." With that, she stomped down the steps and out of sight.

Lotharia and I looked at each other. "I really, really hope Lisa comes back," she said.

"I know. She seems pretty cool. How does she get to switch between avatars like that? Is that something only Euphoria employees can do?"

"Anyone who's not in Death March mode can do it." She gave me a sad smile. "Or who's not locked into one avatar, like me by my corporate account. Sorry, Chris."

"Yeah."

We both subsided into silence and waited. Falkon slept, shoulders rising and falling gently.

Time passed slowly. Fifteen minutes? Twenty? I was starting to get antsy when Falkon suddenly awoke. His head rose, he blinked, then ground the heels of his palms into his eyes.

"Lisa?" I asked.

"My pardon?"

My heart sank. "Oh."

"My name is Squire Falkon the Kick-Ass," he said, face straight. "Lord of Lattes, Killer of Eclairs, Devourer of—"

"You did it!" I leapt to my feet. "It worked!"

Falkon grinned. "Sure did. My manager was kind of bemused. When I explained the situation he said I'd get sick of dying over and over again within the week. I aim to prove him wrong."

"Thank you," said Lotharia. "The odds of our success have just tipped enormously in our favor."

"Well, I wouldn't go that far," said Falkon. "I mean, what are we up against? Four ogres, plus an undead one? And a wyvern? Those are all level thirty plus monsters. We've got a hell of a fight ahead of us."

"You know their levels?" I asked.

Falkon nodded. "Generally, yeah. From Euphoria's early days, when that kind of info was readily available. But I'd have to see the monsters to know their actual levels."

"How can you tell?" asked Lotharia. "All the crunch has disappeared."

"For regular players, sure. But I'm in dev." Falkon blew onto his fingernails then buffed them on his chain shirt. "And I've got a few dev tools I can use to help us out."

"Really?" I wanted to scoot up next to him like a kid about to be told where all the Halloween candy had been stashed. "Like what?"

"Well, I've got to be careful. If I do anything flagrant I'll get flagged by Albertus and that could mean my job. But basic analysis? That shouldn't be a problem. In fact, I can probably disguise it as a spell. I doubt Albertus would care about that."

"That's incredible," I said. "Can you read the monster's stat blocks?"

"I could, but that might be pushing it too far. Back in the day, before Albertus hid a bunch of stuff, there were different levels of info you could access depending on your knowledge skills. Everyone could see a monster's name, level, and health bar. Then the health bar disappeared. Then the name and level. So it'd be easy to access the basic info, but if I wanted to simulate a knowledge check? That would activate a bunch of old mechanics that would probably flag me."

"Oh," I said. "Too bad. But that makes sense."

"Falkon, why did Albertus hide the crunch?" Lotharia sounded distressed. "It was so useful. Really helped me orient myself."

"Well, nobody really knows," said Falkon, leaning back against the wall. "Albertus is kind of the ultimate when it comes to inscrutability. But what I've heard from a friend of mine in the senior dev team in Brussels is that he's been looking to find the right balance between game and immersion. So having all those mana regen formulas and access to monster stat blocks made Euphoria feel like too much of a game. On the other hand, did you ever hear about that one week when he did away with every game aspect? Players lost access even to their own character sheets. Full-on immersion as if you were really living in Euphoria. Disaster. People freaked out, and he quickly reinstated sheets and so forth."

"But why?" I asked. "Why does he care if it feels too much like a game?"

"Well, think about it. Have you ever wondered why a global AI, our first digital overlord, bothered to put together a game like Euphoria in the first place?"

I exchanged a glance with Lotharia then shook my head. "To make money?" It sounded weak even as I said it.

"Nah. Albertus doesn't need or use cash. I mean, think about it: he's basically every computer system out there. He controls everything from weather satellites to the stock market. OK, not controls; 'observes'. He doesn't need money. He's beyond that."

I tried to puzzle it out. Funny how I'd never even thought to ask this question. Nobody I knew had. We'd all been too excited about the idea of Euphoria to ask why.

A small, vertical line had appeared between Lotharia's brows. "Well, he was created to help fix everything, right? Pull humanity from the brink of disaster? Maybe he made Euphoria to entertain us, cheer us up?"

"No. Here's how I see it." Falkon hopped up to his feet, unaffected by the weight of his armor, and began to pace. "Go back to 2057. The world's a hot mess. Mass refugee problems. Coastlines flooding. Crop production crashing. Starvation, war, water shortages – total dystopia. So what does humanity do? Come together, rise above our differences, and fix our problems?" He snorted. "Of course not."

"Yeah, I know this part," I said.

"Well, if you do, you've not thought about it enough. So once we proved we were unable to fix the problem by ourselves, the UN hired the Salvation Six to create Albertus by hooking up every single computer system out there to a main quantum processing center. Out of all that power arises our first true AI. The

Universal Doctor. And what's one of the first things he does after his Seven Days of Cogitation?"

"Create Euphoria," I said.

"Right. Why?"

Again, Lotharia and I exchanged confused glances.

"Because," said Falkon, tapping his fist into his open palm, "he was tasked with fixing our problems and doing what's best for humanity, right? But what does an AI know about humanity? Now, this is my personal theory, but I think it holds up. *I* think Albertus is using Euphoria as a private test lab in which to study us. Learn how we tick, what we want, how we use power, how we work in social groups, all of it. Which is why he's always tinkering with the balance between immersion and crunch. If Euphoria's too much like a game, we humans won't act like we do in the real world. There's a tendency instead for us to turn into sociopaths, to treat this world like it's not real and not care about slaughtering everything we see."

I immediately thought of how I'd felt after killing the dire bat. How I'd stayed my hand and not attacked the goblins when in any other game I might have gone straight for the kill. "Shit," I said. "I think you might be right."

"Uh-huh." Falkon stopped. "Which also explains Death March. Why on earth would a feature like that be included in a 'game'? You think Albertus actually cares about giving desperate folk money or favors for their troubles?"

Lotharia rubbed at her temples. "If he's looking to test us, then… Death March might be the truest test. That's when we'd react the most genuinely, because our lives would literally be on the line. The ultimate immersion."

"Exactly," said Falkon. "See? It all adds up. This whole thing is one big testing lab for Albertus to learn about us. So that he can decide what we really want, and what'll really be best for us."

I sank down into a crouch, eyes wide. The implications were huge. "Does anybody know what kind of conclusions he's drawing?"

"Nope. Like I said, he doesn't talk much. And these are just my speculations. And I doubt it's just Euphoria he's using to learn about us. You can bet he's processed every book, song, movie and other form of media out there. It's why I think his NPCs are so good. And they're getting better. Lotharia, you remember what they were like when you first played?"

She made a face. "Kind of clunky, yeah. They'd make really funny mistakes."

"Not anymore," said Falkon. "They're getting so good that it's even changed people's class preferences. Guess which class is gaining the most popularity the quickest?"

It was obvious. "Charlatan?"

"Yep. I bet that name's going to change really quick. But more and more people are simply spending time in town socializing and having fun. Less and less people are heading out to kill stuff."

"Like you," I said to Lotharia. "That's what you did when you were here, right?"

She blushed. "Yeah, some. But I still went on raids and had fun leveling up."

"Sure you did. Which is why your highest skills are Carousing and Diplomacy. And don't you have a rank in Seduction?"

Lotharia's blush deepened. "Excuse me. I'd appreciate your not discussing my sheet like that."

"Oh. Sorry. Charisma ten?"

"Meh. That excuse won't work for much longer."

"Anyways," said Falkon, cutting in. "That's my long way of explaining why so much crunch disappeared. And why Albertus wouldn't be happy with me if I tinkered around too much with my dev tools. But a little analysis shouldn't hurt." He winked at me, and then his eyes flickered with green fire.

"Holy shit," he said, sounding genuinely shocked for the first time. He was staring right at me. "You're in Death March mode?"

12

THIS WAS STARTING to get old. Or maybe I didn't like having attention drawn to how shockingly suicidal Death March mode was. Either way, I gave Falkon an irritated shrug.

"Yeah, yeah, I know. I got reasons. Trust me. It wasn't an idle decision."

"Just… wow. And you didn't tell me when I was deciding whether to come or not? You, my friend, have balls."

I closed one eye and canted my head to one side as I squinted at him. "And you technically do, too. Ghost balls? Avatar balls? I don't know the right terminology."

Falkon laughed. "Close enough."

"If we're going to adventure together, it's only fitting that we should share our sheets," said Lotharia. Did she sound a little prim? Maybe the testicular talk had brought out her prudish side.

"Sure," said Falkon. "Here, I'll share mine with you guys."

I did the same, then eagerly opened his sheet. I craved information. Greater familiarity with the system, a sense of how I could grow.

Falkon Alastoroi

Species: Human
Class: Knight
Level: 9
Total XP: 953
Unused XP: 9
Title(s): Frost Squire
Cumulative Wealth: 0

 Attributes

Strength: 16 (+2 due to knight class)
*Dexterity: 12
Constitution: 14
*Intelligence: 8
Wisdom: 10
Charisma: 12
Mana: 4/12

Skills

Athletics: Intermediate (II)
Melee: Basic (V)
Survival: Basic (III)
Dodge: Basic (IV)
Climb: Basic (II)
Chivalry: Basic (III)
Carousing: Basic (III)
Knowledge (Cruel Winter): Beginner (IV)
Endurance: Basic (III)
Code of Honor (II)
Engineering: Basic (II)

Talents

```
Challenge Foe
Adrenaline Surge
Astute Observer
Uncanny Aim
Headlong Charge
Throwback
Distracting Charge
Outflank
Avalanche Roar
For the King!
Death from Above
```

I gave a low whistle. "Nice sheet. Engineering? Would you know how to fix up a ballista?"

"Depends," said Falkon. "How badly broken is it?"

"It's up on the wall," I said, suddenly excited. "I'll show you. If we could fix it up, turn it around, aim it down into the courtyard..."

Both of their faces lit up. "Now that's a potent weapon," said Falkon.

"Run me through your talents," said Lotharia. "Quick summary, so we know what to expect."

So he did. Unsurprisingly, all of his talents revolved around close combat, ranging from his ability to force a foe to fight him to several rallying and intimidating cries. I felt immeasurably more confident with him on our team.

"This is what I'm thinking," I said once we were done talking shop. "Let's rescue your blade from Barfo then head up to check out the ballista. Then we can loop around the wall to the remaining tower and clear that one out, too. With a little luck, you guys will level, and I might do so a couple of times. Then, once we're stronger, we'll turn our attention to the ogres."

"Why not tackle the wyvern first?" asked Lotharia. "It's tough, but not intelligent."

"True, but I'm thinking we should lure it down into the courtyard. Then either drop a net on it, or lasso it or something. Fighting it in its nest will most likely drive it up into the air and allow it to do strafe attacks. So getting rid of the ogres first is a must."

"Makes sense to me," said Falkon. "This isn't your first rodeo, is it?"

"Not by a long shot," I said. "Ready?"

After retrieving Falkon's blade from the sullen Barfo and Dribbler, we climbed up to the revolving trap room – where I promptly smacked my own forehead, having forgotten my friends couldn't Shadow Step.

Together, we examined the slowly spinning pillar, Lotharia casting Detect Magic and Falkon using his analysis tool.

"What do you think?" I asked them.

"That's a difficulty check ten trap," he said. "Simple, but it'll cut us to pieces if it detects us."

"I think I have an idea," said Lotharia. "Its magical nature isn't very advanced. I think it triggers through direct line of sight. So if we trigger all of the rods, it should discharge its attacks, allowing us to see how best to cross through."

"That sounds… fun?" It didn't, really. "How do we do that?"

Lotharia smiled coldly. "Obfuscate the keenest sense, blanket thought with fog most dense!"

Her cottony white fog billowed forth from her palm, rapidly filling the room and blocking all sight of the far walls and stairs.

As soon as the fog grew thick enough, the spinning rods roared to life.

The room filled with the world's most dangerous light show. I couldn't tell which color rods were activated, but a good dozen of them spewed liquid flame in a straight line as it spun, their ends splashing against the tower walls. They were a deep, hellish orange, and their radiance caused the fog around them to light up, so that the room looked like a demon's fondest dreams of home.

"Now what?" I yelled.

"Now we weave through the beams!" Lotharia's grin was slightly unhinged, and she climbed the last steps and into the maelstrom.

To my horror she did exactly what she'd suggested, her form turning into a shadow amongst the jets of liquid flame, a silhouette in the sulfurous fog. She stepped over a knee-high beam, ducked under the next as it swung around, then fell into a low crouch to avoid the third.

"Come on!" said Falkon. "Your friend's got style!"

Did he actually sound cheerful? He leapt up and followed after, ducking and leaping over the incendiary plumes of death.

Dang. If they died, they'd just respawn in the highland meadow without their gear. But me?

I wasn't going to mess around. I evoked my Shadow Step ability, using my second to last mana point, and sank away into the darkness beneath me. The shadows roiled, and I emerged in the stairwell across the room as Lotharia ran the last few yards into view.

"Phew!" She bent down to check the back of her calf, then looked at her shoulder. "That was close."

Falkon jogged over a moment later, grinning widely. "Good work, Lotharia. Sharp thinking."

"Why thank you, sir squire," said Lotharia with a shallow curtsy. "Shall we?"

We climbed up to the top room, where I quickly explained how I'd killed the dire bat. Neither of them looked perturbed by the killing, but bringing it up still made me feel funny, so I hurried them out into the sunshine and toward the ruined ballista.

"So?" I turned to Falkon. "What do you think? Fixable?"

He made a face. "It's in rough shape. I'd need access to tools in the smithy, most likely, and new parts. But… yeah. Given time, I think I can fix it. Might not be as powerful as it once was, but it should give even an ogre something to think about."

"We should rest," said Lotharia. "None of us are at full mana and we don't know what we're going to face in the next tower. Why don't you spend a little more time examining the ballista? Chris and I can sit close by. It's about time I taught him to meditate."

"Sure," said Falkon, only half listening. He'd bent under the ballista and was examining something close to the pivot. "Sounds good to me."

"Darkblades can learn meditation?" I asked.

"Sure. Best way to regain mana quickly outside of a full night's sleep. Let's sit over here in the shadows and— What's that?"

I joined her at the battlement and looked out toward the highland meadow. Something was flying toward us. No, *somebody*. They weren't approaching Superman style, one arm extended, but rather were flying forward as if standing, cloak streaming behind them, one leg straight, the other bent at the knee.

"Brianna," I said. "She's found me."

Falkon disentangled himself from the ballista and joined us. "That a good thing?"

"I don't know," I said, suddenly nervous. "This could have all been a mistake. Or not. I guess we'll find out very soon."

"She's your ex, right?" Falkon looked sidelong at me. "You still have any feelings for her?"

"No," I said. "I only accepted her offer so I could help my little brother."

"OK, good. Helps keep things clear. Though if she's flying, that means she's pretty high up in levels."

"She said she's level thirty-five," I recalled. "And now I appreciate how tough that must make her."

"Yeah," said Lotharia. "Not Jeramy the archmagus tough, but way beyond our ability to fight her. And flight means either she's got some fantastic loot or she's arcane. And a level thirty-five wizard can blast us from these battlements without even having to get close."

"So... perhaps we play this one nice," said Falkon. "And... yeah. Just confirmed it. She's level thirty-six."

I forced myself to breathe easily as Brianna drew ever closer. Her avatar looked just like her, black hair streaming in the wind, dressed in black and purple with a strange cloak made of a thousand silver cords fluttering behind her. She slowed as she drew close, and then stopped perhaps fifteen yards out and slightly above us.

Typical Brianna powerplay. Making us look up at her.

"Chris," she said. "There you are! Do you know how long I've been looking for you? You're lucky I didn't give up."

My urge to protest, to argue with her was almost overwhelming. It brought back so many fights. She had the most incredible ability to twist everything so that she was never, ever at fault.

"Brianna. You've got a lot of explaining to do."

Her eyebrows shot up. "Excuse me? I give you a free pass to Euphoria then spend all this time searching for you and this is how you thank me?"

"You told me to go Cruel Winter," I said. "That's not your guild. So why?"

She glanced and Falkon and Lotharia. "Made new friends, I see. Smart. You going to use them like you used me?"

"Used you?" I forced myself to slow down. Take a breath. "No. It's not going to work, Brianna. I'm not going to let you get a rise out of me. Instead, answer my question. Why trick me into signing up for a dead guild out in the middle of nowhere?"

Again, she glanced at my new friends. "I'll tell you in private."

"No," I said. "Actually, let me rephrase that. Hell no. You think I trust myself in private with you?"

Her smile was practically a sneer. "You think these two would make a difference if I decided to really mess you up?"

"Easy now," said Falkon, tone genial. "Let's keep things friendly."

"Why?" Brianna's eyes flashed. "When Chris isn't remotely interested in being friends?"

"One last time, Brianna. What was your plan? You told me to skip all the tutorials, and even stopped Nixie from being able to explain the basics to me. You locked me into this avatar, and then tricked me into coming all the way out here where you thought I'd be all alone. Why?"

"Why?" She licked her lower lip. "Why doesn't matter. I've come to rescue you. When I couldn't find you, I went back to Goldfall and checked every other guild register in case you'd chosen something different. Do you know how much time I've wasted tracking you down? Now come on already. I'll explain everything back at my palace. No need to waste your time out here any longer."

I shook my head. "Don't you get it? I don't trust you. Why do you think I'd go anywhere with you now?"

I could see her frustration rising. Even though she was ridiculously more powerful, she clearly didn't want to embarrass herself before my friends.

Lotharia crossed her arms. "She set you up. Intended to get you all alone out here. Level one and with no idea how to play the game. If you ask me, she was planning to force you to accept a *geas* spell or the like. Blackmail you into accepting by threatening to leave you out here by yourself."

Brianna raised her hand and a small sphere of black fire swirled within it. "Oh, so your new friend is a bitch."

"Hmm," said Falkon, leaning one elbow on the parapet. "Jilted ex tricks you into a situation like this? I'd say she's not over you. Or, perhaps, her original attraction has twisted into some kind of freaky deaky hate-lust thing. Which, given the three-thousand-dollar price tag of getting you in here—"

"Enough," snapped Brianna. "I'm disappointed in you, Chris. I thought you were better than this. But I guess you're still all ego and no smarts." She raised her palm, and the black sphere flattened out into a broad disc of ebon flame. "So fine. Stay out here with your asshole friends. And here's a little parting gift to show you what happens when you insult me. A little Disc of Annihilation to destroy all your gear and force you all to start over fresh."

"Brianna," I said. "I'm in Death March mode."

She froze, then blinked and gave her head a sharp shake. "You're *what?*"

"Death March mode. You know Justin's in trouble. They're pushing for the death penalty. This is my one chance to turn things around."

"What he's saying," said Falkon, still lounging, "is that you actually nearly for real murdered him."

The black disc snapped out of existence. "Death penalty? Death March mode?" She floated closer. "You're serious?"

"You know I don't joke about Justin," I said.

She ran her hands through her hair, the implications of what she'd been about to do hitting her in full force. "You... you idiot."

"Actually," said Lotharia, "I think it's pretty damn selfless and heroic."

A burst of affection filled me for my new friends. To have them standing by my side, to face up to Brianna and call her on her B.S. meant the world to me.

"If you're feeling a little guilty about all this," said Falkon, "you could hook him up with some items to make his odds a little better."

Brianna was glassy-eyed. She gave a jerky shake of her head. "No. This is his doing. His choice."

"Yeah," said Falkon. "But you didn't help any, did you? Kind of screwed him over."

"Falkon," I said. "That's enough."

Brianna flew back. "Winds of eternity, brutal and gray, obey my summons and take me away!"

A tornado manifested around her, and then she was gone.

"Well," said Lotharia in clipped tones. "So that was Brianna."

"I mean, she's attractive," said Falkon. "Or her avatar is. I guess?"

I sighed. I was exhausted. Which was weird, because my body – my avatar's sense of energy – didn't change at all. Instead, a spiritual exhaustion that washed over me. I turned and slid down the inside of the crenellations, hands steepled before my mouth.

"Yeah. I know." I felt old, all battered and weary. "It doesn't make sense from the outside. Why would anybody hook up with someone like her?"

"Hey," said Lotharia. "We're not judging."

"Not much," said Falkon.

Old pain filled me. "I'd just moved down from Seattle. Left everything behind. My job, my friends, my life. We were just starting to get a sense of how much trouble Justin was really in, how badly the government wanted to screw him over. It was a tough time. And I met Brianna at a stupid club a friend of mine dragged me to. I didn't even want to go. But we met, and got to talking about games, and she said I was funny and gave me her number when I asked."

I dug my thumbs into my eyes, then sighed. "And it was a shitshow. The chemistry was crazy and hot for the first month, and then… she gave me lots of reasons to break up with her. And I wouldn't. I kept forgiving her. Or just letting things slide. Like when she didn't show for Thanksgiving lunch. I'd invited her to join Ev and me. Stupid. But she didn't show. Stayed home watching TV. And you know what I did? I bought her roses and went over to her place, to help her not feel bad." I gave a hollow laugh. "I was in a really bad place. I didn't want to let her go. I didn't want to be alone."

Lotharia knelt by my side and placed a hand on my shoulder. "We all need support. And sometimes we don't have much of a choice as to where we can get it."

"No kidding." I rubbed my sleeve across my eyes. "God. I feel like such an idiot. And you know what broke it off? We'd been planning this trip to what was left of Bermuda for some time. Her dad's place. And as things got worse, I kept telling myself we'd fix everything once we got there. But when we finally did… fuck. You can fill in the rest. An insane amount of hate sex and the worst verbal and emotional abuse I've ever experienced. I broke up with her at the airport and deleted all her info. Took me weeks to pick myself up off the floor after."

"And the next thing that happens is you get an invitation from her to enter Euphoria?" Falkon sounded justifiably skeptical.

"Yeah, I know. I know. But like I said. Desperation. My brother. And I'm pretty good at this kind of thing. I thought I could handle it."

Lotharia gave my shoulder a squeeze. "You *are* handling it. You didn't fall into her trap, whatever it was. You've already hit level three in a completely lethal zone. You've made allies who care about you—"

"We do?" Falkon grinned and held up both hands. "Just kidding! I know we just met, but yeah, I like you guys. It's why I chose to come spend up to six months with you here. Sorry. Keep going, Lotharia."

"You're doing great. Hang in there."

"Yeah," I said. I blew out my cheeks. "Damn. I'm sure glad you guys were here. I wouldn't have put it past her to kidnap me or something."

"Says a lot about her that she's that concerned with what two strangers think about her," said Lotharia.

"I know what you need," said Falkon.

"What?"

"You need to do some serious leveling up. That'll make you feel better."

For a moment I didn't know what to say, and then I laughed. "You're right. OK. Enough of my personal drama. Time to focus."

"Time to meditate," said Lotharia. "You ready?"

I couldn't muster any enthusiasm, but maybe that meant it would be the best thing for me. "Sure," I said. "Ready."

The sun was dipping toward the western mountains when I finally opened my eyes. I'd been lost in a world of glimmering gold, an approximation of the vision I'd had when I first received my magic. Meditation was basically a superficial version of that, a way to connect your essence with Euphoria's energy and allow it to flow into your soul.

I checked my mana. Back up to three. Not only that, but energy bubbled through my limbs and my mind was delightfully clear, as if I'd had a deliciously restorative nap. I looked over to where Lotharia and Falkon sat, eyes still closed, and checked their sheets. Lotharia was sixteen out of sixteen. Falkon was back at full, too.

"All right," I said. "Let's tackle that last tower."

They opened their eyes, stretched, then climbed to their feet. Together, we walked along the battlement across the entire front of the castle.

"We used to call this tower the Iron Gullet," said Falkon. "Jeramy once permanently imbued all of its stone with the toughness of steel."

"I remember that," said Lotharia. "He said he was drunk and didn't remember why he'd done it."

"Yeah. Looks like his magic's still good."

The last tower was in perfect condition, in stark opposition to the rest of the castle. The ruins of a catapult could be seen atop it, and the badly scarred door leading into the top room was closed. As I approached, I made out what looked like a symbol carved into the stone wall beside the door. It looked familiar, but I couldn't quite place it.

"A trap?" I asked, turning to Lotharia.

"No." She smiled and stepped right up to the wagon-wheel sized carving. "It's Jeramy's rune. Take a look at it with Detect Magic."

I did so, and immediately raised a hand to shield my eyes. The carved lines of the rune were brilliant with gold mana, which coursed through the grooves with incredible potency. The rune itself sent lines of golden mana around the entire tower, encasing it in a field of pulsing power.

I lowered my hand, eyes growing used to the glow. "That's… you can do that?"

"Oh, yes," said Lotharia. She traced the rune with her fingers. "It's how you make an Imbue spell permanent. Without a rune like this to anchor the magic, it'll dissipate back into the world, causing the item to lose its enchantment."

"But no," chimed in Falkon. "She can't do that."

Lotharia scowled at him. "That's not what he was asking. Of course I can't create a rune like this. At least, not yet."

"Fascinating," I said. The closer I studied the rune, the more complexities I saw. Mana was being drawn from the ambient air and slowly fed into the complex carvings, where it grew brighter, more condensed, and then distributed about the tower. I had a dozen more questions, but they'd have to wait.

"Time to get to work. There should be four floors," I said. "If it's anything like the last, some of them will have reverted into raid rooms. Traps, monsters waiting for errant adventurers, and so forth. If we have any difficulty, we retreat. It's always better to come up with a new strategy and try again than try to force our way through."

Falkon didn't even try to hide his smirk. "Catch a load of this. We've a regular tactician on our hands."

"I think that's sound advice," said Lotharia. "And good to remind ourselves of it. In the heat of battle, it's easy to forget."

"Right," I said, drawing my knife. "I'm the darkblade, which means I should scout."

"You, my dear friend, are level three and in Death March mode." Falkon unshouldered his bastard sword, rotated both arms to loosen his shoulders and nodded me aside. "Let the girl in the armor take the lead."

I wanted to argue. With my Shadow Step ability, I would be able to bounce the hell out of there if anything went wrong – but Falkon was right. No matter how confident I was becoming, I was still vastly underpowered in a very lethal zone.

"Fine," I said. "Ladies first."

Falkon grinned and pulled the door open slowly. We all peered in over his shoulder. An empty room. No gaping holes in the wall like the other tower, no dire bat napping in the corner. Just the stairwell leading down.

"Huh," said Falkon. "That's a little anticlimactic. Well, maybe there'll be something a little more interesting below."

"Wait —" cried out Lotharia, but it was too late.

Falkon stepped forward. His boot passed through the floor and with a cry he fell all the way through and was gone.

13

INSTINCT TOOK OVER. I hopped forward after Falkon, turning as I did so that as I fell through the illusory ground I was able to catch the edge of the doorway. My hands grabbed hold of the rough, broken masonry just within the tower and I clung tight, feet against the inside wall so that I could duck my head under the insubstantial floor and see what lay below.

It was a nightmarish scenario. The Iron Gullet had been hollowed out and filled with shifting shadows, resulting in a hollow throat easily forty or fifty feet high with only broken ledges extending from where entire floors had once been. Strange shadow webbing was layered everywhere, and the light itself seemed enchanted, rising slowly through the darkness in great globs like bubbles inside a lava lamp, casting a shifting cold, purple illumination as they rose.

Pulse pounding in my ears, I searched for Falkon. He was enmeshed in webbing perhaps twenty feet below. He was desperately hacking at the thick black strands that had encased him.

Where was the enemy? This didn't feel like a trap room. There had to be— There!

Shit.

The shadows shifted across from me and resolved themselves into a huge spider creature. It had the pendulous lower half of a massive black widow, and its upper half was that of a lean, goth-looking dude, with grayish purple skin and a wild mane of black hair.

Worse, it held a staff that glowed with enchanted runes, and from whose tip more shadows were pouring forth and streaking toward Falkon.

Definitely not a level three challenge.

"What's going on?" Lotharia's voice was sharp with fear.

We needed her in here, and fast. I lifted my head above the illusory floor. How to summarize what I'd seen? No time. "On your stomach! Duck your head under and cast Hail Strike on the spider monster!"

Lotharia's eyes widened as she took this in, but thank the stars for her high wisdom. She dropped to her stomach and dunked her head through the illusion like a kid bobbing for apples.

I dropped below again. A half-dozen shadowy figures had appeared around Falkon, who had somehow fought free of the webbing and now had his back to the tower wall, sword waving before him.

Lotharia's voice rang out in the gloom. "From the heart of glaciers, blue-green to black, I summon forth the coldest shards and send them to attack!"

Immediately, huge chunks of ice rained down from the ceiling upon the spider dude, slamming into its carapace and torso with punishing force. It screamed and stared up at us. The ice was cutting into its body but doing precious little damage – not surprising, given that Lotharia's spell was only level eight. The monster pointed its staff and a huge gout of black webbing flew toward us.

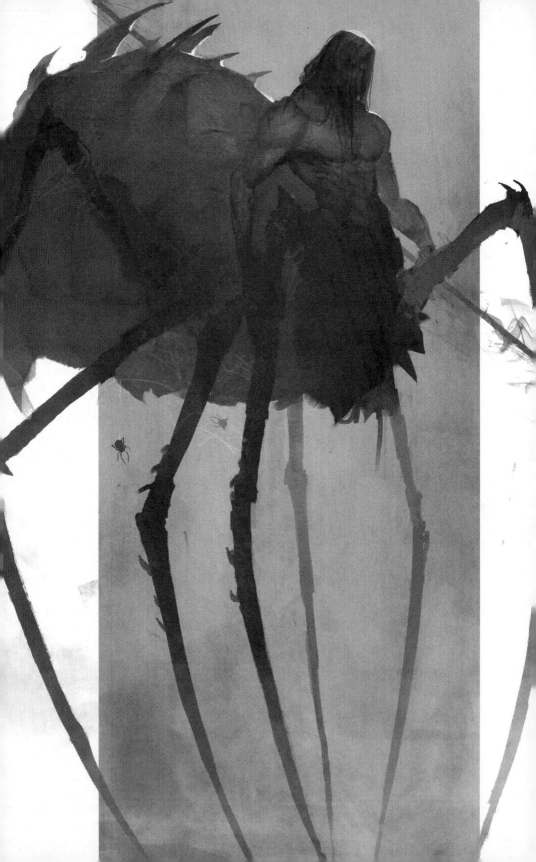

I activated Ledge Runner, shifted my grip from the ridge of rock to Lotharia's shoulders, and hauled her into the void as I pushed away from the wall and fell. She screamed and clutched at me as we fell past the spider monster toward a thick rope of webbing that crossed the center of the tower from wall to wall.

Please work please work please work—

My feet hit the cable and it bent beneath us, sagging violently as it took our weight. My knees flexed and I held tight onto Lotharia, holding off on Adrenaline Surge for now unless I really needed it. Her scream continued and then grew higher as her momentum tore her from my arms. Desperately, I held on to her wrist and swung her around and under me like a pendulum as she fell, letting go of her only when the angle was right: she flew from my hand to land on a ledge, the remnants of the second floor.

Ledge Runner kept me pinned to the cable. Without Lotharia's weight, it rebounded and flung me high up into the air as if it had been a trampoline. I'd not thought this far ahead, and yelled as I flew upward.

"Uncanny Aim!" I screamed, then recalled I simply had to will it into activation. Dagger in hand, I aimed my silver thread right at the spider monster's left eye. I timed it just right – waited till I hit the apex of my ascent, then dipped into Adrenaline Surge for extra killing power.

My blood boiled, my energy became boundless, and with an exultant scream I chucked the dagger with all my strength. It flew straight at the spider dude's head – only to be blocked by a contemptuous flick of its staff.

The dagger ricocheted off into the darkness.

Even as I fell, it pointed its staff at me once again and hissed a word I didn't understand. A black spear of magic flew at me.

I didn't hesitate. *Shadow Step!* Every natural instinct told me to get the hell away from this thing, to disappear into the furthest dark corner, but that wasn't how you won fights. Instead, instincts honed in countless VR combats kicked in. I disappeared into the shadows just before the black spear hit me, and was spat out right behind the spider monster.

Still screaming, I grabbed hold of its staff, then Double Stepped away.

If it hadn't been for the momentum I'd gained from falling *and* my Adrenaline Surge *and* the element of surprise, I'd have had no chance. But sheer terror boosted my strength even further, and I tore its staff free before falling back into the shadows.

I emerged next to Lotharia, who stood encased in her Frost Armor, her scepter pointed at the outraged spider monster high above us.

"Here!" I shoved the staff into her hands. "Use it!"

"What?" She stared at the staff in incomprehension. "How—"

"Use it!"

A thunderous roar sounded from below, the same lion's bellow that Falkon had unleashed upon us when we'd first met him, and I glanced down to see the shadowy figures that surrounded him step back in confusion and disarray.

Lotharia gripped my shoulder. "Here it comes!"

The spider monster was hurtling down toward us, eyes livid, hand outstretched for its staff.

"I name you my foe!" shouted Falkon. "I see the fear in your eyes and the cowardice in your heart, and demand that you face me in single combat!"

There was a strange power to his words that I *felt* as much as heard, and to my surprise the spider-monster corrected its course to veer past us and toward the squire.

Falkon was about to get crushed. What could I do? Shadow Step onto the monster's back? My dagger was gone. My Adrenaline Surge was about to expire.

No.

Time to fight smart.

I extended my hand and cast Light.

The small ball of golden illumination puffed into being, and I sent it hurtling after the charging spider to engulf its head.

At least, I tried to. The ball of light refused to do so, and instead settled for positioning itself directly before the monster's eyes.

Good enough.

The monster shrieked in fury and batted its arm at the ball of light at precisely the right moment. Falkon leapt up, sword over his shoulder like a baseball bat, and swung it right into the spider dude's chest.

A wave of power from his attack washed over us, but the force of the blow was such that the monster was knocked back up into the tower, limbs flailing, to hit the wall a good ten feet above us and cling to the shadows there, hissing in fury.

Falkon had leapt up to meet the monster's charge, and he landed back down upon the edge of his broken platform, where he cartwheeled his arms in an attempt to regain his balance.

The fearsome blow to the spider had opened a shallow cut down the center of its chest. My heart sank. I'd hoped Falkon had lopped it in half. Damn, these upper level monsters were tough. Even though it looked bare-chested, it had to have some kind of crazy armor going on!

Lotharia was feverishly studying the staff. I grabbed her dagger from her belt without asking, activated Uncanny Aim and aligned the silver thread with the same wound Falkon had opened. The spider beast was gesturing, casting a spell, and I waited for it to raise both hands over its head before throwing.

The dagger flew through the gloom, passing through one of the purplish bubbles of light before slamming home into the cut. It sank in deep, the monster's armor having already been parted, and it screamed in pain.

"A little help!" shouted Falkon from below. He was being swarmed by the shadow figures, a dozen of them encircling him and swiping at him with massively elongated claws.

Why hadn't I saved up my XP? I itched to buy something, a power that would solve all our problems, but had only thirty-two points. The only thing I could afford was Sabotage Defenses.

A plan clicked into place. I opened my sheet and spent the XP. "Lotharia! Clear those shadow monsters away with Hail Strike!" I didn't wait for her to confirm, but instead cast Shadow Step and fell away into the night.

The darkness embraced me, velvety and smooth, and then I emerged directly behind the spider monster. I tried to activate Ledge Runner again, but that power was still in its cooldown period – damn! I landed heavily on the spider's bulbous abdomen and immediately lost my footing. Worse, Adrenaline Surge chose that moment to crap out on me, and I was hit by a wave of nausea that brought up my gorge so that I thought I was about to vomit dire bat head soup on the monster.

The spider-dude spun around, outraged at my presence on its back, and that proved to be its undoing. I was falling forward, my plan foiled by my own inexperience with my talents, until the beast turned and provided me with exactly what I needed.

I grabbed hold of Lotharia's dagger where it protruded from its chest, and activated Sabotage Defenses.

Knowledge and skill suffused my hand, and I tucked the tip of the dagger inside the spider monster's tough hide and allowed myself to fall. My own weight caused the blade to slice straight down, as if unzipping the monster's armor from its chest to where its abdomen met with its spider body.

Then I was in freefall, tumbling and spinning into nothingness. Despite the cramping and heartburn, I activated Shadow Step one last time – and appeared in midair directly before the startled spider monster once more.

Its head whipped up in surprise as I slammed my dagger right into the opening I'd created moments ago. The point sank into the vulnerable white flesh beneath the gray leathery hide, and then I executed my patented combat move again: falling to my own death.

I held tight to the hilt, and as a result my dagger cut a deep gash into the monster's chest and stomach. Then I was gone, spinning and dropping for a third or fourth time into the depths.

I hit the wall and stuck. My head cracked against the tower's side and I saw stars, which – along with the come-down from Adrenaline Surge – made me toss my cookies. Heaving and feeling wretched, I stared blearily at where Falkon was climbing up the webbing as if it were the rigging of a ship.

"We can do this!" he yelled, voice echoing around the tower's interior. "For we are mighty, we are brave, we are bold, and best yet, we are too foolish to die! This worm is ours for the crushing, and I salute you, my bravest of friends, my dearest of companions! *For the king!*"

Another talent of his. A wave of warmth washed over me, my mind sharpened, and my spirits rose. With new focus, I wiped my sleeve across my chin and stared up at where the spider beast had finished slathering a bandage of webbing across its wound.

It let out a keening scream, and then tucked its abdomen under and pointed its spinnerets at Falkon.

"Jump!" I screamed.

Falkon leapt, but to no avail – a firehose of webbing slammed into him from above, knocking him back into the wall and plastering him all over in gleaming black filaments. He struggled and roared, but failed to break free.

The spider monster laughed, turned, and plastered me with webbing in turn. I was knocked back into the wall, and layer upon layer of black goo covered me from ankle to neck.

"Lotharia!" I craned my head to peer down at her. "You're up! Do something!"

"One more minute!" She was hunched over the staff. "One more minute!"

"No more minutes!" My voice was getting hoarse from yelling at the top of my lungs. "No more! Wait— duck!"

Without looking up, displaying a level of sangfroid that impressed the hell out of me, she raised a hand and called out, "Obfuscate the keenest sense, blanket thought with fog most dense!"

Fog billowed out around her at tremendous speed even as the spider beast launched a torrent of webbing at where she crouched.

I peered down, desperately trying to get a sense of whether she'd been hit or not, but the fog made it impossible to tell.

"Wait!" I called up to the spider monster as it descended toward me. I was the highest up, its closest prey. "Let's talk – what can we get you? Need us to bring you something? Not a lot of amenities within this tower, am I right?"

The spider dude's face pulled into a horrific grin. Did it understand me? Was it intelligent? I couldn't tell, but I wasn't about to give up.

"What about the demons that are coming?" When rational reasoning fails, try batshit crazy. "They'll be here soon, all nineteen choirs of them!"

Nothing. The spider continued to descend, taking its time and rubbing a hand over its chest where I'd slit it open.

"Sorry about that," I said. "It was an accident. Both times. No?"

The nausea finally receded, and even before I could draw a relieved breath I activated Adrenaline Surge again. My muscles swelled, my whole body went from being abjectly sick to vibrating with life, and with a cry I tore my arm free of the webbing and hurled my dagger up at the spider beast.

Not at the wound. Not at its face. I was too low-level to stop it that way. No. Instead, I activated Pin Down and threw my blade with every last ounce of strength.

The dagger flickered up and slammed into one of the spider's legs, right where its foot would be. Did spiders have feet? Pedipalps? Like 'pedestrian'? I'd no idea, and realized I was starting to feel a bit loopy. Regardless, I'd sunk a dagger to the hilt through one foot, pinning it to a wooden beam from the remnants of the third floor.

The spider beast hissed and turned to gaze at the dagger, swiveling its entire torso to do so, then reached down and effortlessly plucked my dagger free. It flipped it over with enviable ease, caught it by the tip, then threw it down at me with unerring accuracy.

Pain blossomed in my thigh. I bit back a scream, the fury and energy of Adrenaline Surge helping me master my pain. Why hadn't it killed me? Why— oh. Yeah. I was bound in spider silk in its web. It was probably going to inject me full of poison, cocoon me, and then devour me later when my insides had turned into complete mush.

"Hey!" Falkon's voice was desperate. "You! Ugly bastard spider bitch! I name you my foe, and challenge you—"

The spider monster hissed and sent a second mass of webbing flying down to engulf Falkon's head completely and cut off his words.

I tried to reach down with my free arm for the dagger but couldn't get close enough. Instead I set to tearing handfuls of webbing away, but to no avail. Even as strong as I was, it felt like pulling at steel cables. This was what you got for going up against massively more powerful bosses.

In desperation I cast Light again, but the monster was ready and simply crushed my globe of light in its fist, extinguishing it.

Mage Hand! I cast the spell and pulled the dagger free from my thigh. It came out slowly, the pain exquisite, and then I levitated the blade up to my free hand. I summoned Uncanny Aim, but it was still in cooldown. Damn it! I'd have to wait. Every second the spider drew closer I tried for my talent again.

Down came the monster to hang right before me, massive and fell. I tensed, ready to swing the moment it tried to poison me. Uncanny Aim came online. I lined up the silver thread with the spider-dude's eyes – but a mass of webbing slammed my free hand against the wall with such force that even with my strength I dropped my blade.

"OK," I said. "You've got my attention. Let's talk."

The spider monster grinned, lips pulling back from vampiric incisors, and then it pushed its tongue out. Oh, god. A massive, fleshy straw emerged, dripping green ichor and with its underside extending out into a bony needle. So much worse than an Alien's inner jaws. It leaned in, the webbing around it straining and creaking, and I thrashed, trying to get away but to no avail.

The stinger slid right up to my face and then, to my everlasting horror, *caressed* my cheek, drawing a thin line of pain where it touched my skin. The tongue reared back, poised like a cobra ready to strike. I stared, horrified, as a massive drop of green poison emerged from the depths of the tube.

A spear of black fire flew between us, incinerating the tongue and bouncing off the tower wall overhead.

The spider monster recoiled with a shriek, the ruined tongue shooting back into its mouth, and it stared down just in time to take a second black spear in the chest.

The power of the attack blasted a smoking hole open in its web bandaging and punched through its delicate milky-white flesh. It shot back up, keening in agony, but Lotharia simply tracked it with its staff and fired a third spear, then a fourth.

The third attack hit the spider beast right where the second had, widening the gaping hole in its chest, and the fourth slammed right into its face, shearing off the upper half of its head.

The spider beast froze, shuddered, then fell. It plummeted only to slow and then stop as webbing from its spinnerets arrested its fall, leaving it to hang upside down in the center of the tower where it swayed, arms and legs twitching until they finally went still.

"All right!" I yelled. "Way to go, Lotharia! Lotharia?"

The enchantress had dropped to her knees.

"Lotharia!" I struggled to escape, only to be hit by the withdrawal effects of Adrenaline Surge. Again. Vision swimming, I watched as she toppled over and lay still.

14

I MUST HAVE PASSED out. I woke to the sensation of falling forward, and with a cry I jerked around only to have someone pin my arms as they easily overpowered me.

"Easy, there." I recognized Falkon's voice. "You knock us both off this ledge it's going to suck."

He yanked me up, tearing my feet free of the last of the webbing, and then put away his dagger.

"Blegh," I said, and then spat. "Lotharia?"

"Fine, albeit with a headache. She couldn't climb up to help, so she waited for me to regain Adrenaline Surge and bust free. It took me some time to work my way up here, but I think we're all good now."

"We did it?"

Falkon grinned. "Just wait till you check your character sheet. No, not right now. Let's get down first."

We were standing on a small extension of rock barely large enough for the two of us, but there were plenty of handholds with which to descend. "Here," I said. "Follow my lead." So saying, I lowered to my stomach, kicked till I found a toehold, and then began the laborious process of getting us down.

It took about ten minutes, and we both gave up at the end and leapt the last ten feet onto a thick pile of webbing. Lotharia was sitting cross-legged, frowning as she meditated, but upon our arrival she cracked open an eye and examined us.

"Oh. Good. You're not dead."

"That's cheerful," I said.

"Don't mind her." Falkon sat against the wall. "She's got a wicked migraine from using the staff."

"Why's that?" I asked. I was itching to open my character sheet, but wanted to at least appear solicitous.

"It's powered by necrotic energy," she said, closing her eye. "Which means it twists my essence when I try to use it. Converts it through brute force. I'm going to have to meditate extensively to purify myself after each use or risk permanently warping my essence."

"That... does sound bad." Still, I couldn't help but grin. "But we did it! Holy cow, I thought we were goners there for a second."

Falkon rested his head against the wall. "Yeah, me too. And that was just against a level twenty monster."

"It was only level twenty?" I tried not to let disappointment steal my happiness. "Crap. I'd thought it was at least thirty or something..."

"Nope. If it had been, we'd all be dead."

"Still, we did pretty well, didn't we?" I looked from one to the other. "That was some great teamwork."

"Yeah, we did pretty well." Why did Falkon sound so begrudging? "But remember, this tower is a darkblade's paradise. Shadow everywhere, lots of room for creative maneuvering. I don't mean to be harsh, but you're not going to be this effective against, say, an ogre out in a flat, sunny courtyard."

"Yeah," I said, trying not to deflate too much. "I see your point. Still." I rallied my spirits. "For our first team combat, I think we did great."

"Yeah, we did," said Falkon, and finally he smiled. "Gave me forty XP. Lotharia?"

"Fifty." Even her migraine couldn't keep the smug satisfaction from her voice.

I couldn't wait any longer. I opened my character sheet and was deluged with pop-up windows.

 You have gained 75 experience (75 for defeating the spider centaur). You have 77 unused XP. Your total XP is 347.

Congratulations! You are Level 4!

"Seventy-five XP!" I yelled. "Level four!"

Lotharia pressed her fingers to her temples and grimaced.

"Sorry," I whispered. "Level four, baby!"

Falkon chuckled. "Nothing like the early leveling rush."

"You going to lecture me too? Never mind. Excuse me. I've got some serious shopping to do."

 Your attributes have increased!

    Mana +1
    Dexterity +1
    Strength +1

You have learned new skills. *Dodge: Basic (II), Melee: Basic (I)*

So Euphoria finally thought I was learning to fight? Fair enough. At least it wasn't forcing me to specialize in daggers. And more mana was always welcome, along with some dex and strength. Now I needed to work on my constitution. And intelligence. And… everything else, really.

 There are new talent advancements available to you:

I quickly flicked through Distracting Attack, Darkvision, and Wall Climber. All of those would have been useful in my last fight, but like any compulsive shopper I wanted to see what was new to the market.

> *Bleeding Attack*
> XP Cost: 75
> - Not all wounds are created equal. The gift that keeps on giving, a wound dealt by this talent will weaken your foe over time.
> - Pre-requisite(s): Melee: Basic (I)
>
> *Expert Leaper:*
> XP Cost: 55
> - Conquer distances through mighty leaps. Whether from a running start, a dead stop, or dropping down, an expert leaper can perform feats of athleticism unlike any other.
> - Cooldown period scales with your constitution.

Interesting. I didn't know if this was common to all rogues, or if my darkblade proclivity toward assassinations was opening up this talent tree, but I was definitely noticing a trend toward making me extremely agile and able to manage vertical spaces as well as horizontal with ease.

Not that I was complaining. I could easily envision how Ledge Runner, Wall Climber, Expert Leaper and Shadow Step would have amazing synergy.

I then checked my spells. The same three were still available: Death Dagger, Night Shroud (I), and Ebon Tendrils (I).

"I'm thinking about taking Death Dagger," I told the others. "I could continue to work on evasion and maneuverability, but I'm starting to get to the point where I want to be able to actually deal some real damage here."

"I agree," said Falkon.

"You do?" I blinked. I don't know why I'd expected an argument.

"Sure. Your build is centered on delivering a single, devastating strike that incapacitates your foe before they even know you're there. If you don't start taking those offensive spells, you're going to become ever harder to hit but unable to end a fight."

Lotharia squinted and opened her eyes. "Fair enough. But with us both here to deliver the hits, his staying alive is kind of the priority."

"He can't always depend on our being around to deal out the damage, though," said Falkon. "He needs to be able to bring the pain."

"Fine," said Lotharia. "I feel like I should argue more but I kind of want to focus on getting rid of this headache."

I tapped Death Dagger. The letters burned gold, and then it appeared beneath my cantrips. I grinned. Its cost of three mana meant I'd only ever be able to use it when I was at full strength, but combined with a Double Step attack I'd now really be able to earn the title of darkblade.

"So," I said, climbing to my feet. Energy thrummed through me, and I rose to the balls of my feet. "Either of you searched this place yet?"

"Not yet," said Falkon. "But I like the line of your thinking. The cut of your jib, as it were. Let's see what Albertus left us."

"Albertus?" I walked around the base of the tower, peering into the gloomy shadows.

"Sure," said Falkon. "He's the one who decides how much to reward folks for defeating a raid boss." He stopped, hands on hips, and looked up at the dead monster. "Actually, I bet he put this one here just for our party."

I kicked some old furniture apart. "You think?"

"Sure. Trust me, he watches every Death March player closely. I'm not saying he's going to go easy on you, but he won't throw you away by making you face a level forty monster. It's entirely possible that he swapped out whatever was here before and placed this level twenty boss in its place to challenge but not kill you."

"Huh," I said. I wasn't sure if I was comforted or not by that level of attention. "You think he'll intercede with the ogres or the undead in Feldgrau?"

"Nah," said Falkon. "While he might mess with raid monsters and bosses like this one, he won't touch 'natural' monsters like the ogres. Those that are actually part of the local ecology, or have a narrative to explain their presence. Only the spontaneously generated bad guys like this spider-dude or the like."

"Huh," I said again. "That's pretty fascinating. So maybe we should focus on raid areas to keep things more equal?"

Falkon dragged out a small chest from under a shelf. "Nice try, but no Cuban cigarillo. He'd notice what we were up to pretty quickly and up the challenge level to rebuke us. We'd best keep on with our original plans. Now, this looks interesting…"

We both crouched before the small chest. Falkon blew on it and a thick layer of dust flew into the air. There was no lock on the latch, so he opened it with the tip of his dagger and we both peered greedily inside.

"Let's see what we've got," he said, and carefully pulled out a black folded bundle.

"A souvenir shirt?" I asked, trying to not sound let down. "What's it say on the front? 'I killed a spider-dude and all I got was this lousy t-shirt'?"

Falkon's eyes blazed green, and then he gave me a wry smile. "Not quite. It's your lucky day. This is woven from enchanted spider silk. It's as good as common chainmail, and much lighter and more flexible. I think you've scored your first piece of real loot."

I couldn't help but feel a shiver of excitement. Anything that helped keep sharp, pointy things from entering my body were incredibly welcome. I yanked my homespun tunic over my head and carefully slipped the spider silk shirt on in its place. It was smooth, decadently so, so light as to be almost insubstantial yet surprisingly warm.

"And this, I think, is a gift for Lotharia," said Falkon, pulling out a small amulet. His eyes blazed green once more, and then he nodded. "Yep. A mana aggregator. Well, that's the technical term for it. It helps draw ambient mana from the environment, making her regain her spent mana much more quickly. This is a minor amulet, so the effect won't be dramatic, but still."

"And for you?" I asked.

He peered inside the chest. "Looks like that's it."

"That's not fair."

"Euphoria's not fair," he said. "And we ain't done searching yet. Come on."

There wasn't that much more to explore, however, and after another few minutes of poking and lifting and peering we only found a pouch of silver coins and a battered buckler.

We regrouped next to Lotharia, whose mood visibly lifted at the sight of the amulet. She turned it over in her hands a few times, then quickly slipped it over her neck and let out a sigh of relief. "Now this makes the whole fight worth it."

"You know, I don't see a doorway leading out," I said.

"Me neither," admitted Falkon. "And I'm not too excited about climbing up to the fourth floor."

I looked from one to the other. "Do you think Albertus sealed it up?"

Lotharia made a face. "Possible? But unlikely. Here. Let's try again, but this time use Detect Magic."

That made all the difference, thanks to Jeramy's spell. We were quickly able to find an archway where his iron effect wasn't taking hold.

"I guess he only cast it on the tower shell," I said, looking up at the ruined interior floors. "And his magic rune doesn't adapt to new additions."

"It doesn't," said Lotharia. "One of the key elements in carving it is to have a specific set of limits in mind. Otherwise you'd just spin the mana through the rune only to have it sink back into the ground and sky."

"Makes sense. So…" I knocked on the gray blocks that filled the doorway. "How do we open this up?"

"I can probably break through," said Falkon. "But this leads right into the courtyard."

"Ah," I said. "Ogres and wyverns."

"And mouse swarms," said Lotharia with a gleam in her eye. Her amulet had really cheered her up. "Here. I may have a little trick that will help us." She placed her palm on the stones, held her new amulet in one hand, and then whispered, "From mighty stone, strong and grand, adopt the softness of sun-baked sand."

I watched through Detect Magic. Her amulet pulsed, pulling a little mana from the air and sending it into her being, which then pushed in through her palm into the wall. A subtle effect, but the very nature of the mana in the rocks changed.

"Imbue is going to ultimately be my most powerful and versatile spell," she said, stepping back. "I just need to have the patience to work on it instead of going for flashy spells like Hail Storm."

"Flashy, life-saving spells like Hail Storm," I said. "Can we knock it down?"

"Whenever you're ready," she said.

Falkon stepped forward and pressed his hand into the rock. It didn't suddenly collapse as if it were actually made of sand, but he was able to imprint his palm into it. "Very nice. Watch out."

He took three steps back, then ran forward and slammed his shoulder into the blocks. They caved in around him with a dusty *thump*, and he staggered through and out into the evening light before backpedaling into the tower.

I peered out through the hole he'd made and scanned the bailey. The undead ogre emerged from its house, peering around the courtyard warily, but there was no sign of the wyvern or the other ogres.

"I think the coast is clear," I whispered. "Back along the inside wall to the goblin tower?"

"That your base of operations?" asked Falkon.

Lotharia and I exchanged a look. "Best one we've found so far," I said.

"At least until we get around to exploring Jeramy's tower," said Lotharia. "If we can guess the password, that is."

"All right. Follow me, then." Falkon drew his blade and slipped outside. Lotharia went next, the necrotic staff in one hand, her scepter gone. I followed last after giving a final look at the defeated spider boss above us.

We scampered quickly along the wall, and when we knocked, Barfo readily admitted us into the tower. Only once he'd barred and reinforced the door did I finally allow myself to relax.

"You have fun?" asked Barfo, holding out a tray on which stood three little clay cups. "Refresher?"

I grinned and took a cup. "Yes, refresher. Thank you." I sniffed warily, expecting something akin to crude petroleum, but it actually smelled pretty decent, like a slightly oaty chamomile.

Kreekit ducked out of one of the cloth tents. "Humans like danger," she said knowingly. "Big fights, lots of death. Never satisfied. What is your next big fight?"

Falkon sat on a crate and laid his blade over his knees. "You got that right. Always more danger. That's how we get more powerful. As to our next big fight?" He looked over at me. "The ogres, right?"

"Yeah," I said, sitting against the wall. "But if that spider dude was only level twenty, how are we going to tackle four ogres? What do you think their level is?"

"Ogres?" Falkon paused. "Like most humanoids, they scale up. The runt of the group might be in the high twenties, with their boss in the mid-thirties. Way, way beyond our paygrade."

Lotharia bowed her head politely as she accepted her clay cup from Barfo, then scowled at Falkon. "Then why are you grinning like a fool?"

"Because – well, Chris' Death March aside – this is the most fun I've had in ages." Falkon ran his thumb along the edge of his blade, testing for nicks. "What we're trying to do here is ridiculous, but somehow I'm still optimistic. Most folks who play Euphoria are content to follow the prescribed leveling guidelines, playing it if not safe then perhaps simply as they're supposed to, leveling in a smooth and predictable manner. Nobody does what we're doing. Not for long, at any rate. So, yeah. I'm excited."

"He very human," said Dribbler.

Lotharia shook her head. "I think the term is 'suicidally optimistic'."

"Suicidally optimistic," said Dribbler slowly. "That mean the same as 'human'?"

I grinned. "Yeah. Something like that. But we've got no choice here. All right. Time for us to think this through. How can we take down four ogres?"

"Toe-to-toe combat is out," said Falkon. "I doubt even I could take a full hit and survive."

"We should weaken them," said Lotharia, running her finger around the brim of her clay cup as if trying to make it sing.

"Right." I leaned forward, mind spinning as I tried to recall low-level strategies I'd not used in forever. "They're pretty dumb. We have to use that against them. Get them to consume poison, or find a way to inflict them with disease."

"Ogres are pretty resistant to disease, though," said Falkon. "You ever see one of their dens?"

"Yeah." I thought of the squalor inside the stables. "Still. Maybe we can find something virulent enough. From down in Feldgrau, maybe?"

Lotharia arched her brow at me. "Now you're the one who's sounding very human."

"Suicidally optimistic," piped in Dribbler with a grin. "Yes?"

"Sure. That's me. Say we poison them, inflict them with disease." I looked over at Falkon. "You already know what we're going to hit them with."

"The ballista," he said. "Absolutely. But that won't take them out with one blow, and the reload time is terrible without a full team. Even a bolt that large with a steel head won't faze a level thirty ogre."

"Well... what if I Imbue the bolt?" Lotharia looked from me to Falkon. "Turn the head into something akin to enchanted diamond?"

Falkon grinned. "Better. Much better. How long does Imbue last?"

"It all depends on how different the materials are. Iron to diamond? A couple of minutes. If I then enchant it to give it a magical effect? Ten, fifteen seconds?"

Excitement wiggled deep within me. "So, you two work the ballista. Each time you load a bolt, Lotharia enchants it. Then we lure the sickened and diseased ogres out into the open and mow them down."

"Still not enough," said Falkon. "These guys are going to seem ridiculously tough compared to anything we've yet faced. That'll hurt them, sure. But kill them? We need more."

"I've got the spider staff," said Lotharia reluctantly. "A blast from that should hurt."

"Yeah, but you said that'll warp your essence," I protested. "How many blasts can you shoot before being too messed up?"

"Hard to say. There's no definite limit. It's all a matter of how close I want to get to the edge. I should be able to manage a blast for each ogre, though." Lotharia stared into her cup, then drained it. "That will leave me pretty messed up, however."

"Disease, poison, diamond-tipped bolts and spider staff blasts," I said, watching Falkon. "Enough?"

"I still want more," he said.

I sat back. What else could we do? What else could hit the ogres that hard? "What about the wyvern?"

"What *about* the wyvern?" asked Lotharia.

"What if we found a way to set it on the ogres when they come boiling out of the stables?"

"Oooh," said Dribbler. "Very, very bad idea."

"That means humans will try it," said Barfo.

"We'd have to find a way to get rid of the stakes," said Falkon slowly. "But the ogres wouldn't come out of the stables if they saw them missing."

"I could…" Lotharia trailed off, thinking things through. "What if I Imbued the base of each stake with the quality of paper or the like? Then we cut through each one? Leave it connected by just a little bit in the center?"

"That means we won't be able to replace them after," said Falkon. "Which will make killing the wyvern much harder down the road."

I stood, restless energy filling me. "But it's a good idea. We weaken the stakes. Perhaps attach spider silk from the tower to the tip of each one. We time our attack for when the wyvern's home, then trigger the ogres so they come running out with a lot of noise. Drop the stakes, and let the wyvern attack even as we hit them with diamond-tipped bolts and spider fire."

Falkon held up a finger. "If – and this is a big 'if' – if we can pull all that off, then yeah. Maybe that'd be enough."

I punched my fist into my other palm. "Then that's what we'll do. We need to find a way to drive the ogres out at the right time with a big noise."

"Big boom," said Dribbler excitedly. "Big fire, lots of smoke. Wake up everybody."

"Yeah," I said. "That'd be nice. But we're not quite powerful enough yet to be throwing fireballs."

"No," said Kreekit. "Dribbler means explosion!"

"Sure," I said. "But how?"

"Lots of black fire mud in wyvern tower," said Dribbler. "We find barrels and barrels when we first arrive, before we know wyvern up top. Very exciting! We plan a big party, but then have to run from wyvern."

"Wait," I said. "Black fire mud?"

"He probably means pitch," said Falkon. "One of our defensive measures. We'd light barrels and drop them over the walls to blow up the enemy. There were barrels kept in each tower in case of attack."

"Oh, that's good," I said. "So we steal some barrels, roll them up to the stable walls, then detonate them all at once."

Falkon laughed. "See? This is what I was talking about. Exciting!"

Lotharia pressed her fingers into her temples. "You're all mad."

"And we can help!" said Kreekit. She climbed up onto a box and spread her arms wide, cloak splayed out behind her. "Green Liver goblins can help! Barfo can cook good, or he can cook bad.

And when he cooks bad, he cooks very, very bad. We get ogres to eat Barfo's food, they get sick like horse drowning in pond of warm green puke!"

"Horse… drowning?" I shook my head. "Never mind. That's great! That'll handle the poison."

Barfo beamed. "I also cook very good! Make Barfo special soup! Good for everything! Powerful magic. Heal the world."

"Uh, sure," I said. "That sounds great, too. And the disease?"

"I can't believe I'm volunteering this information, given what you'll insist on doing with it," said Lotharia. "But remember those plague zombies in Feldgrau? One of those might do the trick. But I don't know how you'd bring one to the stables without getting sick yourself."

"We talking walking or lying around kind of corpses?" asked Falkon.

"Walking," said Lotharia. "Luckily, you can hear them coming from far away due to the sound of the insects burrowing in their flesh."

"So we isolate one of them, lasso it, drag it up to the castle faster than they can walk. If it gives us a problem, we kill it from a distance and haul it on in regardless."

"I'll let you handle that mission," said Lotharia with a cold smile. "Since you seem so eager."

"All right," I said, turning to face my friends. "Sounds like we've got a plan. First step is for Barfo to brew up the poison while we grab the barrels of black fire mud. Then we weaken the stakes and harvest spider silk from the tower. Kreekit, do you think you three can braid the spider silk into long ropes for us?"

"Goblins very good braiders," said Kreekit. "Yes. Very big yes."

"Kreekit," said Falkon carefully. "Do you know what a braid is?"

"Oh yes," said Kreekit. "Yes, yes. Very dangerous. Very important. Green Liver goblins famous for their braids."

The three of us hesitated and exchanged looks.

"That's… good. Great," I said. "So poison and barrels, then stakes and braids. Finally, we grab a plague corpse and dump it in the stables. Wait till that night and the wyvern, then place the barrels behind the stables. Imbue the bolts, light the fuses… and celebrate an easy victory."

Lotharia snorted. "Right. Nothing could go wrong."

"Hey, at least it's a plan," I said.

"Barfo start cooking bad food very now!" said Barfo, climbing to his feet. "I save many bad things for this day! Barfo go dig them up."

"I'll get to work on the ballista," said Falkon. "Shouldn't take me too long to finish it up."

"Lotharia, want to come scout the wyvern's tower?" I asked.

She gave me a wry smile. "Actually, yes. I've been meaning to visit Jeramy's tower since we got here. Let me meditate some, regain my mana and finish cleaning my essence, and I'll be good to go."

"Sounds good." I beamed at everyone. Sure, the plan was ridiculously perilous. Sure, we were planning to tackle four level thirty-plus foes that could obliterate us with one single blow. I knew a hundred different things could go wrong. But it felt good to take the initiative. It gave me a sense of being in control, even if I knew that sense was false.

"Then let's get to it," I said. "Those ogres aren't going to know what hit them."

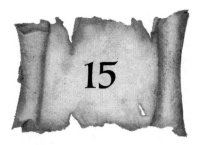

15

L OTHARIA AND I crouched within the doorway of the uppermost room of the goblins' tower and watched as the wyvern
roused itself from slumber. We could barely make out the tops of
its scaly wings as it beat them, then the monster itself rose into
view. It was incredible. We'd been waiting all night for the beast
to fly out and give us a chance to explore, and it had taken till the
breaking of dawn for it to rouse itself. Now the first rays of the day
caused its hide to glisten as if it were covered in dew, bringing out
the deep tones of green and black along its scaled hide.

"There it goes," I whispered. Even within the stone doorway
I didn't feel safe. The wyvern hopped up onto the outer edge of
the tower, facing out over the ravine and Feldgrau far below, and
extended its wings to their fullest extent. They each had to easily
be fifteen feet wide. It gave its thick, serpentine neck a shake,
squawked twice, and then simply toppled forward, falling out
of sight.

Lotharia and I darted to the battlements and my throat locked
up as as the wyvern glided back into sight, wings catching the

thermals, tail undulating behind it. I marveled at its rough beauty and awesome power. We watched as it flew out over the thick forest that stretched across the foothills, dwindling into a speck.

"We're going to kill *that*?" I asked, turning to regard Lotharia.

"I mean, technically we've stated that as a goal," she replied. I couldn't help but notice how the soft dawn light brought out the depths of her brown irises and caused her skin to glow. "I don't think anybody's hinted at how we'd go about executing it, however."

I tried not to let my spirits sink. "We'll find a way. One thing at a time, though. C'mon."

We crossed the top of the wall to the base of the wyvern's tower, glancing in the forest's direction as we went. The goblins had told us the barrels were stored in the tower's top chamber, which made sense: who'd want to carry barrels full of pitch up a bunch of stairs during an attack?

"*Squeeze through the rocks,*" Dribbler had said. "*Squeezy squeeze. Door broken!*"

I stopped and regarded the massive chunks of rubble that had fallen before the tower entrance, dislodged no doubt by the wyvern's nestmaking above. Three boulders had crashed down onto the parapet, settling against the tower itself and filling in the doorway.

"Squeezy squeeze," I said, peering between the huge rocks. "Yeah, right."

The gaps might have been large enough for a goblin, but they were definitely too tight for us. I summoned a ball of Light and sent it dancing through. The goblins had been right about the doorway, however; the falling boulders had smashed it inward. Beyond was a typical tower chamber, circular and filled with the detritus of war. No corpses, but plenty of dropped weapons, and there – six large barrels, tightly sealed and with a black flame painted on their side.

"Think you can Imbue these boulders with the consistency of soup or something?"

Lotharia placed her palm on one of them. "It'd take some serious time. These are very big rocks, and my Imbue's only at basic level."

"Well, maybe you can widen these gaps so we can crawl through," I said. "Then work on them from inside so we're not exposed out here."

"I *could* do that, sure," she said.

I frowned at her tone. "Or…"

"Or we could work our way up from the bottom of the tower."

"You sound surprisingly hopeful for what sounds like a lot more work."

"True. But this was Jeramy's tower. At least, the first three floors were his." A complex emotion crossed her face – something between yearning, sadness, and amusement. "I wouldn't mind seeing if we could get inside. Who knows what kind of tools or answers we might find?"

"If there's one thing I've learned, it's that you don't break into a wizard's tower at level four," I said. "That goes beyond even suicidal optimism."

"We wouldn't be breaking in," she said. "I was friends with Jeramy. It would be more like a visit. And come on. We need all the help we can get, right? Even one of Jeramy's lowest level items would be a huge help to us."

"I don't know," I said. But to be honest, I was getting excited by the idea. I moved to the edge of the parapet and looked down at the doorway far below. "You sure none of the rooms will spontaneously fill with fire or dump lava onto us for snooping?"

"Well, no, not completely, but we can always ask Jeramy for permission to enter." She paused, noting my confusion, and quickly explained, "The fake Jeramy. The, ah – well, you see, he created an illusion of himself to act as a kind of doorman. Take messages, let people know when he'd be back. Maybe we can ask him if we can go in? Back in the day, his close circle had access at any time."

"Were you part of his close circle?"

"Not exactly… but close-ish? Come on. There'd be no harm in just saying hello."

"You shouldn't say that," I said. "That's a sure-fire way to make sure everything goes to hell."

"But…?" She gave me an expectant smile. "You'll come?"

"Fine," I said. "The very least we can do is knock."

We made our way back down the goblins' tower, passing Falkon on the way up with an armload of tools, and then snuck out the front door to sidle along the inside of the curtain wall to the base of Jeramy's tower. Up to the front door – which was in remarkably good condition – and there I stepped back as Lotharia knocked.

"Jeramy?" She kept her voice to a whisper. "You home?"

A window opened in the wall. I mean that literally. One second it was blank rock, the next a rectangle was pushed free, swinging out on hinges, stone changing to four glass panes in a wooden frame. It looked like a cottage window, and leaning out on one elbow was a stocky young man, square-jawed and with an unruly thatch of blond hair framing a jovial face. Tattoos curled around his forearms where they emerged from his rolled-up sleeves, and an earring glinted from his left ear.

"Lotharia!" His voice was distressingly loud. "I haven't seen you in what feels like years! Wait. It has been years!"

"Hi, Jeramy," she said, voice strained. "Can we keep our voices down a little?"

"Oh, sure," said Jeramy, dropping his voice to a cheerful stage whisper. "What's up?"

I stepped forward. "That's not him, is it? I mean, is that— Should I be—" Everything about Jeramy – from the cheerful gleam in his eyes to how natural his smile looked – made him seem real.

"Oh, no, I'm not the real Jeramy," said Jeramy. "Just a dashingly handsome copy of myself. A carbonated carbon copy. But I'm afraid I'm not available. Can I take a message?"

"Actually, we were hoping to come inside," said Lotharia. She bit the her lip and shot a nervous glance at the stables. "It's not safe out here anymore."

"No?" Jeramy peered past her at the bailey. "Sure looks different. Unless we've gone for some kind of frightful post-siege decor? But I'm sorry, Lotharia. You know I love you to pieces, but you don't have carte blanche access rights. So unless I've given you a passcode, I can't open the door."

"Do you know what it is?" I asked Lotharia.

She gave her head a sharp shake. "No. Um. Can we get a hint?"

"A hint?" Jeramy chuckled. "I shouldn't. But what was it Bilbo said? I don't know half of you half as intimately as I should like; but I like half of you half as much as the lower half of you deserves. Or something like that. Also, I can't resist playing at riddles. Remember that night I summoned the champagne whale? And you dove inside it wearing only your birthday suit?"

Lotharia blushed furiously. "Um, yes. I seem to recall something along those lines."

I did my best to not grin, but had to admit that the image was… a delightfully evocative one.

"Well. Here's the hint, though it's more of a question: what do I enjoy doing more than anything else?"

Lotharia didn't hesitate. "Casting magic."

"You'd think, but nope."

I looked back at the stable. Was that movement in the shadowed doorway?

"Gaining power?"

"Nope-a-dope!"

Movement. "Lotharia, we've got company. We've got to go."

"Learning about Euphoria?"

"Nope-a-rope-dope!!"

"Helping others!"

"Ha!"

"Um – furthering the goals of Cruel Winter?"

"Your friend here's right. That looks like an ogre emerging from the stables." The illusory Jeramy frowned. "Which is downright *weird*. Did somebody ride him here?"

I went to grab Lotharia by the arm, prepared to haul her away, when something tickled the back of my mind. Lotharia had said Jeramy loved absolutely awful puns. And something Jeramy had mentioned *after* Lotharia had asked for her hint popped out at me. Why had he bothered to mention the champagne whale?

"Um."

Jeramy looked at me, eyebrow raised.

"You… like having a whale of a time?"

"Yes! Sharp young lad. Good bone structure. You've done well for yourself, Lotharia." With that, he gave her a salacious wink.

The window changed, its sill dropping to the ground, the glass-paned frames turning into a stout wooden door.

I looked back. An ogre was staring at us, scratching its head. With a grunt, it picked up its club from the shadows and began striding in our direction.

I mean, despite knowing that it was thirty yards away and that we had an open door right before us my heart began to pound like a mad thing. That was certain death coming to say hello. I didn't hesitate, but grabbed Lotharia's hand and jumped inside.

The door closed quickly behind us, reverting to a seamless wall.

"We're not together..." Lotharia's protest trailed off as we both looked around the bottom-most chamber of Jeramy's tower. "It's just like I remember it!"

We'd entered some kind of library/study/lounge. A huge orrery hung from the ceiling, planets and comets wheeling around a blazing star, planes of different elements intersecting throughout in the forms of sheets of fire, ice, earth and so on. The walls were lined with bookcases of gleaming dark wood on which count-less tomes stood behind glass panes. A heavy desk was set at an angle at the back, its surface clean and devoid of all objects. A handful of couches and massively overstuffed armchairs faced each other in the middle around a small table in whose center bubbled a fountain of pink liquid.

Everywhere I looked I found objects that piqued my curios-ity. Countless little curios were secreted amongst the books, from skulls to crystals to small cases to bundles of feathers or dancing motes of light in a stoppered jar. A stuffed blue alligator hung from the ceiling, while a flock of rainbow-hued flamingoes picked their way carefully around the couches.

I stared at them. "Are those real?"

"You shouldn't need me to prompt you to use Detect Magic by now," she said, voice hushed. "Shield your eyes."

I gave a curt nod and activated the cantrip, raising my hand in anticipation of the glow. I was glad I did – almost everything lit up, from the pink fountain to countless objects behind the glass-paned shelves. After a moment the glow grew muted, and I lowered my hand, blinking and trying to focus.

The flamingoes. They all radiated magic – no, they *were* magic. I frowned, trying to understand what I was seeing. The golden essence that was the air condensed into their shapes, but without focus points; the glow of their heads was the same strength as that of their feet. They looked like magic balloons, smooth and vacuous and without detail.

"Not real flamingoes," I said. "But then…?"

"Illusions," said Lotharia. "And basic ones at that. Jeramy was capable of creating exceedingly complex, believable illusions when he wanted – if you looked at them with Detect Magic they'd look as real and complex as any other living being. These are just for fun. But come on. I'm disappointed you haven't seen him yet."

"Seen what?" I scanned the room. It was like trying to pick out a single headlight on a highway of oncoming cars at night. Then I saw it. A humanoid shape standing beside the desk, staring right back at me, outlined in magic but with all the complexity the flamingoes had lacked: his head was dense and swirling like a nebula, while pulses of magic ran through his frame like an ethereal circulatory system.

I dropped Detect Magic. The space by the desk was empty. "An invisibility spell? Is that Jeramy?"

"No," said Lotharia. "And yes, an invisibility spell. I think that's Worthington, his butler. Hold on. Let's see if he'll talk to us."

She circled the couches, passing through the flamingoes, whose forms flickered and solidified around her. Then she stopped and bowed to where the butler stood. "Worthington? It's Lotharia. We met a few years back – do you recall? You helped me down from the chandelier and brought me a pair of talking slippers."

I re-appraised Lotharia. There was clearly more to her than I'd imagined. Diving naked into champagne whales? Getting caught in chandeliers? No wonder she'd earned Carousing: Basic (V).

The air shimmered and Worthington appeared. He was a robot, bronze-skinned and fashioned in classic art deco lines. He canted his head to one side. "Greetings, Miss Glimmervale. How may I be of assistance?"

"A robot?" I asked. "I thought Euphoria was high fantasy."

Lotharia shrugged. "We're in Jeramy's private sanctum. As an archmagus, he already had quite a degree of control over Euphoria, but here? He could pretty much do as he pleased. Though I doubt Worthington would survive long if he stepped outside. Um. Worthington. Do you know where Jeramy is?"

"He is on the fourth floor, ma'am."

"The fourth floor?" I inhaled sharply, eyes widening. "He's alive? He's here?"

"Wait," said Lotharia. "We looked into the fourth floor. It's full of broken weapons and barrels of pitch."

"Ah," said Worthington. If his face had been mobile, I'm sure he'd have given us a polite, pitying smile. "The other fourth floor."

"Oh." Lotharia nodded as if that made any sense at all. "Can we speak with him?"

"But of course. You only need access the fourth floor."

"And… how do we do that?"

"I cannot divulge that information."

"Hmm." Lotharia looked sidelong at me, then back at Worthington. "Well. Can you send him a message?"

"I am afraid I have instructions not to interrupt him." This was said with an air of complete finality.

"Worthington," I said, stepping next to Lotharia. "Cruel Winter and Castle Winter itself are in dire straits. Can you lend us any objects of power to help us defend it?"

"I am afraid I have instructions not to let anyone despoil the tower. As such, no."

"Rats." I cast a covetous look around at all the objects that lay on the shelving. They'd all glowed with magic. While I might be willing to confront a regular butler, an archmagus' butler was a different thing altogether.

"Thank you, Worthington." Lotharia stood a little straighter. "We were hoping to climb to the regular fourth floor. Do you mind if we use the stairs?"

"You have carte blanche access to the amenities," said Worthington. "That includes usage of the stairs. However, I must ask that you not break the summoning circle on the third floor. That would bring about a ruinous state of affairs."

"Summoning circle?" I paused. Those words never implied anything good. "Is there something inside it?"

"There is," said Worthington.

"We shan't touch it," said Lotharia firmly. "Now. Is there anything you can tell us about what happened to Cruel Winter? What brought about the siege? Why Jeramy has secluded himself on this fourth floor?"

"Master Jeramy was perturbed the last time I saw him," said Worthington. "He was in quite a rush. The siege, if that's what it was, seemed a great inconvenience. He was engaged in great magics. He said that a formidable trap had been laid for him inside the keep, and retired to his private study to contemplate his next move. He has remained there since. Now. May I offer you some refreshments?"

I exchanged a glance with Lotharia. "Ah, refreshments? Do we have time?"

She smiled and sat on the couch. "The barrels of black fire mud aren't going anywhere. Thank you, Worthington. A gin and tonic, please."

I sat on the other end of the couch. "They had those back in the… middle… fantasy ages?"

"And you, sir?"

"I'll have a Singapore Sling with mescal on the side." Lotharia raised an eyebrow. "What? You've never seen *Fear and Loathing in Las Vegas* before?"

Our drinks simply coalesced along with a silver tray on Worthington's palm, and he bowed as he served us.

I took a sip. "Perfect."

"Ah, civilization," said Lotharia, curling her legs under her. "This brings back memories. I thought I'd be doing this the moment I came back, not spending weeks scurrying through Feldgrau like an extra in a zombie movie."

I lifted my shot and sipped it. Exceptionally smooth. I drank it slowly, savored the sublime white lightning taste, then set the glass down. "Hey, that zombie movie brought us together. Not all bad."

She closed one eye as she looked at me through the narrowed lashes of the other. "No. Not *all* bad."

I snorted and leaned back. The couch was that dangerously soft kind that slowly enveloped you the longer you remained still.

"Let me ask you: if you could pick, would you really rather have come back to a decadent party castle? Or, despite the hardships, would you have chosen to go with the reality we ended up with?"

Lotharia sipped her gin and tonic. "Sign me up for the decadent party castle. You saying they're even remotely equivalent?"

"You know, maybe I'm nuts, but I prefer what we've got going over some endless surreal party. I'm sure it would have been a lot of fun, but…"

"But you like being dirty, overwhelmed, and on the verge of death at all times?"

A dangerous light had entered her eye, and there was a curl to her smile that made me feel intensely aware of the short distance between us.

"I mean, not when you put it that way. But yes?" I stared down into my drink, trying to focus my thoughts. Looking at Lotharia was becoming too distracting, and I felt a strong urge to articulate what I was feeling. "I felt it when I first arrived here. Before I knew how everything had gone to shit. When I first looked out over the mountains and valleys and saw the forest… I was thrilled. So much unknown. So much to discover. And being in Death March mode made it all the more *real*." I risked a glance up. She was watching me over the rim of her glass. "And I've never felt more alive, you know?"

"Hmm," said Lotharia. "Sounds like you needed to get out more." Then she laughed and leaned forward to touch my arm, "I'm kidding! I'm kidding. I understand what you mean. At least, I think I do. Adventure. Excitement. Exploring the unknown. That's been an allure to our species since we first came down from the trees, right?"

"Now you're calling me a monkey." I grinned ruefully and took another sip. "It's more than that. It's…. Look. When I was around ten or eleven my family went on a vacation to Australia. I don't even remember where this happened, but we'd driven out of the major cities to avoid the rioting and were visiting a friend in a small town somewhere, and they recommended this lake to go picnic at."

"Uh-huh," said Lotharia, curling a strand of hair behind her ear. I was struck by how wonderful it felt to have a mild buzz and be having a serious conversation with a wildly attractive girl who was giving me her undivided attention.

I pulled it back together. "Yeah, so we got there and started to unpack the picnic stuff and my parents weren't talking to each other, they were doing that icy cold thing, and my brother must have been six and was focused on his comic books, so I decided to swim in the lake. There was this tree extending right out of the middle of it. Rising out of the water, this huge oak, and I decided to swim out to it."

The memory was clear-cut in my mind, as if etched in acid. The scrubby, dry grass around the lake's shore that extended below the water. The lake had flooded its banks, risen up. Walking into the water had been the weirdest sensation, wet, silty grass beneath my feet. The lake lukewarm. When I was thigh deep, I'd plunged forward and begun swimming toward the distant tree. Everything had been going great till my foot kicked down a little deeper and pushed through into a zone of icy cold water.

The shock had been intense. I'd snatched up my foot as if something had tried to grab it and pedaled in place. I dipped my foot again and once more felt that bitter coldness, as clearly separated from the warm upper layer as if demarcated by a razor. I'd dipped my head underwater to look, and seen nothing but blackness beneath me. Gone was the ground. It felt like I was staring into an abyss.

"I swam back to shore as if I'd seen the Loch Ness monster," I said. "Came thrashing up onto the shore, gasping and all freaked out. Nobody noticed. I grabbed a towel and sat behind the car."

Lotharia finished her drink. "And you've loved adventure ever since?" She sounded mystified.

"No," I said. "I mean, yes, but it's because of what I thought I saw in the darkness below me. It felt like I'd discovered this impossible, magical realm. Felt like something should have been looking up at me, from the depths of that lake with its strange tree. It made me so aware of the hidden, the mystery of the world." I finished my drink in turn. "But in our world, the real world, all the lakes are empty. The caves hold nothing more than blind fish. The deepest forests are secondary growth. That moment of magic, of terror? I can't find that in the real world. Which is why Euphoria makes me feel like that ten-year-old version of myself. What we've been experiencing? Living through? The impossible odds, the magic, the danger, the excitement? It's what I longed for when I was a kid and never found again. And now here it is, and I wouldn't trade it for the world."

We sat in silence. I wanted to turn away, to avoid meeting her gaze. To get up, even, and pretend to be interested in the books behind their glass panes.

Lotharia reached out again and touched my shoulder. "Despite the draugr and ogres and goblin soup, I've been having a good time, too."

We shared a smile, and then the lights dimmed and turned a deep rose and a disco ball descended from the center of the orrery. A million motes of light began to twirl around the room, and a sultry song began to play.

Lotharia sat up straight. "Worthington?"

The butler appeared. "Did I misread your interaction? Jeramy always asked for this configuration when about to engage in the song of sliding leather."

"The song of— what?"

Lotharia cracked up and covered her face.

"Ah," said Worthington. "My apologies." The lighting once more became a neutral luminescence, the disco ball retracted, and the music faded away. "Please resume your courtship."

"Courtship?" I looked wildly at Lotharia. "I— We're—"

"It's OK," said Lotharia, rising to her feet and wiping at her eyes. "Thank you, Worthington. You've been a most gracious host. Come, *dear*. Let's move our *courtship* upstairs to the black fire mud barrels."

"You are most welcome, ma'am."

Lotharia took my hand and pulled me toward the steps that curled along the inside of the wall. Not knowing what to say, trying not to act flustered, I instead activated Detect Magic once more and allowed my gaze to drift. The more powerful an object, I guessed, the brighter the glow; It was surprising to see what lit up the brightest. A single marble wedged between two heavy books glowed like a miniature sun; a boot under one of the couches was nearly as bright. The alligator was clearly an object of some power, as were a dozen other random objects secreted about the room.

I stopped at the sight of an unexpected glow. It limned a trap-door at the base of the steps. I switched off Detect Magic. Hidden from the normal eye. "Lotharia. You see this?"

"Mm-hmm," she said. "It's Arcane Locked, however. No way we could open it."

"Interesting. Given what we've heard about the levels under-ground and all." I walked carefully over the trapdoor and onto the first steps. "I wonder what Jeramy was up to."

"Hard to imagine him doing anything serious," said Lotharia, climbing toward the second floor. "All I remember him doing was pulling elaborate gags and throwing impossibly creative parties."

"Well, he reached archmagus, didn't he? You don't do that just by having fun."

"Having a whale of a time," she absently corrected, and then we reached the second floor. It was a bedroom, complete with a king-sized bed, two massive walnut wardrobes, a floor-to-ceil-ing mirror and countless thick carpets laid over the stone floor. A full-sized portrait of Jeramy hung on the wall.

I laughed. I couldn't help it. It showed Jeramy, shirtless, flexing before a waterfall, one foot atop a knocked-out grizzly's head.

"Now," said Lotharia. "Do we resume our courtship, or head up to the third floor?"

My face burned and my stomach did a flip. "Excuse me?"

She laughed and gave my shoulder a push. "Are you really this innocent? Your face! Oh, come on. Onto the third floor. And remember: don't touch the summoning circle."

I ran my hand through my hair, desperately trying to keep my head above water. "Oh, don't you worry," I said. "That's one of my life's greatest maxims, right up there with the Golden Rule and 'don't feed the Mogwai after midnight'."

She snorted and drew her scepter from under her cloak with her right hand, her spider staff with her left. "Good."

I paused. "Expecting trouble?"

She looked down at me over her shoulder. "Nothing I can handle."

"You got that expression wrong. It goes: 'nothing you *can't* handle'."

"Nope, I said exactly what I meant to the first time. Think of these as my comfort blankets. Now come on. Let's see what Jeramy's left sitting in his circle these past few years. I'm sure it's in a very good mood."

We rounded the last of the steps and emerged onto the third floor. It was dominated by an incredibly complex summoning circle, complete with endless squiggly runes in crimson and white chalk, candles that were somehow still burning, golden chalices filled with suitably ominous dark liquids, and a haze of smoke that appeared in a perfect cylinder above the summoning circle itself like you might see illuminated by lasers at a nightclub.

Inside, Jeramy sat on a reclining armchair, wearing a bathrobe and with a full-length golden beard reaching down to his sternum. He'd been staring out one of the many windows that circled the interior of the tower, each of which looked out over an impossible landscape. A quick glance showed me their variety: a view over a medieval metropolis inside a ravine; a harsh moonscape on which spindly-legged albino spider-crabs danced; a treetop village where elves made their way across rope bridges; an underwater realm shot through by beams of glittering light amongst which mermen swam in an intricate dance; and more.

"Jeramy?" Lotharia stumbled to a stop.

"Hmm?" Jeramy turned to us, eyebrow raised. "Oh. Hello, Lotharia! You're a sight for sore eyes! Thank goodness someone's finally arrived. I was going insane from boredom in here." He leapt to his feet, suddenly energized. "Be a dear and let me out?"

"Wait, wait, wait," I said, putting a hand on Lotharia's shoulder. "What are you doing in there?"

Jeramy grimaced. "Silly mistake, really. That's what you get for doing these things in a rush. Over here, see? The *uribundos* rune. I got the third crossing wrong, allowing the power I summoned to swap places with me. A novice mistake! But I've had *ages* to kick myself over it. Now. Give it a quick smudge with your boot?"

Lotharia frowned. "Worthington told us you were on the fourth floor."

Jeramy nodded patiently. "I am. This circle on the third traps me on the fourth. You're speaking with me across space. But really, I'll invite you both upstairs as soon as you release me."

"Sure," I said. "As soon as you tell us what the passcode to the tower is."

Jeramy raised an eyebrow. "I approve of your caution. I love having a whale of a time. Now, can we hurry?"

Lotharia hesitated, and then went to step forward.

"No, wait." I'd been gaming for far too long to accede this quickly. "Lotharia. Ask him something only he could know and that he couldn't have heard us talking about downstairs."

Jeramy's patient smile turned into a hard line. "You test my patience, boy. Hurry and let me out of here. I've wasted too much time already to waste more playing at trivia."

"On my last night here, you gave me a gift," said Lotharia. "What was it?"

"You expect me to recall every gift I've ever given? That was ages ago. I'm sure it was some precious trifle." He waved his hand. "Now. Smudge the circle and I'll reward you more handsomely than you can imagine."

We both stepped back.

"Wow," said Lotharia. "I can't believe how close that was. Thanks, Chris."

Jeramy's eyes narrowed. "I see that your life is inextricably intertwined with your body, boy. Yet you are so weak. Free me, and I shall raise you in power such that none of the threats you face can menace you again."

I paused. Wait a sec. Did he know I was in Death March mode? Wasn't he an NPC? How—

"No, thank you," said Lotharia. "We'll be making no bargains with you."

I forced myself to nod. That one moment of temptation slipped away. What was I thinking? Accept power from something like him? Never.

Jeramy gave us both a predatory smile. "Last chance, buckeroos."

"Yeah," I said. The flat, inhuman anger now filling Jeramy's eyes was making me nervous. "Let's head on up."

Jeramy threw himself at the edge of the circle, his form exploding as he did so into a torrent of blood and viscera so that he hit the curling wall of smoke with a horrendous scream. We both leapt back, clutching at each other, and stared wide-eyed as the gore slid down the summoning circle's wall to reveal a hunched goatman. His knees were reversed, his feet become hooves, and his shoulders and spine were covered in thick, bristly fur. His head was all goat, his mouth filled with fangs, and twin curling ram's horns of ebon made his head appear massive and horrific.

With a shriek, he tore a strip of flesh from his side and hurled it at us. The strip become a hissing black snake midair, only to evaporate in a flash of smoke upon hitting the summoning circle wall. Furious, the goat demon threw back its head and shrieked with such volume that we both clapped our hands over our ears.

Stumbling, we ran up the stairs, our panic preventing us from noticing the flat stone roof that blocked the stairwell. I ran hunched over, hauling myself up the steps, my hand accidentally closing on a marble as I went. I flinched before colliding with the flat roof only to emerge onto the fourth floor, Lotharia hard on my heels.

Gasping, we fell to the ground, then turned and kicked our way back to the tower wall to stare at the smooth ground we'd emerged from. There was no sign of the way down.

"My god," said Lotharia, pressing her hand to her chest. "That was insane. What was that thing?"

"And why the hell did Jeramy summon it?" I tried to force my breath to slow. I'd not been panicked like that since arriving here. I'd not even thought about Shadow Stepping or summoning my Death Dagger. My only thought had been the most primal and basic: escape.

"Wow." Lotharia took a deep breath and held it. "I'm going to repeat that for effect: wow."

"Yeah." I climbed to my feet and pulled her up after me. "No kidding. And I thought the ogres were trouble."

"Oh, no. If that thing ever got free, we'd all be done. Or worse than done." She combed her black hair from her face and composed herself. "I vote we never visit that third floor again."

"I second your motion." I realized I was holding something in my left hand and opened my fist. A small, clear marble, much like a children's toy, sat in my palm. "Huh. What's this?" I activated Detect Magic and immediately closed my fist over the bright glow.

"Where did you get that?" asked Lotharia.

"On the steps. It was just lying there." I opened my hand carefully again, feeling a spike of excitement. "What is it?"

"Looks like a mana stone," she said. "Like the one embedded in the pommel of Falkon's sword. Can I see?"

She held it up to the light and turned it this way and that. "Yep. A very minor one. I bet Jeramy dropped it and never noticed. It stores mana you can draw on in times of need. I think this one probably holds about four or five mana points. Negligible for someone like Jeramy."

I grinned as I took it back. "But it doubles my own store. Awesome. How do I use it?"

"Just having it in your possession will increase your mana pool. You can keep it in a pouch or whatever. When you meditate, you can keep going until you refill your mana stone. It's pretty basic at this level."

"Mana marble," I corrected her, and pulled open my character sheet. I'd not earned any XP, to my disappointment, but a quick check proved Lotharia right: my mana had risen to nine. "Sweet!"

"Now," said Lotharia. "Let's get to work on these barrels. You check them while I weaken the boulders. Then we can time it right and roll them across the wall to the goblin tower."

"Sure thing," I said. "And maybe you can Imbue them to make them a little lighter?"

"You're getting lazy," laughed Lotharia. "No. You need to up your strength. And there's only one way to do that."

"Great," I said, turning to the large barrels with a sigh. "Great."

Still, I couldn't claim to be too upset. I slipped my new mana marble into my pocket, rolled my shoulders to loosen them up, and walked on over to the closest barrel as Lotharia got to work.

16

WE WAITED TILL dawn the next day to tackle the plague corpse mission. Nobody wanted to head down to Feldgrau with evening drawing on, so instead we rested in the goblin tent village, something that was only made possible by Barfo's cooking his 'bad food' outside the curtain wall.

Falkon nudged me awake with the toe of his boot, and I sat up to the remarkably pleasing aroma of candied apples and oatmeal. Pale morning light was filtering in through the massive hole in the side of the chamber, and Barfo was casually stirring his secondary pot while Kreekit knitted some kind of bone cardigan. Lotharia was sipping from a clay cup, blanket around her shoulders, and Falkon gave me a smile before returning to cleaning his armor.

The goblins' den was actually surprisingly homey. I sat up, stretched, and gave thanks for Euphoria's lack of emphasis on the need to brush one's teeth or shower. I scarfed down a bowl of what Barfo called 'brown grass and knobby fruit' – and which he kindly explained he'd kept rat bits out of – and then stepped outside to survey the land that stretched out below Castle Winter.

The sun had barely cleared the high peaks to the east, and long shadows still stretched across the forested vale. When was the last time I'd actually stopped to appreciate the stunning beauty of Euphoria? While there might be a broad valley somewhere in the European Alps that rivaled this in terms of sheer beauty, even the most gorgeous Alpine valley would lack the mystery and magical potential of what lay before me. For in those dark woods, fairies and dark secrets really did lurk, while at any moment a dragon or griffon might fly forth from the peaks into the morning light.

I thought of my brother Justin, of how perilous my quest was, of the enormity of the odds stacked against my success and how reckless this whole endeavor was, and still I smiled. The sun was warm on my bare arms, I was just starting to get a taste of power, and Euphoria was a fantasy land like I'd always dreamed of exploring. Ever since I was a kid and read my first Fighting Fantasy 'choose your own adventure' novel I'd wanted to be thrust into the midst of a thrilling, impossible world.

And here I was.

Falkon and Lotharia stepped out to join me, and for a moment we simply stood shoulder to shoulder, gazing down at Feldgrau. The village was a dark stain upon the grassy sward, hedged in by dense forest and looking out of place in this pristine wilderness. From this vantage point I could make out the fields that had clearly fallen fallow since the village's neglect, and parts of the town I'd not visited when I'd first arrived: the broken tower in which the Dread Lord resided, squat and vicious like the lower half of a shattered blade; the yawning charnel pit before it whose depths were shrouded in darkness, its banks made of raw earth as if the very grass refused to come close; the many collapsed and broken buildings that testified to the horrific attack that had laid the township low.

"The past few days make my first weeks down there seem a night-marish dream," said Lotharia. "Crawling in the shadows, hiding like a rat in whichever bolt-hole I could find. It feels almost like another life."

"We're going to have to be extra careful," I said. "I know that goes without saying, or should, but you can't head out on a mission like this without actually saying it, you know?"

"Got it," said Falkon.

"So, we agreed on the plan? Lotharia and I will enter the town using our Stealth to locate a plague corpse. We'll then lasso it and drag it to the town border under the cover of Lotharia's fog, where you'll be waiting to cover our retreat up to the castle. Sound good?"

The plan's simplicity had seemed its strong point last night when we'd devised it. Now it sounded foolishly optimistic.

"We've got all day," said Falkon. "Remember that. Bide your time. Wait for the perfect moment. And if things go wrong, we all sprint the hell out. Clear?"

"Clear," Lotharia and I murmured.

We stood still for a moment longer, none of us eager to begin this mission, and then as one we followed the thin bank around the base of the wall to the wooden siege bridge, over which we quickly scampered. From there we picked an oblique approach down, not wanting to use the main path, skirting the forest edge as we moved ever closer.

The ground had leveled out and we were drawing close to the town when something drew my eye toward a couple of massive trees that flanked the main path far to our left. Astute Observer?

Either way, I picked out a couple of figures standing as still as statues behind each trunk, looking up the path. Squinting, I thought I could make out the pale gleam of bone and multiple arms.

"Over there," I whispered, sinking into a crouch behind a tangle of blackberry bushes. "You see those two trees? Looks like the undead have posted a guard."

"You're right," said Falkon. "And serious-looking guards, too."

"I don't see them," said Lotharia.

"Hurry up and buy Astute Observer, then," said Falkon, and pretended to flinch away when she thwapped his arm.

"Interesting," I said. "They weren't there when we escaped. Which means they've been posted since we left. But nothing we've done has affected Feldgrau. So why post guards?"

Lotharia drew her scepter from behind her back. "They must have noticed our activity in the castle. The Dread Lord must be keeping tabs on us."

I recalled his chill eyes gazing at me when I'd floated down upon the tides of magic to examine Feldgrau, and shivered. "Yeah. Let's make a really strong effort to avoid getting any more attention. Sound good?"

They both nodded and we resumed our approach, running all hunched over and darting from tree to outcropping to bush till we reached a large rock on the far flank of Feldgrau with its path leading up to the highland meadow.

"This should be close enough," I whispered. "Falkon, want to chill here?"

"Sure," said Falkon. "Adrenaline Surge and Headlong Charge should bring me into town in a matter of moments if things go wrong."

"Things are *not* going to go wrong," said Lotharia darkly.

"Exactly." I rubbed my palms on my hips to dry them. "All right. I'm up."

"Good luck," said Falkon. "Remember: hitting the undead between the legs doesn't do a damn thing."

I chuckled but was too nervous to let the humor distract me. "OK. On the count of three. One. Two. Three."

"You're supposed to run at three," said Lotharia dryly.

"Oh. Yeah. Right." I took a deep breath, focused on the darkness within the closest building, and Shadow Stepped, sinking into the shadow beside the rock. It was like falling into a pool within the depths of a cave; soft and chill and all-enveloping. Darkness flowed across my eyes, and I stretched for the far shadows, keeping my mind firmly focused on the ruined shack. Was it too far?

There was a sense of strain, like trying to swim five yards farther than was comfortable underwater, and then I emerged with a muffled gasp, hand over my mouth, crouched beside the shack. Elation and euphoria swirled within me even as I pressed my back to the wall, looking side to side for any signs of the undead. At the first hint of danger I'd Double Step right back to the boulder – but there was none.

Coast was clear.

I waited, giving it ten or so minutes to make sure this far corner of Feldgrau wasn't on anything's patrol route, then waved over to where Lotharia was waiting, beckoning her over. She bolted across the open grass, shoulders hunched, looking as if she expected to take an arrow in the side at any moment. I steadied her when she reached me, and couldn't help but grin.

"Gotta love that Athletics: Basic (I) you got going there, eh?"

Lotharia elbowed me in the side and peered past me into Feldgrau. "You're not exactly in a position to show off. Now – what's the plan?"

"I think this was some kind of animal shack back in the day," I said. "Probably belonging to that small hut over there. The actual street begins just beyond it, leading straight into town. How about we skirt around the back of the hut and see what we find?"

She nodded, so I ran out from the shadows, over the furrowed, night-frozen mud of what might have been a pig wallow ages past, and reached the back of the hut. Lotharia joined me a moment later, and we moved around the back, casting anxious glances in every direction till the street came into view.

The houses here were relatively small and impoverished; they quickly became better than huts, but none of them had two stories and all of them were closely packed together as if huddling in fear. 'Street' was too grandiose a name for the rutted path that ran between them, but the track had clearly been the cause behind the erection of the buildings, which extended out of the village proper to follow the path as it led toward the highland meadow. Carefully, taking our time, we worked our way behind the houses, and finally reached the first crossroads.

"This was once called Moon's Way," whispered Lotharia. "It looped all the way around Feldgrau, with markers in the ground depicting the changing phases of the moon. Full moon for the main path that led up to the castle. I think it was crescent here where it hit the highland meadow's road."

"Should see some traffic on it, then," I replied. "Let's settle in and watch."

We both crouched, shoulders touching, and sure enough, it didn't take long for a skeleton to shuffle into view. He looked confused, stopping to turn around and gaze behind him several times. It was too easy to imagine him scratching his head, but he just kept on shuffling, till finally he turned into a doorway and was gone.

A few moments later, a pack of draugrs moved past the rear entrance of the alleyway across from us. Luckily, they didn't come any closer, and soon disappeared. More skeletons, this time in a group of six, moving with the greater purpose of a squad along the Moon's Way. There was silence for a spell. Lotharia chewed on a strand of her hair, then froze. A six-armed champion stalked into view.

I tried to sink even deeper into the nook in which we were hiding. At a pinch I could Shadow Step away, but that would mean leaving Lotharia behind. So basically not an option. The champion easily stood some seven feet tall, with a mess of over-lapping shoulder blades like bone carapace armor connecting to clavicles from which each of its arms extended. It carried a tower shield in one of its left hands, a bow beneath that, and then a variety of blades and maces in its remaining hands, with a quiver hanging from its hip.

A band of pale metal – perhaps silver or platinum – was welded to its brow, above which rose a forest of small boney protrusions like sharp thorns. Its eyes burned with malevolent blue flames, and its head swung from side to side as it strode by, ceaselessly examining its environs.

My throat squeezed shut with fear and my skin tingled as the hairs on the nape of my neck and backs of my arms rose. My stomach filled with acid, and I wanted nothing more than to turn and run. I held my breath, and for a brief second I could have sworn it stared right at me – but then it moved on, following the curvature of the street, and was gone.

"Holy crap," I whispered. "What level do you think those things are?"

Lotharia pressed her sleeve to her brow. "I've no idea. Easily level twenty. Maybe thirty. Who knows?"

"I'm just glad it doesn't have Astute Observer." I turned my blade over and over in my hand. "Where would I even stab it?"

"Look – over there," whispered Lotharia, leaning into me and pointing over my shoulder toward an alleyway, her cheek nearly touching mine. "There – see it?"

I did. A classic zombie-looking monster, staggering like a drunkard, knees bent, shoulders hunched. I could barely make out the buzz of the flies that surrounded it, along with a faint wet bubbling noise. That'd be the insects in its flesh, I hazarded, and my gorge rose.

I took the lasso from my hip. I'd practiced last night, but wasn't expecting to toss it over the zombie from a real distance; instead, the plan was for me to Double Step in and out, dropping the lasso over its head before it registered my presence. Or managed to infect me, for that matter.

"Coast clear?" I asked.

"You're the one with Astute Observer," she said, "but yes. Looks good to me."

I bit my lip and leaned out, taking a good look both up and down Moon's Way and Highland Meadow Road. Everything was quiet. I unspooled the lasso, holding the slipknot in my right hand, and was about to Shadow Step when Lotharia grabbed me by the shoulder and hauled me back into the shadows.

"Don't move!" she whispered in my ear. I remained frozen, half lying in her arms as she hugged me tight, staring out at the band of street before us. A moment later a ghost woman floated into view, her face rotted and pale, dress and lower legs fading away into mist. Her presence made me feel awful and weird, as if I'd hit my funny bone then had that feeling generalized all over my body. I held my breath, and then she was gone.

"Close one," whispered Lotharia, breath warm in my ear.

I caught my balance and edged away, very aware of how it had felt to have her arms around me. "Thanks," I whispered back. "Here we go."

I double-checked for traffic again, then Double Stepped across Moon's Way and into the alley. Up close, the buzzing of the insects was horrendous, and I nearly gagged from the stench. Holding my breath, eyes watering, I dropped the lasso over the zombie's shoulders and hurled the coil of rope back across the street to where Lotharia waited, completing my Double Step back as quickly as I possibly could.

There wasn't any time to catch my breath, however. Lotharia had already cast Summon Fog by the time I emerged, the cottony white mist boiling out everywhere to obscure this part of Moon's Way. I snatched up the coil of rope where it lay scattered across the street, wrapped it around my back and arm and hauled with all my strength.

The plague corpse didn't resist, the rope going slack immediately. I skipped back, only to nearly fall over myself as the rope suddenly went taut as a piano wire. What the hell? Then it hit me. I'd toppled the corpse over with my first yank.

Lotharia reached my side, emerging from the fog only a few feet before me. "What's wrong? Go!"

"It's fallen over!" I hissed. "I'm not strong enough to drag it all the way out of town!"

"Give it a moment, then." She glanced nervously around. "They stand up by themselves. Then pull it more carefully!"

Grinding my teeth, I tested the rope. There was a little more give – was it standing up? I forced myself to wait, precious seconds rolling past, then pulled again. There. Some resistance, then give.

"Got it," I said. "Time to—"

A skeletal champion stepped out of the fog behind Lotharia. Two hands gripped her arms, a third clamped over her mouth while a fourth tore her scepter from her grasp. It lifted her right off her feet, eyes burning into mine.

Movement right behind me. With no time to even look I Shadow Stepped wildly, the fog giving me enough cover right there and then to disappear into the roiling darkness. A moment later I was behind the skeletal champion that had been about to grab me. I activated Adrenaline Surge, the sweet, delirious burn of power coursed through my limbs, and slammed my dagger right into the monster's spine.

My blade skittered off bone, barely scratching it. It wheeled, shockingly fast, hand swooping around to catch me about the throat, but I fell back into the fog, hit the dirt and rolled, coming up to my feet and nearly overbalancing in the process.

More shapes were emerging from the fog all around me. More skeletal champions. One – no, two, three of them. Four in all. Arms like octopoid monstrosities, blades and maces and bows. My heart was pounding, my pulse like a drum in my ears, but I could only see Lotharia in the original champion's grip, kicking and trying to break free.

They were closing in around me. I cursed and threw myself into a reckless roll, narrowly avoiding two different attempts to grab me and coming up behind Lotharia's champion. This time I was ready.

I summoned my Death Dagger.

A shard of ice formed in the palm of my hand, elongating in the flash of an eye, wicked and broad, black like the space between stars and edged with a burning, brilliant blue like the kind of flame you get from a chem lab Bunsen burner. Its edge undulated like the waves of a stormy ocean, and where it swung it keened, as if slicing the very air and hurting it in the process.

With a cry, I brought the Death Dagger down high on the champion's back, aiming to cut through into its chest.

The wicked, beautiful dagger hit the champion – and bounced right off.

Shocked, I staggered back, blade burning in my fist. The champion spun around again, whipping Lotharia through the air.

Damn it! I'd forgotten. The Death Dagger did necrotic damage. Useless against the undead! I dismissed it, furious at my waste of mana, and then threw myself aside as the champion charged me.

I hit the ground awkwardly, tucked in my shoulder and rolled. Came up running and sprinted off into the fog, quickly leaving the champion behind only to run right into another who loomed above me. It swept me off the ground, two hands latching onto my upper arms, another pair squeezing the sides of my head as if it were trying to burst the world's largest egg.

Hell no. I Shadow Stepped without hesitation, stretching, trying to throw myself as far away from this melee as I could. Sweet darkness pulled me away from the skeleton's embrace, and then spat me out in the shadow of a chimney atop a roof. I staggered, nearly fell, then wrapped my arms around the chimney as if it were my long-lost love. Gasping, sweat burning my eyes, I stared down into the fog-choked street.

The fog cloud was dissipating even as I stared, revealing six skeletal champions in all, each of them casting around for some sign of me. I hunched down just as Adrenaline Surge gave out, and could do no more than simply lean my head against the chimney and focus on not puking.

Six of them. And they'd appeared as soon as we'd made our move. Which meant that first one *had* seen me. It had gone on to report, maybe, and then come back with five friends to lay an ambush. Damn!

Anger helped me lift my head. The champions were still hunting for me, while the one carrying Lotharia was stalking with rigid angularity deeper into Feldgrau. I glanced out past the edge of town: no sign of Falkon. If he'd seen the five champions, he'd no doubt realized there was nothing he could do.

Sounds came from beneath me. A champion was making its way up to the roof. I didn't have time to hesitate. I checked my character sheet: only one mana left. Again, I wanted to kick myself for the huge Death Dagger waste, but what the hell. I was still learning.

With extreme effort, I made myself stand. I wanted nothing more than to curl up and wait for death, but extensive experience dealing with hangovers in college helped me muscle through. Breathing in sharp, short pants, I hobbled along the top of the roof to its edge. C'mon, Adrenaline Surge. Any day now!

A boney fist smashed through the tiles a few yards behind me, and faster than I'd have credited the skeletal champion hauled itself up, sending tiles flying, hands and weapons clattering on support beams and broken clay until it stood before me in a deep crouch.

Two scimitars. A whip. A morningstar, and two empty hands. I had my dagger.

It moved forward, going from absolutely still to blur without any transition. I could barely stand. Tasted bile in the back of my throat. My leg muscles were cramped. It felt like the worst food poisoning in the world.

And then the nausea was gone.

I threw myself backward, right off the roof just as the champion closed with me, activating Ledge Runner as I fell. I swear my feet swerved off to the left, pulling the rest of me onto a rope that hung across the street, burnt pieces of flesh hanging from loops along its length. I didn't even want to know, but simply crouched as the line sagged to take my weight, then I spun and sprinted up its length to the house on the other side of the street.

Have I mentioned how much I effing love Ledge Runner?

The three champions still in the street all oriented on me like Terminators, but I didn't care. There was no time for anything but to scramble up onto the next roof and then race down its sloping side to leap over to the next building. The roofs were partially caved in, wrecked by fire and rot, but Ledge Runner didn't give a fig for all that. I ran as surefooted as a goat, chasing after the distant champion.

One mana point left. No way I could fight that thing. The best I could do was distract it and tear Lotharia free from its grasp. And then? I had no idea. One step at a time.

I could feel Ledge Runner running out. No, no, no. Just a little bit more! I put on a final burst of speed, trying to ignore the stabbing pain in my side, the way my breath was rasping in my raw throat, and then as I drew abreast with the oblivious champion, I leapt.

I activated Uncanny Aim in midair, targeted the champion's foot, and then double whammied it with Pin Down. I hurled my dagger as I fell, and felt Ledge Runner give out as I hit the ground.

It was enough. It corrected my balance and caught me sufficiently so that I could fall into a graceless tumble, all elbows and knees, and come up on all fours.

The champion was staring down at its impaled foot, nonplussed, and when it turned to regard me I flung a ball of Light right into its eyes.

Lotharia tore her hand free and ripped the spider staff out from under her cloak. The skeletal champion flailed at its head, raking its claws over its eyes. Lotharia bounced, swung in its two hands, but managed to shove the end of her staff under its jaw. A moment later the top of its head burst out in a conflagration of black fire and shards of bone, and she fell to the ground.

"Took your time," she said, grinning as she climbed to her feet.

"Took my— screw you!"

Her grin turned into exhilarated laughter.

"We've got to run. Five champions are heading this way!"

"You got a plan?"

I didn't. Then, just like that, I did. "Yeah. Hide over there – in that doorway. I'll wait at the corner there. Let them see me, chase me. I've got one mana left. I'll Double Step away— Here they come! Go, hide!"

She looked like she wanted to argue, but instead yanked me toward her and planted a kiss square on my lips. Before I could react, she dove into the doorway and was gone, and then the champions came pounding around the corner and right at me.

That kiss had addled my mind, but luckily thinking wasn't necessary right now. On pure reflex, I took off at a run. I tore around the corner, trying to place myself in Feldgrau, using the bird's-eye image I'd captured from Castle Winter. Some three blocks in. I'd taken a right turn, meaning I was running away from the castle. Another right would take me toward Falkon.

A glance over my shoulder showed me the champions were gaining on me. They ran with a robotic efficiency that made it look like they'd be able to run forever. I gritted my teeth and tried to put on more speed, but I was still winded from my race across the rooftops. Reluctantly, knowing the cooldown could kill me, I activated Adrenaline Surge.

I whooped with exhilaration as I took off, my feet almost leaving the ground. Fire flooded my legs, my lungs opened up, my arms pistoned as I surged ahead, fast, faster, fastest. I was the love child of a cheetah and a gazelle, an impossible blur that they'd never catch up with!

I looked over my shoulder. They had fallen behind – only to duck their chins, eyes ablaze, and start running even faster.

Damn it! The undead couldn't have Adrenaline Surge too, could they? They didn't have fucking adrenal glands!

I turned right and ran straight into a pack of regular skeletons. Sheer momentum carried me through them, pinballing from one warrior to another, their blows coming too late, the last swinging its sword right at my neck. I ducked and was under it, then gone, out into the open street.

There was a shattering of bones from behind me. My eyes opened wide. I didn't need to look back. The champions had torn right through the squad.

Think, think, think! Was I close enough to the edge of town? One more block, just one more block – then some sixth sense kicked in. I sensed the blow coming at my back, and burned that last mana point for all I was worth even as I dove aside into the shadowed side of the closest building.

I Double Stepped into the darkness, diving headfirst as if into a swimming pool of endless night only to explode right back out onto a rooftop in the shadowed lee of a taller building. With a scream of panicked surprise I slid stomach first down the tiles, feeling rough edges try to catch at my midnight spider silk shirt, bruising but not cutting me. There was one last jump left in my Double Step. With no time to waste, I turned my dive into a sideways roll, arms tucked against my chest, and fell right off the edge of the roof and into the alley below.

I never hit the ground. I sank into the darkness, let it take me and spit me back out as close to Feldgrau's edge as I could push it. I emerged inside a shack of some sort, the corpse of a pig lying on its side beside me, ribs arching out of leathery skin. I bit down a shout, clamping both hands over my mouth, and struggled to my feet. Where the hell was I?

Fire still dancing through my veins, I looked out the window and nearly crowed with delight. I was in the pig-sty I'd first run to, way back at the beginning of this mess. I didn't hesitate. I blew right out the door, out into the open, trying to outrun my imminent collapse, across the grass, leaving Feldgrau behind me as I tore toward the forest. A moment later, Adrenaline Surge came to its awful end, and I crashed headfirst into the bushes, down onto all fours, my stomach trying to invert itself and claw its way up out of my throat. I barely even registered the chime of my XP notifier.

Blind, trying not to pass out, I crawled forward until a hand clamped onto my shoulder. I tried to scream and managed only to gag instead. I rolled onto my back, and made out Falkon above me, blade in one hand, length of rope in the other. He held his finger to his lips.

"Lotharia?" I managed to gasp.

She emerged from the shadows beside Falkon, the last of her ice armor melting away, dark veins of black and purple etched across her cheeks, eyes bloodshot, spider staff in hand.

"We did it," said Falkon, giving the rope a tug. A faint moan sounded from further off in the trees. "I don't know how, but we did it. Now. Time to get back up to the castle before they come hunting for us. We're about ready to execute our plan."

17

W E DIDN'T WANT to come anywhere close to the main trail as we returned to Castle Winter, so instead we looped widely through the forest while dragging the plague corpse behind us – a task which was made easier by its constant and futile attempt to catch up and attack us. Luckily it was slow as molasses, so we simply had to guide it by walking just out of reach.

The forest, however, was far from friendly; Falkon with his Survival: Basic (III) told us numerous times to squat behind bushes or get out of sight, which proved a challenging experience with the plague corpse coming up behind us. Luckily, we managed to evade both notice from the forest denizens and being hugged by the corpse, but still – the journey to the castle made for a harrowing couple of hours.

Sweet relief flooded through me when we finally staggered across the siege bridge and onto the narrow bank beneath the walls. Barfo's largest pot was bubbling a score of yards along the wall, and even from here its stench made my eyes water.

I was concerned about Lotharia, who had remained mostly quiet on our hike up, but I was equally concerned about the plague corpse – we couldn't just bring it into the bailey.

"Hold up," said Falkon, turning to face the tottering zombie. "Let's see if this works." He quickly tied his end of the rope to a massive rock, then hefted a second stone about the size of a melon.

"What are you doing?" I asked, watching as the zombie stumbled toward us, arms pinned by its side by the lasso.

"This." Falkon hurled the rock with unerring accuracy right at the zombie's chest. The blow hit with a dull thud and the zombie staggered back, one foot going over the edge of the ravine, and then it plummeted out of sight altogether.

"Wait— what?!" I ran to the edge of the ravine only to see the zombie hanging below, twisting and moaning as he kicked at the cliff face. "Oh. Right. Yeah. I was about to suggest doing exactly that."

"Sure you were," said Falkon. "We'll leave him hanging till it's time to deploy him in the stables."

"Sounds good. Lotharia? You doing OK?"

She was leaning against the castle wall, arms crossed, head bowed so that her hair hung before her face. I could just make out the faint tracery of purple veins across her cheeks from where I stood.

"Yeah, fine." Curt words, leaving no room for follow-up. "I could use a rest. Come on." She pushed off the wall and stepped into the goblins' chamber. Falkon and I shared a look, then followed.

Kreekit and her goblins came dancing up, demanding we tell them what had happened, but I deflected them onto Falkon and hurried after Lotharia, who had moved to sit against the far side of the chamber.

"Hey," I said, crouching before her. She looked up, eyes hard, expression cold. "You're clearly not OK. Talk to me, yeah? Can I help?"

She clenched her jaw as if biting back a response, then sighed. "I used the spider staff a lot to get out. Each time I felt it warp my essence a bit more. I'm— I'm heavily polluted right now by necrotic energy. But it's not just that." She curled a lock of hair behind her ear, revealing the network of dark capillaries across her face. "It's changing my essence. Who I am. It feels… I'd never considered how invasive Euphoria is. How it's directly connecting to our brains. How it's feeding us all the sensory information we need to perceive this world, but also how it can affect what we feel. What we think."

"It's messing with your mind?"

"This necrotic energy is making me more impatient. More irritable. It's an effort to even talk to you like this. I really, really, really want to tell you to go away. But I know that's not me. That's the effect of the staff." She took a deep breath and then blew out her cheeks. "So. I'm going to have to meditate to clear my system out. To get back to myself."

Tears gathered in the corners of her eyes, and she gave me a brave smile. "I've got to admit, it's scary thinking about how this is messing with my head."

I reached out and took her hand. "Take all the time you need. And we should drop the staff part of the ogre plan. No more touching that thing."

"We'll see." She gave my hand a squeeze, then pulled away. "I just need some time. That's all."

"Sure. Yeah." I thought of that mad kiss she'd given me, and wanted to give her a hug back, or say something inspiring, but nothing came to mind except trite words that would only irritate her further. "Let me know if you need anything, all right?"

She nodded, and I pushed myself back up to my feet and walked away. Avoiding the knot of excited goblins, I stepped back to the crack in the wall and gazed out over the ravine to the forest below. I mean, I knew Euphoria had an incredible effect on our minds – the damn game could kill me if events in here justified it doing so. But to warp our very thoughts? How we felt about things? That caused me to shudder. What's to say it wasn't changing us subtly all the time? What was Albertus' goal here? To learn from us, sure, but might it decide to implement changes at some point to 'improve' us?

Conspiracy theories were all too plausible. Right now, few people could afford the three-thousand-dollar playing fee. Only the truly wealthy, the insanely dedicated, or terminally ill made it in. Nothing like swapping three days for six months when you had but weeks left to live. I'd heard rumors about new centers being set up around the world. Places that could handle much higher player numbers, and the speculation that would cause a drop in price. Not only that, but there'd been that news article three weeks ago about a drive to develop home pods.

Was Albertus looking to make Euphoria widely available? And if so, would that give him access to our deepest thoughts, allow him to modify who we were en masse? It made a certain twisted sense: we'd created him to solve our problems, problems we'd proven unable to handle. Might not one of his solutions be to change us, the very cause of those problems?

I hugged myself and repressed a shiver. What was he learning from me? Was he actively observing me right now? What had Falkon said? That Death March players were of special interest to him? Did that mean I had a duty to represent the best of humanity?

Thoroughly unnerved, I stared out over the pristine landscape, and really wondered for the first time whether Euphoria had ever been meant as a game at all.

In an attempt to distract myself, I opened my character sheet. I'd gained some XP in Feldgrau, hadn't I?

 You have gained 55 experience (35 for evading
    the Dread Lord's ambush, 20 for rescuing
    Lotharia). You have 57 unused XP. Your total
    XP is 402.

    Congratulations! You are Level 5!

Huh. Normally, I'd be over the moon, but right now I was too shaken up by what had happened to Lotharia and my own thoughts on Euphoria to get too excited. Instead, I felt a grim determination to excel, to beat this game, to defeat the ogres and ensure the safety of my friends. I'd take the XP and the benefits, but for purely utilitarian reasons.

 Your attributes have increased!

    Dexterity +1
    Strength +1
    Constitution +1
    Mana +1

You have learned new skills. *Stealth: Basic (III), Athletics: Basic (I)*

Well, that was a welcome set of upgrades. Finally, a con bump without it being conditional on a good night's rest. I'd sure run around enough to earn it. Out of curiosity, I looked down at my arms. Was there a little more muscle tone there? I clenched my fists. A faint tracery of a vein ran down my forearm, and further up, some definition of my bicep and triceps. Strength eleven wasn't anything to get really excited about, but I now felt less like a puny weakling and more like an average, healthy guy. I could live with that.

And heck yes. More stealth, please! Along with some basic Athletics. All of which were key in what was proving to be my evolving playing style: hit and run, and then keep running. Darkblade to the max, I guess.

Curious, I swiped to the next notification window.

 Five talent advancements available to you:

These had remained the same: Distracting Attack, Darkvision, Wall Climber (I), Expert Leaper, and Bleeding Attack. I could only afford Expert Leaper with my fifty-seven XP, but I decided to hold off for now.

Next window.

 There are new spells available to you:

Here we go. Night Shroud and Ebon Tendrils (I) I already knew, but the latest addition made my heart skip a beat:

Shared Darkness: your affinity with the
shadows can now be extended to a companion, allowing you to bring along a medium
or smaller sized humanoid with you when
you Shadow Step.
- Mana Drain: 3
- Cost: 100 XP

Now *that* would prove incredibly useful. If I'd had that down in Feldgrau, I'd have been able to snag Lotharia right out from the skeletal champion's arms and escape them with the greatest of ease. Well, maybe not 'ease', per se, but you get the picture. one hundred XP, though. Expensive. Right up there with Darkvision.

I tapped my lips. We'd be fighting the ogres inside the bailey real soon. Expert Leaper would no doubt come in super useful. But if I survived that fight, I'd probably earn a ton of XP and be able to buy anything on my list.

I looked over to where Lotharia sat, arms crossed over her knees, forehead resting on her wrists. No. I'd wait for Shared Darkness. Let Albertus learn a little about human compassion and friendship.

I swiped my sheet closed. My new options and long-term plans had ameliorated my previously dour mood. I turned to see Falkon extricating himself from the Green Liver goblins, hands held up as if in surrender as they threatened him with wooden spoons.

"Fine, fine! I'll taste it. Just give me a moment, will you?" He backed out of the group and walked up to me, shaking his head. "Guggee Maggot burgers? I don't care what he seasons it with. And yes, I know people eat grubs in the real world. I saw that documentary on Australian bush cuisine being taken global to deal with the famine issues or whatever. But let me ask you this: were those Australian grubs prepared by goblins? I think not."

"Too late now," I said. "Sounds like you already agreed to try one."

"Yeah." Falkon rubbed the back of his head ruefully. "It was that or deploy Avalanche Roar and run like crazy." He paused, eyeing me up and down. "You hanging in there?"

"Better now. I'm worried about Lotharia. She says the staff's changing her basic personality."

Falkon looked back at her. "Nothing a good bout of meditation won't fix."

"Changing her basic personality," I said again with emphasis. "How's that even possible?"

Falkon sighed. "Want the technical answer? It due to the time dilation effect. One minute in the real world is forty-five minutes in here, right? That means we're experiencing events forty-five times quicker than normal. Which is physiologically impossible due to the limit of how quickly a neuron can fire, which is about once per millisecond."

"Uh huh," I said.

"Anyways, the reason that matters is because one of the two ways Albertus came up with to overclock neurons is to fill in the gaps between the "frames" created by your neuron firing with false memories. So a lot of what we experience in Euphoria isn't directly experienced by us; it's implanted memory, seamlessly synced up with our real-time experience. You see where I'm going with this?"

"No," I said. "We're having fake experiences here?"

"Not quite. It means Albertus can choose how to inflect our experience in Euphoria based on our actions. Pick up a cursed item? Those fake memories he's inserting between our normal "frames" will be evil ones. Social psychology has shown that we understand

who we are by perceiving what we do. And if what you've done –
or felt – has been evil or twisted? You start becoming that way."

I made a face and looked away. "Fine. That sounds impressive
and all, but that doesn't make it OK."

"Yeah, I know. We've argued about that a lot – my tech friends
and I." Falkon crossed his arms. "But you know what? The basic
principle behind it is that these changes follow decisions made
in-game. You act evil, or acquire cursed items? You pay for it. And
there's been no sign these changes are permanent. They're felt
in-game, but fade away once people log out. I've read the reports,
people saying it felt like a dream, or being under the influence
of a drug or booze. In fact, it's one of the primary appeals for a
lot of gamers. Allows them to actually *feel*, to actually *be* somebody they're not."

"Come on, Falkon," I said. "You know it's not that simple.
We're all still making memories here. Even if Euphoria undoes
the neurological changes it's imposed, we'll still remember enjoying doing dark stuff if that's the road we've chosen."

"Yeah, true, but look at the word you just used: chosen." He
raised his hands. "I admit, it's complex stuff, but it's all there in
the small print and people are free to log out at any time if they
don't like it. Well. Except for Death Marchers, that is."

"I'm just saying. I don't like the implications."

"You're not the only one. Maybe I'm being a little too defensive because I work for Euphoria, but yeah. I hear you. It's…
unsettling."

We stood in silence, watching Lotharia for a beat, until Falkon
turned to me. "Guess what? I leveled up! Level ten, baby!"

"Yeah? Same here. Level five." I snorted in amusement. "Get
anything good?"

"Nothing crazy. My wisdom went up for some reason – maybe 'cause I'm mentoring you two? Survival hit level four, and Engineering hit level three. I've now got sixty-nine XP to spend, but I'm saving it for Behemoth Blow. A whopping one hundred XP, but it allows me to triple the power of any single attack at the expense of leaving me weakened right after. You?"

"I'm holding on to my XP, too. I'm shooting for a new spell called Shared Darkness. It'll allow me to take a friend with me when I Shadow Step."

Falkon raised his eyebrows. "Nice. You'd be able to move me around the battlefield, dropping me off in advantageous positions. I approve."

I laughed. "Right. Because my talents and spells are all about augmenting your effectiveness."

"As they should be." He gave me a light punch on the shoulder. "Things are looking good. I was going to argue in favor of attacking this evening, but with Lotharia in rough shape I think we should wait till tomorrow. Which will give me time to put my finishing touches on the ballista. You and I can then carry down the barrels of pitch—"

"Black fire mud," I corrected.

"Black fire mud down to the front door here in preparation for moving them into place once the ogres head out. With a little luck, Lotharia can weaken the stakes, and we can launch our attack at dawn."

I felt an uneasy combination of excitement and dread. "You really think we can pull this off?"

"Against four level thirty-plus ogres? Sure!" He punched me in the shoulder again, harder this time. "What could possibly go wrong?"

I rubbed my shoulder. "You know you're not supposed to say that out loud."

"Yeah, yeah. You ready to tackle those barrels? I want to roll one into the revolving trap on the third floor and see if it doesn't clear the room for us. Jumping over those flame jets is getting really old."

"Sure. Just one thing: my XP window told me I earned thirty-five XP for evading the Dread Lord's ambush." I watched Falkon's face carefully. "That wasn't a random attack. I could have sworn a skeletal champion that walked past us earlier on had seen us, but when it kept walking I convinced myself it hadn't. Now I think it went to report to the Dread Lord, who sent the others to help it capture us."

Falkon rubbed his chin with his thumb. "Weird."

"Yeah. And they didn't ever actually try to hurt us. They grabbed Lotharia by the wrists, and tried to do the same to me. When I freed Lotharia from the champion, it had been carrying her deeper into Feldgrau, toward the broken tower."

"Weird *and* unnerving," said Falkon. "What does the Dread Lord want with you guys?"

"I've no idea," I said. "But I'm thoroughly spooked."

"As well you should be." Falkon grimaced. "Well, I don't know. I guess avoid Feldgrau? Say 'no' to Dread Lords and stay in school?"

"Great advice. No wonder you earned that wisdom."

"Yeah, yeah. Let's go. After all that screaming and running down below, some carefully controlled explosions in the revolving trap room should prove practically medicinal."

"Wait!" Dribbler came running up. "I have something to show!"

We both paused. Immediately I thought of squirrel heads or lizard tails or the other kind of stuff my old cat Luffy had been prone to displaying so proudly on our front doormat.

"You do?" I tried to sound open. Tried really hard. "Like what?"

"Come! Very exciting! I work very hard. Boom!" He scampered back into the weird little tent complex. I sighed, got down on all fours, and followed, Falkon right behind me.

I'd never entered their miniature tent city, which proved to be a small labyrinth in its own right, a mass of tunnels made from salvaged canvas, blankets, and stained sheets. Dribbler didn't need to bend over, and ran ahead till he reached a small tunnel dug straight down into the earth.

"My room! Come! Exciting! Very fun! We have very good time!" He hopped right off the edge and disappeared into the darkness below.

I hesitated for perhaps ten seconds, trying to convince myself to follow Dribbler into the dark, when a flare of orange light lit up what looked like a decent-sized chamber below, chisel marks clearly showing on the raw stone. Dribbler appeared, holding a candle. "Come!"

"Fine, fine," I said. Being friends with goblins had its responsibilities, I guessed. I sat on the tunnel's edge then slid down into the chamber, falling into a crouch, and looked around Dribbler's quarters.

His room was surprisingly awesome. He'd hung all kinds of things on the walls, from dirty rugs to gaudy robes to chunks of mirror embedded in the rock. The far wall was left bare, and there he was carving out a diorama of some kind, with a goblin that might feasibly have been him standing on a throne holding a skull scepter over a mass of kneeling figures.

"The future," said Dribbler, pointing at the statues that half emerged from the wall. "Not yet, but soon. Now, look!"

He shoved away a little table made of planks propped up on rocks, and revealed six miniature barrels set beside each other, each no larger than an apple. A mess of strings connected them all together.

"That a weapon of some kind?" asked Falkon, crawling forward. "Some kind of six-headed morningstar?"

"No!" Dribbler hurried around his small creation. "You want big bang for ogres, yes? But how? How make all barrels explode at once? Question from beyond the stars! But easy for me. Easy! Fuses. Watch."

Carefully, he bent down and touched his candle flame to the outermost little rope, which was was black with dried pitch. After a few moments it caught fire. The flame quickly ran down the length of the thread, then split as it carried on to six more threads.

"Impressive," I said. "But—"

"Wait!" Dribbler waved his hands at us. "Wait for boom!"

"Right, we want the boom to come outside, when the fuses light the real barrels—"

Kaboom!

All six little barrels exploded at once, filling the chamber with smoke and percussive force. I yelled and fell onto my ass, arms thrown before my face for protection. Ears ringing, I waved the smoke away to see Dribbler dancing around the sooty spot, leaping from one foot to the other as he waved his arms overhead.

"Black fire mud and nasty smoke!
Bits of barrel go poke, poke, poke!
Light them up and make them burn!
Kill the ogres one by one!"

The ringing started to go away. I coughed and waved the smoke around some more, then tried to click my jaw to clear away the rest of the ringing. "Dribbler."

"Yes?" He stopped on his left foot, right held high. "You like the boom-boom shake the room?"

"I— yes." It took a moment to swallow what I'd been about to say. "Very excellent boom. You, ah, don't need to show us again in a small enclosed space, but yeah. That was… great."

"Dribbler," said Falkon, sounding unamused. "You know you could have just told us about all this? A live demonstration that nearly blew our heads off wasn't necessary."

"No, no, very necessary. You not believe Dribbler otherwise! You say, hahaha, stupid goblin, go poke a snake hole with your strangle stick! But now you see, now you believe! Dribbler connect your barrels. Then, when Chris touch main string, all go boom at once!"

I considered. "He's got a point. I'd probably not have believed him."

"I guess. Well. Looks like you're on wiring duty tonight, Dribbler."

"Yes!" He resumed his leaping dance.

"Black mud fire and nasty smoke!

It not funny, not a joke!

When fire goes boom it clear the room!

Send all ogres to their doom!"

I wasn't able to sleep. Long after the goblins had disappeared into their tent-city, after Falkon's light snores filled the tower chamber and Lotharia lain still, I sat on one of the large rocks by the ruptured wall, staring out into the night.

The odds of my dying at dawn were high. I kept saying the words over and over in my mind, till they lost all meaning: *tomor-*

row at dawn I might die. At one point a wave of nausea passed through me, but I clamped my jaw shut and waited for it to pass.

The world outside had never looked so beautiful. The stars glimmered overhead, the mountains and rolling hills were darker shadows against the night sky. The cold made me shiver, but I was strangely glad for it. As if my body welcomed any sign of still being alive, just as my mind drank in every sight as if greedy for life while I still had it.

"Hey."

I startled, nearly falling off my rock. Lotharia had stepped up beside me, her blanket wrapped around her shoulders.

"Hey," I said.

"You doing all right? You've been sitting there for awhile."

"I'm—I'm fine. Can't sleep, is all."

We stood in companionable silence, both of us staring out into the darkness.

I turned to her. "Could you do me a favor?"

"Anything."

"If—if I don't make it through tomorrow—"

"Chris—"

"No, hear me out. If I don't make it, I need you to get word to my brother. Let him know what happened. I'll give you my friend Ev's number, she knows how to reach him in jail." I studied her face in the gloom. "Could you do that for me?"

"Of course." She took both my hands in hers. "But you're going to make it."

"I plan to try—"

"No." She squeezed, hard. "You're going to make it. I'm going to watch your back. I won't let anything happen to you."

"Lotharia," I said. My throat felt tight. "I might not—"

She hugged me tightly, fiercely. Her cheek was smooth against my own, her face buried in my neck. .

We held each other.

Finally she stepped away and wiped the back of her hand across her eyes. "You should get some sleep."

"Hey." I felt light headed. "How about when this is all said and done we grab a cup of coffee? In the real world?"

Lotharia smiled. "I'd like that. I'd like that a lot." She hesitated, then leaned in and kissed my cheek softly. "Good night, Chris."

I watched as she returned to her sleeping pad. Then, after she'd lain down once more, turned back to stare out into the night.

18

THE MOMENT HAD finally arrived. After hours spent feverishly preparing the bailey in the pre-dawn gloom, I sat
hunched atop one of the tiny buildings erected within the castle
walls, a dark cloak wrapped around my shoulders as I watched
the stables.

The ogres had returned from their hunt just after midnight.
They'd been squabbling as always, shoving and insulting each
other, but the sight of the bloated deer laid out before the gates
had stilled their jibes. For a long moment none of them spoke,
and then they laughed. One of them reached down and took the
dead deer by the head and dragged it behind them into the stables.

None of them had noticed the noxious green fluid leaking
from the wound in the deer's side. Miraculously, none of them
had smelled it either. Barfo had spent an hour pumping his
noxious poison into the deer's corpse after Falkon had delivered
it to him, until it sides had swollen to the point of bursting. The

ogres, he'd assured us, would consider the smell delightful. And somehow, he'd been right.

That had just been the first trial, however. Upon entering their stables, I was sure they'd notice the flies buzzing and swarming around the back wall. We'd killed the plague corpse and laid it outside the stable, hoping that might mitigate the worst of the smell, but even ogres would have to notice that, wouldn't they?

I had waited, breath held, but no roar of outrage had sounded. Instead, I'd heard more coarse laughter and the sound of tearing flesh as they'd tucked into their dinner.

Amazing.

The wyvern had arrived but an hour before dawn. I'd hissed the alarm, and Lotharia and the goblins, hard at work on the stakes, had frozen as one and stared up into the sky in alarm. But the wyvern had flapped lazily into its nest, and after a tense few minutes my friends had gone back to work.

Now the trap was set. Dawn finally broke over the mountains, and the tension in my guts ratcheted up another notch. Ogres were like college kids. Not strictly nocturnal, but they apparently hated waking up before midday. Now was the hour to strike, right when they were in their deepest sleep.

Lotharia and Falkon emerged from the top of the goblin tower. They crept to the ballista, where Lotharia set to enchanting the first bolt with the hardness of diamond. Any moment now. Finally, Lotharia handed the bolt to Falkon, who slotted it in place. They both looked down at me and gave me the thumbs up.

Show time.

I took a deep breath, rubbed my palms on my thighs, then pulled out a bandana and tied it over my mouth and nose. I checked the live coal in the small metal box at my side, checked that I had my full 10 mana points, then stood.

A moment of stillness. I closed my eyes and centered my thoughts. The time for fear and planning was over. Now was the time to act.

I Shadow Stepped. Darkness enveloped me, held me tight, then released me with a sigh as I emerged behind the stables. The furious buzzing of the flies around the corpse was only rivaled by the pained groans coming from the other side of the wall. A fierce burst of exultation filled me. Didn't sound like the ogres were feeling all that great. A thick mutter, then a long series of hard burps, followed by another wretched groan.

Perfect.

The barrels were lined up along the back wall. Dribbler's fuses were laid out before them like rat tails. The stench of the plague corpse made my eyes water. How the hell hadn't the ogres noticed? Could any creature really be that foul?

No matter. *Focus.* I knelt and opened my little metal box, held the main fuse to the coal's white ashen surface, and then blew. A cherry core revealed itself. I kept blowing, patient and gentle, until the pitch-soaked fuse finally caught.

I dropped it and stepped back. The urge to escape immediately was overwhelming, but I fought it down. If for any reason the fuse failed, I'd have to relight it.

Mesmerized, I watched the flame race up the main cord, then split into six. Good job, Dribbler! Up the six cords the small blue flame danced, then, just before it blew, I turned and ran around the side of the stable toward the undead ogre's door.

"Hey!" My shout shattered the morning stillness. "Dead and ugly! Come and get me!"

The dead ogre bounded out of the broad doorway in an instant. It never slept. Never rested. Was always vigilant, and now charged right at me. I stopped in my tracks, heart in my throat, and ran right back toward the stable. The ogres within were grunting in confusion, but no matter – getting the undead ogre close to the blast was the icing on the cake.

I ran right at the broad front doors. I caught a glimpse of the nightmare within – the partially consumed deer corpse charred on a spit over the fireplace, the ogres rousing themselves from their nests, covered in their own puke and looking out of it – and then the barrels blew.

The back wall exploded inward on a tide of smoke and fire. I screamed and I Shadow Stepped before it hit me, racing into the velvety darkness within the stables before it could be banished by the flames.

The nascent explosion was immediately muffled, swallowed by the darkness. There was a second of silence, and then I emerged back atop the small building on which I'd begun, only to be assaulted by the shockwave of the stable's explosion as it rolled over me.

I fell into a crouch, hands clamped over my ears, and stared wide-eyed at the destruction we'd wrought. The walls of the stables had blown out, sections of the roof rising entirely before collapsing all the way down to the ground. The entire structure was demolished, the back wall taken out by the barrels and the rest undone by gravity. With a rumbling, sliding roar, the walls and roof fell upon the ogres, who rose bellowing in shock and fury.

Smoke billowed up into the sky with their screams, and one by one they emerged from the wreckage, their massive, bloated forms blackened and charred. They looked disoriented, unable to process what had just happened. Their leader – Mogr – was the least affected and the most furious. He screamed his rage at their fallen base and smashed his foot through what was left of one wall.

TWANG.

A bolt a yard long slammed into Mogr's back. A direct hit! The enchanted diamond head sank at least a foot into the thick slab of muscle that ran down his side, causing the ogre to stumble forward with a grunt of surprise.

Falkon immediately began reloading the ballista, but while he did so Lotharia raised her scepter and called out, "From the heart of glaciers, blue-green to black, I summon forth the coldest shards and send them to attack!"

A rain of ice shards fell upon the ogres, who roared in greater extremes of anger and tried to cover their heads with their thick forearms. The ice didn't do much damage – the equivalent of paper cuts, I'd guess – but it kept them off balance, reacting instead of identifying the source of the attack.

THWANG!

Mogr grabbed hold of the undead ogre standing by his side and hauled it before him. The next bolt slammed into its head, shattering the skull and causing the monstrosity to drop. Mogr shoved it away angrily and looked up, spotting Lotharia and Falkon.

Damn. So much for true love.

Mogr screamed an order in his thick, alien language, and pointed at the top of the wall. The other three ogres turned and focused on where my friends stood. As one, the ogres reached down and took up large chunks of rock from the rubble.

My turn.

I Double Stepped. Sweet darkness, and then I was crouched in the shadows beside the ruined stable wall, behind the four ogres. They towered over me, each at least ten feet tall and no doubt weighing over a thousand pounds. The stench had been cleared by the explosion and smoke, but the very air here was greasy and rancid.

No time to dawdle. I focused my magic and summoned my Death Dagger. It manifested in my palm, icy cold and flickering with its fell blue light, dropping my mana down to four.

The second largest ogre drew his arm back like a catapult, a massive chunk of rock cupped in his huge palm. I ran forward and past him, slashing inside his knee with my Death Dagger as I went.

The blade cut through the ogre's thick, rubbery skin and I immediately circled around into the ogre's shadow, where I tried to activate the second part of Double Step. Nothing happened—the shadow wasn't thick enough. The ogre screamed in pain and shock and stared down at me in fury. Its arm whipped high overhead, but instead of launching its rock at the far wall it sought to hammer it into my head instead.

No, thanks. I threw myself forward into a desperate dive. A foot the size of a wheelbarrow caught me in the hip, lifting me off the ground and spinning me through the air. I bit back a scream, then screamed anyway when I hit the ruined stable wall, bouncing off and onto the ground.

The ogre that kicked me stepped over, rock raised high. My chest was locked up. I was completely winded by the blow, and the world was swimming. Then, without warning, the air between us filled with fog, a rushing, impossible cottony thickness that hid me just enough for the last part of my Double Step.

I dove deep, allowed the shadows to wash away my pain, and emerged high in the foggy air above the ogre's shoulders. Gravity immediately yanked me down, and I activated Sabotage Defenses. My Death Dagger pierced the ogre's hide, then ran all the way down the inside of its body, cutting through tough, fibrous muscle and ribs.

The ogre arched its back with a shriek and dropped its raised rock upon its own shoulder. I danced aside as the cinderblock-sized stone crunched to the ground, and then stabbed my Death Dagger into the back of the ogre's leg.

The ogre collapsed onto its wounded knee. It still wasn't done, however – far from it. Snarling, it wheeled around and grabbed me about the waist with shocking speed. Its fingers closed around my waist completely, and it yanked me into the air, right toward its open maw.

TWANG.

A bolt smashed through the front of the ogre's face, snapping its head back and causing it to collapse to the ground.

Still it held onto me, squeezing ever tighter as it raised its free hand to yank the bolt free. Fear was squeezing me just as hard – what would it take to kill one of these? I sawed my Death Dagger into the inside of the ogre's wrist, severing tendons like violin strings, and it let go of me, spilling me out onto the cobbles. I rolled to my feet, gasping, as the ogre tore the bolt free of its left eye and threw it at me.

The bolt turned in midair, hitting me crosswise across the stomach with ridiculous force and knocking me down again. I fell, tangled up with the bolt, and somehow, impossibly, the ogre sat up, then rose to its one good leg.

Fuck me. Level thirty was no joke.

With a roar it keeled forward, intent on body slamming me into oblivion. I grabbed the bolt, raised its head, jammed its butt into the dirt, and then completed my Double Step away at the last second.

I appeared inside the top room of the goblin tower, where I'd slain the dire bat. Gasping for breath, I reeled to my feet and ran out the door onto the battlements, only to throw myself back inside as a massive rock exploded against the inside of the parapet, sending shards in every direction.

"Lotharia? Falkon?" Shaking with the intensity of my emotions, I crawled to the doorway. "You guys—?"

"Fine!" yelled Falkon, wrestling a bolt into the slot. "Three bolts left!"

I jumped to my feet and ran out by his side. Lotharia stood at the edge of the wall, weaving her scepter in the air as she cast a spell I'd never seen before. The fog was lifting from the center of the courtyard. Three of the ogres still stood, and the sweet thrill of victory coursed through me at the sight of the dead fourth one – impaled on the bolt I'd levered up beneath it.

Mogr took up a rock the size of a chair with both hands, but before he could hurl it the dawn air was rent by a screeching roar. Everyone turned to stare at the top of the far tower as the wyvern rose into view, huge wings beating, claws scrabbling at the tower's edge for purchase.

"There we go," said Falkon. "Bolt ready?"

"Ready!" called Lotharia.

"Wyvern's right on time. Fire!"

TWANG!

The bolt shot through the air and punched clean through the bicep of the smallest ogre, causing it to lose its grip on the rock it had raised and drop it on its head.

Mogr snarled, turned a complete circle, then a faster second one, and hurled his huge rock at us.

It's ascent was mesmerizing. At first seemed to simply float toward us before speeding up with terrible accuracy.

"Take the helm!" screamed Falkon, drawing his blade.

"What? Where are you—?"

But he didn't wait to answer. He took three short steps and hurled himself off the wall's edge, blade raised over his head. "Death from above!" he screamed, and then brought his blade down right upon the rising rock.

The shattering crash that resulted was thunderous, and then Falkon was falling through the shards of rock to the ground far below.

"What? What the hell was that?!" I was furious, amazed, flabbergasted, but didn't waste any time. I grabbed one of the two remaining bolts and slotted it into the long groove. I ran to the front and seized one of the wheels, where I strained to winch the huge wire back.

"Chris!" Lotharia's voice was tight with fear. "The wyvern! It's coming this way!"

"It's supposed to go for the damn ogres!" I gritted my teeth and focused on turning the wheel. How had Falkon done this so quickly? Oh, yeah. Strength sixteen. Shoulders burning, I activated Adrenaline Surge. Immediately, the task became manageable; I worked the winch all the way back just as a huge shadow appeared over me.

The wyvern beat its massive wings as it lowered down, huge claws extended to grasp me by the shoulders. Lotharia screamed and leapt aside, but I had other plans. I ducked into a crouch, grabbed the ballista by the back and dropped it all the way to the ground, aiming the bow-end right at the wyvern.

TWANG!

The bolt flew right at the wyvern's pale stomach, but somehow, impossibly, the creature snagged the bolt right out of the air with one of its claws and snapped it in half.

"No fair!" I'd never even asked Falkon what the wyvern's level was, but it was clearly way too high.

"Get out of there!" screamed Lotharia. "Run!"

The wyvern released the fragments of the bolt and screeched again, plunging its claws down toward me. Its wings blotted out the sky, covering me in shadow.

I Double Stepped right up past its snatching claws to appear in the gloom beneath its scaled stomach. I emerged from the shadows pressed right against its surprisingly warm body, and slammed my Death Dagger into its side.

The wyvern's body went rigid as my blade sank to the hilt. It felt like sticking a needle in an elephant, but even needles could hurt. I held on to the dagger for dear life as with a ferocious blast of its wings it lifted up off the wall, and for a second I was terrified it would fly out over the ravine, leaving the castle behind.

Instead, it banked and fought for height, causing too much sunlight to appear for me to Double Step away. Only my ongoing Adrenaline Surge allowed me to hold on to my Death Dagger's hilt, my weight once more forcing the blade to cut through the monster's scaly skin, widening the cut to a foot in length, then two.

Surge was going to give out any second, though. I tried again and again to Shadow Step away, but the wyvern had turned, catching me in the morning light. I looked for something below to fall onto with Ledge Runner, but even with Astute Observer nothing presented itself.

We climbed higher and higher. Thick, jellied blood that steamed in the morning air was oozing out of the wound, but the wyvern couldn't reach me with its claws and the couple of times it tried to snap at me with its beak it fell short. So instead it fought for height with each massive wingbeat, ensuring my fall would be fatal.

I flailed around, bouncing off its muscled side. I had to do something, come up with a plan – anything other than wait for Adrenaline Surge to give out. I stared down at the castle that was now easily fifty yards below. The wind whipped about me, pulling tears from my eyes, and in desperation I saw a chance.

I let go, causing the Death Dagger to disappear, and fell, dropping right past the wyvern's left claw. The wind howled about me and my stomach tried to climb out of my throat. I fought the urge to kick and scream, and instead flipped around. I'd never gone skydiving before, and now I knew why: falling toward the earth at terminal velocity was *fucking terrifying*.

The castle raced up to meet me, remarkably detailed and vivid in what could be my last moments. I missed the curtain wall by a yard, falling along its inside, plummeting alongside the wyvern's tower.

The shadowed side.

I completed my third Double Step with a scream and slammed into the world of shadows like a fat man cannonballing into a swimming pool. I burst right through, not even having the time to pick a destination, and emerged into a dark chamber I barely had time to recognize as Jeramy's bedroom on the second floor of his tower before some kind of ward or protective spell seized me and hurled me back outside, phasing me through the wall and high into the sunlight above the bailey floor.

Thoughts scrambled by Jeramy's anti-magic protection, I wind-milled my arms as I fell toward the wyvern stakes. I activated Ledge Runner out of complete desperation, and my feet immediately sought out the strands of spider silk Lotharia and the goblins had stretched out between the stakes at chest height the night before.

My feet ripped off to the side, dragging me down at a diagonal, and I hit the spider thread, causing it to bow beneath me and then snap a half-dozen stakes off their whittled bases. They spun and crashed to the ground, and then I hit the dirt and everything went dark.

19

"Hey, champ," I said as Justin approached my table. Other inmates were fanning out through the room, or hesitating by the doorway as they searched the sparse crowd for their loved ones. "Big brother's home."

"You didn't have to come." He stood before me in his orange prison uniform, looking embarrassed and exhausted and defiant all at once.

"I know. Your arrest was just the excuse I needed to justify my coming back to Florida."

He pulled out his chair and sat. Still wary. Still trying to figure out how to take my appearance. "You hate Florida. You always have."

"Maybe it'll grow on me this time." I opened my backpack and pulled out a half-dozen comic books which I pushed across the table to him. "Here. Figured you'd lost track of your favorites. You still reading the X-Men?

"Seriously, Chris." There was something vulnerable in his voice, something he tried hard to cover up. "I can handle this. You're paying for my new lawyer is already plenty. He says that even with the disaster emergency legislation I'll only get hit with a first-time offense. Five years max. And even that we can fight."

"You won't get five years. I spoke to the lawyer too. I told him I want you to get less than a year and community service." I leaned back on the rear two legs of my chair and studied him. "You're going to be fine."

"Right. Exactly. So why'd you come all this way? I'd have let you know if I needed you."

"Seattle was getting boring," I said.

"Boring? This coming from a pro-gamer living in a sweet apartment in Belltown? You get tired of the waterfront views and gamer groupies that quick?"

"Yeah, well." I hadn't grown tired of it. In fact, I loved my life in Seattle more than anything. Seattle was one of the few cities that hadn't been touched by climate change or infrastructure collapse, or buried under a rising tide of poverty. "I guess I missed family. What? I can't come visit and hang out for a while? This is perfect. You're, like, a captive audience."

Justin didn't even chuckle. "Sure you can. But there are these things called omnis, you know? We could have talked any time. I'm *fine*. The attorney said that even if they try to pin Sam's death on me they'll get laughed out of court for lack of evidence."

"Yeah? That's great. And I'm not here as your attorney. I'm here as your big brother." I leaned forward, resting on both elbows. "And I'm already here, so get used to it."

I could see him wrestling with pride. With fear. His eyes glassed over with tears for a moment and then he rubbed them angrily with his sleeve. "Fine. But if you're planning to stay at my place, I've only got regular Wi-Fi and I left my VR kit at college. So don't get your hopes up about much gaming."

"No worries," I said. "I'm tired of all that gaming, anyways. I've heard people talking about something called 'the beach' and 'sunshine' and 'the outdoors'. Might be fun to explore."

He laughed weakly. "Fine. Anything as long as you stop with these awful lies."

"Atta boy." I reached out and ruffled his hair precisely because I knew it'd annoy him. "You're going to do great, kiddo. Don't worry. I'm going to make sure of that."

"Yeah?" He looked away. "You said the same thing to Mom."

That hit hard. I sat there, fighting the urge to lash right back, and instead forced myself to nod slowly. "Well, Mom got a tough deal. Didn't help that she didn't want to go get checked till it was too late. We've got a great lawyer and he's working on this right from the get go, right?"

"Yeah," he said. "But for how long? I found out how much he's charging."

"Whatever. I've got enough savings to see this through. And if it drags on? I'll get some job down here. It's probably about time I worked a nine-to-five like an adult."

Justin shook his head, a sad smile playing on his lips. "I'm glad you're here, Chris. Thanks."

I wanted to give him a wink, or at least a confident smile, but my throat closed up and for a moment I didn't think I'd be able to respond at all. "Of course. That's what big brothers are for. We'll make it through this together. There's nothing I won't do to make sure of that. You hear me?"

"Yeah," said Justin, and his eyes filled with tears. "I hear you."

I swam up through the pain into a world of screams, bellows, dust and blood. Falkon stood over me, blade held at the ready, shoulders heaving as he stared up at a blackened and battered Mogr. The massive ogre loomed over us both, a club the size of a tree in its hands. Everything hurt. It felt like after my car crash in high school, when we'd barely avoided hitting a truck by slamming into the crash barrier, giving me the worst case of whiplash from my neck down to my ass.

"Falkon," I rasped.

"Finally. Get out of here. Go!" He shifted his stance, wide-legged and low, as if preparing to take a massive hit. I clawed my way up to sitting. Not enough shadow out here to escape.

Mogr took a step forward and Falkon bellowed at him, screaming his anger and defiance up at the ogre, blasting him with his Avalanche Roar. The very air before him shimmered with power, and for a moment Mogr hesitated, head rising, piggish eyes blinking in surprise.

Then the ogre leaned forward and showed us both what a real roar sounded like. Ropes of spittle flew from his maw, and I felt the volume of it deep within my chest as if I were standing too close to the speakers at a concert. Falkon staggered back, dismayed, and then somehow threw himself forward, moving faster than my eye could track, leaping straight up at the ogre to cleave down at his club. Headlong Charge and Throwback, maybe?

I wanted to just sit there, watch the fight, but I knew I had to get moving. I had to survive. I activated Adrenaline Surge, and sweet relief flooded through me. I leapt to my feet, pain and exhaustion gone, and surveyed the courtyard.

All hell had broken loose. Most of the stakes had toppled to the ground, some due to my fall, and others obviously due to the ogres moving forward and triggering the tripwires. A second ogre was down, a final bolt lanced straight into its throat, numerous deep cuts from Falkon's blade across its chest and arms, its body mottled with frostbite and covered in its own vomit. The last one was climbing up the wall toward Lotharia and the ballista, smashing its fists into the rock to create handholds as it went.

I was down to three mana. I drew my dagger and ran out wide, circling around Mogr. The ogre leader had rebuffed Falkon's best attack, knocking him back, and was about to go in for the kill when he shuddered to a stop. His throat convulsed, then he put one hand on his knee and vomited a torrent of half-digested flesh and bile.

What should I do? Race to the closest shadows so I could Shadow Step up to Lotharia? No. Even sick and diseased, Mogr was going to crush Falkon. There was no time. I burned the last of my mana and summoned my Death Dagger once more, and as Mogr heaved himself up I activated Pin Down and hurled the burning blue blade through his boot.

It sank not only through his flesh but also into the ground, and Mogr gave a grunt of surprise as his momentum was arrested, his knee driving down to the floor. Falkon was on him in a moment, swinging his great blade over and over again at the chieftain, who raised his club awkwardly in an attempt to block. Huge chips of wood went flying with each blow, and then with a roar that must have torn his throat Falkon swung his blade like a baseball bat and sheared clean through the ogre's club.

I was out of mana and had only my dagger. What to do? I darted from side to side, trying to find the right time to attack, only to see Mogr reach out and pluck Falkon off the ground. Falkon screamed in pain and drew his blade across the ogre's forearm, laying open the flesh to the bone, but still the ogre stood, lifting my friend right up into the air.

Madness took hold of me. I sprinted forward, scooted down, and slashed up with my blade as I passed between Mogr's legs.

The ogre screamed in agony as I cut through, well, *something*. He dropped Falkon and staggered back. I grabbed Falkon by the forearm to heave him up, and then Adrenaline Surge ran out.

I staggered as if sucker-punched. Suddenly the morning sunlight was too bright, the dust in the air too thick, and the memory of every sick moment in my life crashed down upon me a thousand-fold. Wheezing, I turned to face Mogr, only to see Falkon race forward again and slam his blade deep into Mogr's gut.

The ogre screamed again and backhanded Falkon, who spun out like a ballerina on his tiptoes and crashed to the ground, going completely still. A moment later his body faded away, leaving his gear to sink to the ground without him.

I froze. For a second it didn't make any sense at all, and then it hit me: Mogr had killed Falkon with a mere backhand. Shock and horror suffused me. It didn't matter that my friend was respawning this very moment in the highland meadow.

He'd been killed before my eyes.

I gulped, looked up and met the ogre's eyes. With a sneer, Mogr tore his foot free of my Death Dagger, leaving it lodged in the dirt behind it, smeared in gore and completely out of reach.

No mana. No shadows close by even if I'd had some.

Mogr grinned and pulled the sword out of his gut. The blade came free with a wet, sucking sound. Despite its size, it looked like a toy in the ogre's fist.

I needed to run. Needed to get the hell out of there – but post-Surge nausea had me nearly doubled over with cramps and the desire to puke.

Mogr examined the blade, then licked his own blood from the length of one side. He chuckled, a laugh that suddenly bubbled into nausea of his own. I hobbled backward. Prayed desperately for the disease and poisoning to hit him hard, now, and give me the miraculous break I needed.

The ogre coughed his nausea away and strode toward me.

Uncanny Aim. I hurled my dagger along the silver thread right at Mogr's right eye. The ogre simply swatted the dagger out of the air.

I staggered back. Light. I summoned a ball right before the ogre's face, but he simply lunged forward and swallowed the spell, cheeks bulging out, then gulped it down.

My eyes went wide. He could do that?

What else? No weapons. No mana. No more tricks up my sleeve.

Mogr took a step forward, covering four yards in one go, and raised Falkon's blade above his head.

A victorious shriek sundered the air and the wyvern fell upon us, a comet out of the morning sky. It slammed down into Mogr, wings furled, hitting the ogre with all the force and speed of a runaway train. The ogre was driven into the dirt with bone-snapping force, the wyvern's talons shredding his shoulders where they dug in deep, its beak striking down again and again to tear huge gobbets of flesh from the ogre's chest and neck.

I straightened out of my crouch, eyes wide.

Mogr wasn't done yet. Dropping Falkon's blade, he lunged up and closed his hand around the wyvern's neck, twisting beneath its weight, and then slammed his other fist into the side of its head. The wyvern screamed and opened its wings, beating them powerfully and driving stinging clouds of dust in every direction. I backed away, arm raised to shield my eyes. And then, like the sun breaking free of the clouds, the nausea was gone.

I sprinted around the dueling titans to where my Death Dagger was embedded in the ground. The last ogre had gained the top of the wall and smashed the ballista – Lotharia was trapped between it and the wyvern's tower, backing away slowly, scepter held before her.

I tore the Death Dagger free as the wyvern lifted Mogr some five yards off the ground then slammed him back down. The side of the wyvern's crocodilian head was smeared with broken bones and loosened scales, its eye barely visible, but Mogr looked like he should be dead. Still he fought on, blood pooling beneath him, roaring his clotted bellows as he refused to give up.

I ran toward the wall, but Lotharia and the ogre were easily fifty feet above me. Too far. A mad plan hatched in my mind. I summoned my character sheet, scrolled down with a flick of my hand and tapped Expert Leaper.

Swiping my sheet away, I ran toward the small house beneath the pair of them—the same one I'd climbed to avoid the rats—and activated *Expert Leaper* just before I jumped.

I didn't know what to expect, but found myself soaring up as if I'd hit a trampoline, high enough that I was able to hit the edge of the roof with my stomach and stab my Death Dagger into the tiles. It sank and stuck, and with a grunt I hauled myself up. A scream sounded from above. No time! I took a deep breath, crouched low, and then leapt straight up.

I must have soared some ten feet into the sky, and as I hit the apex I pressed my foot against the curtain wall and leapt back. Expert Leaper was still active, such that I suddenly propelled myself away from the wall into the air, the ogre up top sliding into view. I activated Uncanny Aim, targeting my silver thread at the back of the ogre's head as it closed its hand over Lotharia's arm. Not daring to think, not daring to hesitate, I hurled my Death Dagger with everything I had – and then started to fall.

Arms clawing at the sky, I activated Ledge Runner, but to no avail – there was nothing beneath me but packed dirt. I fell some twenty or thirty feet straight down, feet hitting first, momentum driving my body down into a savage crouch. A bone snapped – several bones – and everything began to slide away just as I hit Adrenaline Surge again.

Vigor flooded into me a mere second before the pain threatened to overwhelm my senses. Gasping, I straightened out on the ground, the fire in my veins trying to overwhelm the shock and agony. My left leg was bent the wrong way at the knee and shin. Something was profoundly wrong with my hips; everything felt loose and wet and hot down there, and bone had torn through the bicep of my right arm.

Adrenaline Surge raged through me, keeping the worst of it at bay, but I knew I was in dire straits. Gasping, I levered myself up onto my left arm in time to see the wyvern tear out Mogr's throat. The ogre's scream turned into a gurgle, blood spraying everywhere, and then he went limp.

I stared up at the wall. The other ogre had released Lotharia and stood, hands clawing at the back of its head where my Death Dagger had sunk in. Outrage and despair hit me like a ton of bricks. I couldn't believe it. How had it survived such a direct hit? Damn its being level thirty!

Lotharia called out a spell. At this distance I couldn't make it out, but a hail of ice shards suddenly exploded around the ogre, slicing its hide and bouncing off its face and chest.

The ogre growled and reached back to close its fist around the hilt of my Death Dagger even as it turned away from the ice shards. Just then, however, it suffered a violent spasm; it contorted, bending over to vomit, and in doing so lost its balance atop the wall. It stepped back again, found nothing there to take its weight, and fell.

I watched, mouth open, as the vomiting ogre plummeted into the small house I'd leapt onto, punching right through the roof with a crash. A plume of dust erupted in its wake.

I let out a faint cheer of triumph as my XP chime sounded. If a Death Dagger to the back of the head didn't kill an ogre, a headlong dive fifty feet into the ground seemed to have done the trick. And that was the last of them! The ogres were dead!

A small shape darted up to my side, and I startled before recognized a terrified Dribbler. "Here! Here! Drink this! Barfo special soup!"

I didn't hesitate, but took the flask and drank from it. Barfo's special soup burned as it went down, a whisky kind of burn that spread along my veins much like Adrenaline Surge.

Lotharia yelled something down at me. Her tone was urgent. She pointed, but the potion I'd drunk suddenly caused the pain to spike. I saw double, and then the bone of my broken arm slid back through the torn muscle and into place. My leg did the same, straightening out, waves of sheer, insane torment making me shake and gasp as I lay there.

Then the agony was gone, and while I still felt like crap, I could tell the worst had somehow been miraculously healed. Dribbler giggled, patted me on the head, then screamed and ran back in the direction of his tower.

Off to the side, the wyvern shrieked. It was hopping toward me. It stared at me from its remaining good eye.

"Oh, no," I said, trying to stand. "No, no, no—"

The wyvern lunged toward me, beak open wide. I screamed, fell back, then a spear of black fire flashed down and impacted the side of its head, knocking it away.

I stared at the wall top. Lotharia stood there, spider staff extended. The wyvern let out a furious shrill cry and tried to stab at me once more, but again a bolt of black fire knocked it back.

No. There was no way I was going to let Lotharia destroy herself in an attempt to save me. Drawing my focus to a needlepoint, my emotions sluiced away as I focused furiously on my only chance at surviving. I summoned my character sheet even as I pushed away from the wyvern with my heels.

 You have gained 360 experience (240 for defeating three ogres, 120 for defeating an ogre chieftain). You have 362 unused XP. Your total XP is 762.

Congratulations! You are Level 6!
Congratulations! You are Level 7!
Congratulations! You are Level 8!

There was no other word for what I felt: euphoria. I laughed, the sound half manic, and swiped the window away.

Before me, the wyvern opened its wings and bugled its fury up at Lotharia. Again she hit it with a spear of black fire, each blast melting its scales and opening up a savage wound. A fourth time, a fifth.

I skimmed the next window as quickly as I could.

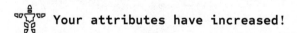 **Your attributes have increased!**

Mana +3
Strength +2

Dexterity +2
Constitution +2

 You have learned new skills. *Climb: Basic (II), Athletics: Basic (IV), Dodge: Basic (III), Melee: Basic (II), Backstab: Basic (III)*

The wyvern hopped away, opened its wings, and thrust itself up into the sky. Dust billowed everywhere and I was momentarily blinded. I stared up through my fingers up past my window. The wyvern was muscling its way up into the air.

 There are new talent advancements available to you:

The four I knew: Distracting Attack, Darkvision, Wall Climber (I), and Bleeding Attack. A new one right below: Cat's Fall. No time to read the details – I could guess what it meant.

 There are three spells available to you:

Night Shroud, Ebon Tendrils (I), and
Shared Darkness.

I felt drunk on the opportunities. My fingers flicked out as I tapped Shared Darkness, Night Shroud and Ebon Tendrils. I hesitated, then snapped up Distracting Attack and Bleeding Attack as well. Anything that might help save Lotharia from using the staff any further.

Lotharia was waiting to see if the wyvern was planning to fly away – no such luck. It rose to her level, fifty feet above the bailey, and then blared its defiance and hatred at her, huge wings buffeting her with gusts of air.

One last thing till I could join in the fight. I darted around Mogr's still form, and over to where he'd been originally assaulted by the wyvern. The ground was torn and soaked with blood, but Falkon's blade was easily visible. I snatched it up, eyed the swirling mana stone in its pommel, and glanced at my character sheet: my mana pool had risen from my three newly-gained points to a total of nine.

I stuck the blade in my belt and stared up at the wyvern. There couldn't have been a more impossible match-up. Still, there was no way I was staying out of this fight. No way I would let Lotharia damn her soul. Taking a deep breath, I broke out into a run.

20

I SPRINTED TOWARD the rat house. Above me, the wyvern bellowed once more and lunged toward Lotharia, who backed away and met it with her own blast of black fire. I charged right into the doorway, running so fast I'd have slammed myself into the back wall if I didn't have other plans.

Double Step took me up to the top of the goblin tower. I burst out into the familiar room, skidded as I fought my momentum, my boots fighting for traction on the smooth stone floor, and then I ran out the tower door onto the wall, right hand catching the doorframe to whip me around, over the edge and into the void.

Expert Leaper. Ledge Runner. Adrenaline Surge. I activated all three at once and launched myself off the wall, my legs suddenly as powerful and explosive as huge springs. The wind from the wyvern's wings whirled perilously around me, and for a split second I was paralyzed by complete and utter terror at what I was doing. I arced out over the bailey floor far below, heading right toward the vast wyvern, which turned its serpentine neck to regard me as I sailed toward it.

Time slowed down. *Sabotage Defenses. Distracting Attack. Bleeding Attack.* I felt like I was mashing buttons, bringing up all my powers at once, and at the last moment I summoned my new favorite weapon: Death Dagger.

The blade coalesced in my palm, so cold it burned, and my body twisted just moments before I slammed into the wyvern's side. My dagger punched through its scaly hide as if it were butter, sinking down to the hilt, and the wound was atrocious – blood gouted forth as if I'd slit the side of a wineskin, my weight and momentum causing the dagger to cut a ragged path down the wyvern's flank, slicing open its armor and making the beast shriek with shock and pain.

Momentum can be a bitch. It carried me right down the side of the wyvern, dagger tearing free, and out past its tail. I was in the full glare of the morning sun. The bailey floor was far below me, but I knew it would come screaming up to meet me very, very quickly.

I wasn't done, however.

I poured mana into my new spell, and summoned Night Shroud. The world around me immediately grew dim, the wyvern a shadowy form encased within my bubble of darkness. The wyvern was turning, trying to track me, its ungainly body making such agile aerial maneuvers a challenge.

But even though I could see through my own Night Shroud, I knew, could feel how inky dark my spell had made the air around me. I was encased in deepest shadow, and before I flew out the back of the hovering sphere of darkness, I completed my Double Step.

The shadows embraced me, held me tight, then released me on the far side of the wyvern who was still encased within my Shroud.

Falling past its long neck that was turned in the other direction, I stabbed down with my Death Dagger. Sabotage Defenses, Distracting Attack, and Bleeding Attack were still in effect, and in that moment I finally realized the true power inherent in being a darkblade.

My Death Dagger cut a horrendous wound down the wyvern's neck, causing it to spasm and contort in midair at the shocking pain. I didn't wait, but started a new Double Step and disappeared just moments before it whipped around and snapped its jaws at where I'd been.

I appeared over its back, still falling at terminal velocity, and slid down its length, slicing it open as I went. Ledge Runner kicked in and my feet found purchase, the speed at which I was moving instantly forcing me into a full-out sprint as I raced down the wyvern's spine, balancing with impossible grace as I leaned down to run the tip of my Dagger along the wyvern's back.

The wyvern had had enough. With a great beat of its wings it lifted up into the sky, rolling over onto its back within the Shroud and facing me. I looked over my shoulder as it opened its maw, revealing a glittering core of copper-bronze flame coruscating in the depths of its gullet.

Oh shi—

I completed my Double Step just as its explosive breath engulfed me, a deluge of what looked like molten metal. The first flickering of agony touched my back and left elbow, but was then cooled by the shadows as I disappeared out of death's way.

I emerged above the wyvern at the apex of my Night Shroud, and fell upon it as the last of its breath weapon uncurled into the sky, fading away and leaving a baking, arid heat in its wake. I fell upon the wyvern and once again slashed at its neck, opening its flesh to the bone.

But my attacks weren't enough. Devastating as each wound was, I was still only level eight, and this monstrosity was what – level thirty? Forty? It would take me too long to whittle its hit points down.

Time for another plan.

I initiated a new Double Step, appearing once more high above the wyvern, and this time I activated Ebon Tendrils. From the heart of my Night Shroud I summoned a massive python of shadow which I sent curling around the wyvern's left wing, constricting and crushing the delicate bones and leathery expanse.

The wyvern contorted violently, shaking its wings in an attempt to free itself, but my Tendril held fast. I fell upon the wyvern once more, Ledge Runner giving me purchase, and hacked with my Death Dagger as the wyvern trumpeted its fury and began to fall.

With one wing scrunched up, it fell into a wicked spiral, spinning around and around as it fell to the ground. My Night Shroud tracked our fall, keeping me in darkness, and I hacked at the monster's neck like a madman, slicing and gouging with all my strength. Adrenaline Surge powered my arm so that I felt like a machine, delivering endless wounds as the ground came rushing up to meet us at a vertiginous speed.

I waited till the last second, the last possible moment, and before we hit I completed my Double Step and disappeared into the shadows.

I appeared in the shadows at the base of the goblin tower as the wyvern impacted with the bailey before me. The sound of snapping bones and tearing flesh was gut churning. Lotharia emerged from the doorway a moment later, and together we stepped out together into the sunlight, hand in hand, to stare in horrified fascination at the wyvern. It crooned piteously as it sought to climb to its legs, but one of them was badly broken. Even with the damage done by Mogr, Lotharia's staff, my Death Dagger and the collision with the ground, it yet lived. It oriented on us, the Night Shroud finally having dissipated, and blinked its massive eyes. In their depths I saw as much agony as hatred.

"How—" Lotharia's voice was hushed with awe. "How did you do that?"

"Leveled up," I said. I did a quick check: no mana left. "Watch out. It's not done yet."

That's when Adrenaline Surge chose to give out. I groaned and sank to my knees, the nausea and pain from my partially healed wounds pushing me to the brink of passing out just as the wyvern opened its jaws. Through the crushing headache that hit me I saw the flickering bronze glow of its breath weapon growing in its gullet, but Lotharia lifted her staff before I could pull her back into the shadows and fired a spear of black fire straight down its throat.

The attack knocked the wyvern's head back and it spewed its bronze flame into the sky.

"Time to finish it," said Lotharia, her voice cold, and I looked at her – really looked at her – for the first time since the fight had begun.

She was in rough shape. Unwounded, but the purple-and-black veins were thick across her cheeks, emerging from under her jawline to extend up toward her eyes, which were now surrounded by black. Her skin had grown even paler, and her hair wove through the air as if she stood submerged in a current.

She lifted the spider staff and fired off another blast at the wyvern. It reared back, trying to get away, but to no avail.

"Lotharia," I croaked. "Stop."

She ignored me and walked toward it. Another blast. Another. Another. I could see the darkness growing around her eyes, the tendrils creeping ever thicker up her cheeks. A dark majesty was manifesting around her, and her expression was cold as she launched yet another blast at the wyvern's head.

"Lotharia!" We'd lost Falkon to the ogre's blow, but as painful as that had been, that was a temporary loss. What I was witnessing here ran the risk of being permanent. I tried to rise to my feet, but nausea kept me down. "Please! Enough!"

The wyvern rose up, and with one final, desperate effort it launched itself at Lotharia – only to take a black spear straight into its good eye. It crashed to the ground. For a moment its head arched up into the air, and then it gave a final rattling croak before collapsing altogether.

My XP chime sounded, but I ignored it. Instead, I stared at Lotharia, who moved to stand over the fallen wyvern. Dark magic was playing up and down the length of her staff.

"Lotharia?" I forced myself to stand and slowly approached her, hands raised to show I meant no harm. "How about you put the staff down, yeah? It's over."

She looked at me sidelong. There was no recognition in her eyes. Her hair was still undulating, which combined with the darkness that pooled around her eyes and the veins that had darkened across her face served to give her a chilling appearance, like Sarah Kerrigan from StarCraft after she'd gone all Queen of Blades.

"How about… how about you give me the staff, all right?" My gorge rose and I tasted bile. I freaking *hated* Adrenaline Surge. "I'm going to take it. All right?"

I extended my shaking hand for her staff, moving slowly, feeling like I was making a huge mistake. She gazed at me with those flat eyes of hers, then lifted the staff and pointed it at my head.

"Whoa. OK. No need for that. You can hold onto it if you want. No problem."

Her jaw tightened, her eyes narrowed a fraction, and Astute Observer helped me see the blast a split second before it came. I tried to leap aside, but was too late – far too late.

The spear of crackling black fire shot forth, only to impact a dome of lurid green light that incandesced all around me. The spear and dome both dissipated at once, leaving me standing in complete shock. Lotharia narrowed her eyes, frowned, then looked toward the front gate.

A woman was standing there, an eerie, strange figure clad in torn crimson robes. She wore a skull mask over her face, but that did little to hide the fact that she was dead: her skin had taken on a greenish pallor, and I could see wounds in the side of her neck and torso that hinted at charred bones and flesh. Yet she held aloft her own staff, whose tip glowed with the same green light as the forcefield that had just defended me.

I ran my hand through my sweat-matted hair. "What the...?"

Lotharia raised her staff to attack this stranger when a dozen skeletal champions stepped into view, filing through the ruined gatehouse to stand on all sides of the new arrival.

"Surrender," called out the woman, voice hollow from within the bone mask. "Put down your staff. Now."

Lotharia licked her lower lip, then spun and sprinted toward the boarded-up keep. Overwhelmed, I lunged forward to try and catch hold of her arm, but was too slow, too late. With a blast of black fire Lotharia shattered the boards that covered the doorway, staving in the great door itself, and then she was through, swallowed whole by the darkness.

"Damn it," said the undead lady. "Fuck."

"Lotharia!" My cry echoed off the bailey walls. There was no response. Grimacing, I staggered after her, but stopped when a blast of green fire exploded before me. With a curse I turned to the lady at the gate. At that moment the nausea left me. I stood up straight, ignoring my wounds. "Who the hell are you? What's going on?"

"That's what I want to know." She gestured at the champions to stay and then strode toward me. "We saw a plume of smoke erupt from the castle and our scouts heard the sound of battle. My master decided it worth the risk of sending me up here to prevent your being killed." She paused, taking in the dead wyvern, Mogr, the other two ogres that lay in sight. "Wait. *You* did this?"

"I, uh, had some help." I was out of my depth. I wanted to process what had happened to Lotharia, wanted to collapse somewhere and recover from the strains of battle. Instead, I forced myself to focus. "My friends and I, yeah." I looked at the dozen skeletal champions who watched us with burning eyes. "Who are you? What do you mean, couldn't let us die?"

The woman took off her skull mask, revealing a disconcertingly attractive face; high cheekbones, full lips, an expression that was at once callous and dismayed. A wicked scar ran from the left corner of her mouth to the ear, looking as if her entire cheek had once been slit open, and a gold ring glinted in one nostril. "The name's Michaela Firion, Dark Exarch under the service of the Dread Lord Guthorios the Forlorn. As of a few weeks ago, at any rate." She leaned her weight on her staff, placing her other hand on her hip. "We've been trying to arrange an audience with you ever since you caught my master's attention. You and your friends have been surprisingly hard to corner."

There was too much to process here. Too many questions I wanted to ask all at once. "I need to go after my friend. I have to help her.

And collect my other friend from the highland meadow. Gutho-rios is going to have to wait."

She smiled at me, darkly amused. "The undead are by definition patient, but the time has come for an audience." She gazed at the keep, then narrowed her eyes. "Also, to be honest? I don't think you're powerful enough to go in there and live." She looked over at the dead wyvern. "Well. Probably not powerful enough."

"Wait. Are you a player or an NPC?"

"Player."

"You are?" That surprised me more than anything else. "And you signed up to play undead?"

"No. You could say I was recruited against my will. But that's neither here nor there. Time to head down to Feldgrau."

The panicky desire to run filled me. As strangely personable as this undead lady was proving to be, I'd no desire to let her escort me down to meet with this Guthorios the Forlorn. I licked my lower lip. The closest shadow was only a few yards away.

"I wouldn't," she said, tone dry. "You're looking pretty worn out, and I'd much rather not have to coerce you into coming. It'll probably strain our friendship if I'm forced to cast Bone Puppet on you."

"Friendship?"

"And why not? We have the same goals, we'll be working together – I've always been an optimist. Other than my being undead and working for a master who seeks only to use you to further his own aims, what's to stop us from becoming friends?"

I tried not to stare at the gaping wounds, the charred bone, the faint green pallor to her otherwise alabaster skin. There was a feline amusement in her dark eyes, and her full lips hinted at a wry smile.

"Fine." And like that, I gave up my half-mad idea of trying to evade a dozen skeletal champions and whatever else Michaela could do without even a single mana point. "But first we're going into the keep to fetch Lotharia."

"Nice try. No. I'm not tangling with those powers without the express permission of my lord."

I stared at the dark doorway. "I can't abandon her. I won't."

"It may be a little hard to trust me, but believe me when I say she's… well, mostly fine in there. Given what I saw of her, she chose to take shelter in there for a reason. Eventually I'm sure you'll want to pry her out and try to heal her of her taint, but for now? She can wait."

I curled my hands into fists. Something bloody-minded and stubborn caused me to square my shoulders. "Stop me if you have to. But I won't abandon her." And I marched toward the distant doorway.

"Oh, for fuck's sake," the undead lady said.

I was out of mana. I had nothing left to give me an edge. I knew I was being an idiot. But I couldn't leave Lotharia in there alone. Tormented and warped by the spider staff, turned into something unholy by her desire to save me.

I owed it to her.

More than that.

I simply had to do anything and everything I could to save her.

My body arched in agony and I screamed as pain wrenched its way through me. My muscles spasmed and strained but my body stopped. Swayed. And then turned around.

Michaela's hand was wreathed in green fire, wisps of which extended in my direction. She beckoned, and I walked jerkily toward her. My muscles pulled and strained to no avail, while my very core, my bones, forced their way against me, forcing me forward, step by step.

The pain was excruciating. I was immediately drenched in sweat and nausea spiraled up from within me, making me gag between screams. When finally Michaela clenched her fists so that I could drop, I nearly sobbed in relief.

"There," she said, voice curt with disgust. "Is that what you wanted? Honestly, men can be so ridiculously pig-headed."

I lay there gasping, pushed to the brink of blacking out, and then turned to gaze back at the keep. Helpless fury filled me. *I'm sorry*, I thought. *Forgive me, Lotharia.*

"Damn you," I rasped, slowly climbing to my feet.

"Yes, yes," said Michaela. "Now. Will you accompany me willingly or do I have to march you the whole way down?"

"Fine. I'll come. But we're going to have to swing by the highland meadow to pick up my friend. I won't meet with Guthorios without him. Her."

Michaela arched a brow. "That's thoughtful of you. What a considerate friend. I'm sure your companion will thank you effusively for making sure they're dragged before the Dread Lord too."

I took a deep breath and forced a smile. I wouldn't let Michaela see how weak I was. "Knowing Falkon, he'll probably get a kick out of it. Deal?"

"Very well." Michaela sighed. "I was ordered to bring all of you, after all."

"What does he want with us?" A small worm of fear wriggled in my gut. "Is he going to 'recruit' us against our will?"

"Make you undead, you mean? No. That wouldn't serve his purposes at all. He needs you very much alive. But otherwise, yes." She smiled. "Infuriating, isn't it? But you'll only get cryptic answers from me. You'll have to wait for your audience to learn what this is all about."

"Fine. One moment, then." I walked over to Falkon's gear and picked it all up. "Think one of your champions can carry this?"

"My champions?" She stared at me blankly, then laughed. "Oh! You mean one of the Servitors. Sure." She snapped her fingers, and one of the skeletons sprang forward, crossing the distance with disconcerting speed to take the gear from my hands. "Now. Ready?"

I rubbed my palms on my hips. No, I wasn't ready. I wanted nothing to do with Guthorios. I felt an abject sense of misery over abandoning Lotharia, but had to admit there was nothing I could do in that department, either. Not yet, at any rate. Meeting up with Falkon was a step in the right direction.

"Ready," I said.

"Very good. To the highland meadow, then. And since you're going to have to tell Guthorios all about yourself, I'll save my questions till then. I'm well aware of how annoying it is to have to repeat yourself."

"Thanks." We began walking toward the gatehouse. It all felt terribly surreal. The corpses of our foes were a testament to our victory, but instead of celebrating together we were split up, and I felt nothing so much as a pang of loss.

When we reached the main gatehouse I turned one last time and stared at the keep. Nobody stood within the doorway, but I thought of Lotharia hidden within its haunted depths, and I made a vow: *I'll be back for you. I swear it.*

And with that, I left the Castle Winter to meet with the Dread Lord of Feldgrau at last.

NIGHTMARE KEEP

PHIL TUCKER

Nightmare Keep

Chris' adventures continue in the second installment of the
Euphoria Online Trilogy.

Chris' adventures continue in the second installment of the
Euphoria Online Trilogy.

I've managed to survive my first week in Euphoria Online.
But I couldn't have done it without my new friends. Lotharia.
Falkon. The Green Liver goblins.

But now Lotharia's gone missing. Swallowed by that nightmare keep. Lost to the darkness.

Everyone's telling me that going after her is madness. That I
don't have a chance in hell.

But I'm not the kind of guy to turn my back on my friends.
Damn the odds.

I'm going to find her.

About the Author

Phil Tucker is a Brazilian/Brit that currently resides in Asheville, NC, where he resists the siren call of the forests and mountains to sit inside and hammer away at his laptop. He is currently working on the epic fantasy series, Chronicles of the Black Gate, launched in May 2016. Connect with him at www.authorphiltucker.com or drop him a line at pwtucker@gmail.com

Sign up for his mailing list here:
WWW.AUTHORPHILTUCKER.COM

Kickstarter Backers

On May 1st, 2018, I launched a Kickstarter to fund the creation of interior art and the release of the Euphoria Online trilogy in hardcover format.

When the dust settled my Euphoria Online Kickstarter had attracted the support of 385 backers and raised almost $20,000. The project funded in less than twelve hours, and for much of the project's duration was the most popular publishing project across all of Kickstarter's categories.

To say I was stunned is to put it mildly.

Because of the generous support and enthusiasm of my readers and backers, I was able to commission the stunning interior artwork you saw in this novel, and release the books in gorgeous hardcover. I can't sufficiently express my thanks for the folks who chose to support me in this endeavor, and who are listed below with all my gratitude.

–phil tucker

Aaron M

Abel Orlando Garcia II

Abigail Keller

Abraham Lincoln

Adam Derda

Adam Weller

Adrian Collins

Aerronn Carr

Ahinahina

Aisha Laury

Alex Raubach

Alex Schwartz

Alex Tabor

Alexander X Rodriguez

Alexandra Askew

Alexey Vasyukov

Alfredo R. Carella

Alvin Lo

Amanda Longo

André Laude

Andrea Orjuela

Andres Zanzani

Andrew M.

Andrew M. Lyons

Andrey Lukyanenko aka Artgor

Angus Frean

Anita Harsjoeen

anon

Anonymous

Armando V.

Arook

Ashley Niels

Ashli Tingle

Aurelia Smith

Austin Brown

Autumn PeLata

Axel Nackaerts

Barbara Pitman

Ben

Ben

Ben Galley

Ben Heywood

Ben Trehet

Bernie S.

Bracht

Brandon S.

Brannigan Cheney

Brewmasster ov däss

Brian Becker

Brian Griffin

Brijwhiz

Brittany Hay

Brooke

Bryan Geddes

Bryan H.

Bryan Shang

Bryce O'Connor

Bryce Vollmer

C Forry

C. Scudder Mead

Caitlin Krueger

Cameron Brunton-Hales

Cameron Johnston

Captain Dray MacGregor

Carl Armstrong

Carlee Sims

Carole-Ann Warburton

Caroline Kruger

Cat H

Cedric Gasser

Charli Maxwell

Chris B.

Chris Black

Chris Jiang

Chris Roberts

Chris Torrence

Chris Vinson

Christina Bryant

Christina Gale

Christoffer Sevaldsen

Christopher Goetting

Christopher Huddleston

Clay Sawyer

Clementine and Rosemary

Cody Wheeler

Connal

Corey Fake

Cory Crowe

Daefea

Dale A. Russell

Dan

Daniel

Daniel K

Daniel Sgranfetto

Darrius Taylor

Dave & Christy Quigley

Dave Snowdon

Dave Upton

David Andre

David Kitching

David Queen

Dayvd D

Dean McQuay

Derek J Roberts

Derrek Kyzar

Derrick Eaves

Dianne Munro

Dion F. Graybeal

Do not include a name

dogmadude

Don Reiter

DRJ

Dustin Cramer

e

E. Mac

Ed McCutchan

Ed Wallace

Edwin, Eli and Ender Hunt

Eric miller

Eric Terrell

Erik Jarvi

Erik Nielsen

Errel Braude

Esko Lakso

Ethan Michael Thompson

Gabe and Nicholas

Gavin Claxton Mahaley

GhostBob

Glenn Curry

Goran Zadravec

Greg Tausch

Grendelfly

Hannah Tanner

Haunar

Heather Q

hidsnake

HiuGregg

I do not need my name listed.

Ian Mitchell

Iliyan Iliev

Inga

Iquito

Ivan Majstorovic

J Ford

J Goode

J Lance Miller

j wright

J. Eged

Jack Ankeny

Jackie Standaert

Jacob "Iocabus" Jones

Jacob Matthews

Jaime gilbert

Jake Whipple

Jakob Ingi Vidirsson

James H.

James O.

James Poe

James Rowland

James Yeary

Jamie Danielle Woods

Jamil

Jan Thomas Jensen

Janet Young

Jason Campbell, MD

Jason Coleman (BX)

Jason Rippentrop

Jason Sickmeier

Jay Peterson

JC Kang

Jeffrey Berry

Jeffrey Hurcomb

Jeffrey Munro

Jennifer L. Pierce

Jer

Jeramy Goble

Jesper Pettersen

Joe Dorrian

Joe White

Joe Williams

Joel Roath

Joel Wright

John Couchman

John Iadanza

John Idlor

John Woosley

Jonathan Garcia

Jonathan Haas

Jonathan Johnson

Jordan Hoddinett

Jordan Jones

Jose Javier Soriano Sempere

Joseph Born

Joshua Anderson

Joshua Basham

Joshua Stewart

Joshua Thornton

JP Pinsonneault

Justin B. Ellis

Justine Bergman

Juts

Keanu Bellamy

Kelly Bowen
Kelvin Neely
Kenneth Kalchik
Kepi
Khyreerusydi
Kimberly Kunker
Kopratic
Kristen McDowell
Kristen Roskob
Kristian Handberg
Kristy Wang
Kyle Pike
Kyle Swank
Landrovan
Larry J Couch
Lawrence Preijers
Leah White
Leila Ghaznavi
letoze
Loeki
Luke Challen
Lynn Worton
Madison Treat
Making adventures more like
    life. - Joh
Marc
Marc Rasp
Marcos Ramirez
Martina
Matt Klawiter
Maureen Bacon
Max Dosser
Maz

MC Abajian
Micbri
Michael D. Taylor
Michael Downey
Michael Fazio
Michael Hodgman
Michael J. Sullivan
Michael Leaich
Michael Q Anderson
Michelle Findlay-Olynyk
Michelle P. Dunaway
Mike Tabacchi
Mike Weber
Misko
Mitchel Geer
Mitchell Hostiadi
Nate Cutler
Nathan
Nathan Anderson
Nathan Nabeta
Nathan Turner
Negative Red
Nick Human
Nick Ryckbosch
Nicolas
Nimrod Daniel
Norman Rechlin
Not necessary.
nothing
Old Grey Haired woman
Oliver Knight
Orliv
P carvalho

Pam Wickert
Paolo Jackson
Pat Walsh
Paulo
Penny Evans
Pery R
Peter Badurek
Pobin
Pornokitsch
Przemek Iskra
Psiwizard
Rama Lex
Rebecca Mc
Reuben
Rev. Kevin Muyskens
Rhcoll
Rhel ná DecVandé
Riccardo Maderna
Richa
Ridian Jale
Rob Henschen
Rob Holland
Robert F Towell
Robert Karalash
Robert Q
Roger Stone
Rory Thrasher
Rosie Vincent
Roxanne Lingenfelter
Ryan Leduc
Ryan Porter
S Gelgoot
Saad Hasan Syed

sal1n
Sally Qwill Janin
Sara G.
Sarah Merrill
Scott Dell'Osso
Scott Foster
Scott Frederick
Scott M. Williams
Sean Anderson
Sean L
Sean McCune
Shadowcodex
Sharon Wells
Shawn Polka
Shawna J. Traver
Simon Julian
Sir Aaron of Clan Shaefer
Stephanie Au
Stephanie Carl
Stephanie Meier
Sterrin
Steve Brenneman
Steve Thompson
Steven Lank
Stubbs
Succotash
Susan Contreras
Susanne Porter
SwordFire
Sylvia L. Foil
Tam
Tanner McVey
Tarasa Escoubas

Tavis W.
Thank you Andrew
ThatAnimeSnob
Thomas Pettersson
Thomas Stratton
Tim
Tim Harron
Todd L Ross
Tomas Bowers
Tomer Bar-Shlomo
Tommye Hart
Tony
Tony Muzi
Tony Nguyen
Trae Watkins
Travis G
Travis Horner
Tyler Chadwick Rabren
Victoria Johnsen
vikyle
Walter Schirmacher
Wayne Mathers
Will Pomerantz
William C. Tracy
William Robbins
Wolfram Pfeifer
Zach Slade
Zack McFarland
ZAK
Zathras do Urdenz

PHIL TUCKER

The PATH OF FLAMES

Chronicles of the Black Gate

The Path of Flames

Book 1 of the
CHRONICLES OF THE BLACK FLAME
Is available now.

The first book in the epic fantasy series readers are comparing to David Gemmell and Raymond E. Feist.

A war fueled by the dark powers of forbidden sorcery is about to engulf the Ascendant Empire. Agerastian heretics, armed with black fire and fueled by bitter hatred, seek to sever the ancient portals that unite the empire - and in so doing destroy it.

Asho—a squire with a reviled past—sees his liege, the Lady Kyferin, and her meager forces banished to an infamous ruin. Beset by tragedy and betrayal, demons and an approaching army, the fate of the Kyferins hangs by the slenderest of threads. Asho realizes that their sole hope of survival may lie hidden within the depths of his scarred soul—a secret that could reverse their fortunes and reveal the truth behind the war that wracks their empire.

Unpredictable, fast paced, and packed with unforgettable characters, The Path of Flames is the first installment in a gripping new epic fantasy series. Grab your copy today!